TALES OF THE
OTHERWORLD

ANNE DOYLE

PRESENTS

TALES OF THE

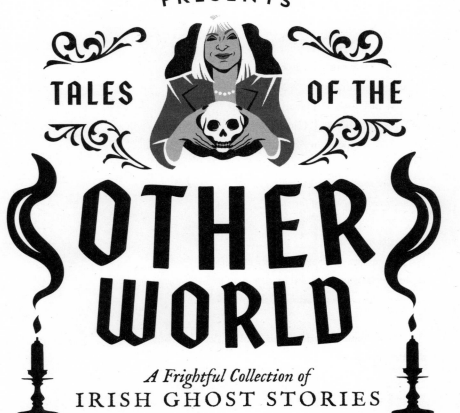

OTHER WORLD

A Frightful Collection of
IRISH GHOST STORIES

GILL BOOKS

Gill Books
Hume Avenue
Park West
Dublin 12
www.gillbooks.ie

Gill Books is an imprint of M.H. Gill and Co.

Story introductions © Anne Doyle 2023

978 07171 97385

Editorial consultation by Dr Sarah Cleary
Designed by Bartek Janczak
Print origination by Sarah McCoy
Printed and bound in Great Britain by
CPI Group (UK) Ltd, Croydon, CRO 4YY
This book is typeset in Adobe Garamond Pro.

*The paper used in this book comes from the wood pulp
of sustainably managed forests.*

A CIP catalogue record for this book is available from
the British Library.

5 4 3 2 1

CONTENTS

TALES OF THE
OTHERWORLD

PRESENTED BY

ANNE DOYLE

INTRODUCTION

HOSTS HAVE ALWAYS BEEN a part of my life. This isn't something I acknowledge easily, nor is it something by which I'm best pleased. I believe in ghosts, and they sometimes frighten me. But, I suppose, a shiver or a scary thrill now and then is no harm – maybe it helps keep you young at heart.

When I was a child, ghosts were a part of the fabric of the everyday. Back then, people accepted their presence and spoke openly about them with a mixture of superstition, warmth, wariness and respect. I know, for sure, that my grandfather believed in them. He once met the ghost of a neighbour on a summer's day with the sun noon high. But, of course, ghosts generally moved in darkness and shadows. The lack of electricity probably helped, and, certainly, it was a while before electricity reached my family's home, outside Ferns in County Wexford. Many spine-tingling evenings were spent around the fire outdoing each other with the stories we'd heard, dreamed or invented. When you're a little girl with a wild imagination, lamplight casts long shadows. Those evenings probably ensured that my interest in ghost stories remained. I have sought those stories out and, at various times in my life, found comfort, escape and surprise in them.

I remember like yesterday, walking along a winding road near home. I was probably about eight at the time. As the youngest child I was well used to wearing hand-me-downs and, with five brothers, the pickings were slim. But this day I was wearing my pride and joy: a little waisted coat with a velvet collar – a treasured gift from an aunt in England. Oh, and I had a duck egg in my pocket. A takeaway supper! Probably not the wisest place to carry it.

At that time rumours were circulating about the end of the world, with talk of nuclear warnings and atomic weaponry. Suddenly there was a huge peal of thunder, so very close that an electrical storm was almost upon us. I got such a fright I squeezed the duck egg. It did little for my lovely coat.

Then, just rounding the corner towards me came a little girl. She was my size, equally plain, with short dark hair, and she was wearing a waisted grey coat with a velvet collar. There weren't many children in that isolated townland; certainly no other little girl. The fetch was often spoken of in local lore – a supernatural being who comes to 'fetch' you. Was I looking at mine?

Of course, the little girl was quickly followed by her mother. They were visiting relatives. Nor did a scrambled duck egg decorate her coat. But that encounter, with the fear of the end of the world thrown in for good measure, triggered my lifelong fascination with doppelgängers. Some of the stories in this anthology have a similar sense of the uncanny – disquieting moments of uncertainty, a stirring of the curtain between this world and the possibilities of the other.

The ghost stories we scared each other with were often locally based and steeped in the history of the area. Close to home, at the top of Milltown Hill, there was a fine field known as the Bell Field, so named because a ghost bell was said to toll there. When I was ten or eleven, I was one of the children who stayed back after school for extra tuition. This was preparation for a scholarship and a generous act by the teacher. But it was pretty harrowing for a child walking a couple of miles home in the dark. I remember that it would be pitch black dark – the road home from the village very quickly ran out of houses and lights.

My heart would race walking up that hill. It was steep; that was nothing to a child. But near the top, to the left, lay the Bell Field. A mad rush past, willing the bell to stay silent. It never tolled for me – well, not yet!

One evening, about six o'clock, in a dense dark, I was scurrying past the field when I became aware of a presence. I couldn't quite see the outline, but I knew it was large, looming and very close to me. Just when I thought my heart would stop, I heard a loud 'moo'.

Silly, now, but the fear was almost paralysing. The same can happen when you read a good story. It settles like a blanket over your shoulders. You get wrapped up in its suspense and atmosphere until your heart pounds and the hairs stand on the back of your neck. Then some everyday occurrence brings you back to soothing reality and all is well.

When I first moved to the house where I now live, I was surprised and a little perturbed to discover there was a ghost in the basement. She was small, with grey hair in a neat bun, and she wore a rather drab dress with a sort of pinny. She seemed to move about constantly as if preoccupied with some matter of urgency.

I saw her a number of times, always in the basement. It made me a little reluctant to go down there at first – but the vodka is down there, too, so needs must! Fortunately, I wasn't the only person she favoured with an appearance or I might have doubted myself – nothing to do with the vodka! We house-shared with her for about three months, and then she was gone. It's a bit alarming to think I saw off a ghost. I hope she left for good reasons. Maybe she was just minding an empty house.

By an odd coincidence, an acquaintance of mine lived in this house when he was a small boy. His parents were caretakers. I told him one evening about the little lady and, as she had given me quite a start that day, I was a bit cranky about her. The next time we met, he had a photograph album with him, with pictures of his mother. It had occurred to him that his mother might be the ghost. I was mortified to think I had been so insensitive. Thankfully, there was no resemblance – his dear mother was a glamorous and elegant woman. My little lady was simply herself. I never felt any ill will from my ghost – she paid me no attention at all, really. I was, after all, a stranger.

One sunny summer afternoon in 2000, my eldest brother took his dog for a ramble in the fields. He came back ashen-faced. So shocked did he appear that my other, very laid-back brothers inquired as to what had happened. 'I saw Mammy down the field,' he said.

My mother had died in 1979, more than twenty years previously. He described what he believed he had seen, and what I believe he saw: a sort of freeze-frame image of my mother, not three-dimensional. Neither spoke, he was too shocked, but she looked straight at him. If I'm honest, I was a little put out that our mother hadn't appeared to me when she died, after an overnight illness while I was abroad. But he was her eldest son. I asked him how she looked. He said he thought she had looked 'very concerned'.

Shortly after that, my brother collapsed and was taken to hospital. He was diagnosed with late-stage multiple myeloma, and he died less than three months later. The trees were only shedding their leaves when we brought him home to Ferns to join our mother in the grave.

These are just some of the memories reawakened in the past year as I put this anthology together. Good stories can work that way – like chance meetings, stolen glances and unexpected interactions. Dusting off old memories was like meeting old friends as I went through my collections of stories, often on suitably grey and drizzly days. And I've had the pleasure of finding writers new to me, too. This way I have been able to build new memories and I look forward to getting better acquainted with the wealth of their great tales.

My dreams have been wonderfully weird and wild since putting together *Tales of the Otherworld*. I have loved dipping into the spectral zone, letting my thoughts linger a while in the flicker of a candle or the sheen of a mirror. As the nights begin to draw in once more, I hope the stories selected here give you an enjoyable shiver, a certain thrill. And, just occasionally, on a dark night, maybe they'll cause you to glance over your shoulder.

Happy reading.
ANNE DOYLE, 2023

THE HAUNTED CELLAR

THOMAS CROFTON CROKER

(1825)

This is not a story that will give you particular shivers. The spirit here is naughty but jolly. If, like me, you have a fondness for the contents of the cellar, you might regret the presence of Cluricaune Naggeneen – that little rip would drink you out of house and home! Quite different to the ghost I met in the basement of my own home – a faded and silent little lady who seemed always to be anxiously busy and on the move. Rather unsettling. Thankfully, she left us (as far as I know), but the Cluricaune loves the drop and will stay with you wherever you go.

HERE ARE FEW PEOPLE who have not heard of the Mac Carthys – one of the real old Irish families, with the true Milesian blood running in their veins as thick as buttermilk. Many were the clans of this family in the south; as the Mac Carthymore – and the Mac Carthyreagh – and the Mac Carthy of Muskerry; and all of them were noted for their hospitality to strangers, gentle and simple.

But not one of that name, or of any other, exceeded Justin Mac Carthy, of Ballinacarthy, at putting plenty to eat and drink upon his table; and there was a right hearty welcome for everyone who should share it with him. Many a wine cellar would be ashamed of the name if that at Ballinacarthy was the proper pattern for one. Large as that cellar was, it was crowded with bins of wine, and long rows of pipes, and hogsheads, and casks, that it would take more time to count than any sober man could spare in such a place, with plenty to drink about him, and a hearty welcome to do so.

There are many, no doubt, who will think that the butler would have little to complain of in such a house; and the whole country round would have agreed with them, if a man could be found to remain as Mr Mac Carthy's butler for any length of time worth speaking of; yet not one who had been in his service gave him a bad word.

'We have no fault,' they would say, 'to find with the master, and if he could but get anyone to fetch his wine from the cellar, we might every one of us have grown grey in the house and have lived quiet and contented enough in his service until the end of our days.'

''Tis a queer thing that, surely,' thought young Jack Leary, a lad who had been brought up from a mere child in the stables of Ballinacarthy to assist in taking care of the horses, and had occasionally lent a hand in the butler's pantry, ''Tis a mighty queer thing, surely, that one man after another cannot content himself with the best place in the house of a good master, but that every one of them must quit, all through the means, as they say, of the wine cellar. If the master, long life to him, would but make me his butler, I warrant never the word more would be heard of grumbling at his bidding to go to the wine cellar.'

Young Leary, accordingly, watched for what he conceived to be a favourable opportunity of presenting himself to the notice of his master.

A few mornings after, Mr Mac Carthy went into his stableyard rather earlier than usual, and called loudly for the groom to saddle his horse, as he intended going out with the hounds. But there was no groom to answer, and young Jack Leary led Rainbow out of the stable.

'Where is William?' enquired Mr Mac Carthy.

'Sir?' said Jack; and Mr Mac Carthy repeated the question.

'Is it William, please your honour?' returned Jack. 'Why, then, to tell the truth, he had just *one* drop too much last night.'

'Where did he get it?' said Mr Mac Carthy, 'for since Thomas went away the key of the wine cellar has been in my pocket, and I have been obliged to fetch what was drunk myself.'

'Sorrow a know I know,' said Leary, 'unless the cook might have given him the *least taste* in life of whiskey. But,' continued he, performing a low bow by seizing with his right hand a lock of hair, and pulling down his head by it, while his left leg, which had been put forward, was scraped back against the ground, 'may I make so bold as just to ask your honour one question?'

'Speak out, Jack,' said Mr Mac Carthy.

'Why, then, does your honour want a butler?'

'Can you recommend me one,' returned his master, with the smile of good humour upon his countenance, 'and one who will not be afraid of going to my wine cellar?'

'Is the wine cellar all the matter?' said young Leary. 'Devil a doubt I have of myself then for that.'

'So you mean to offer me your services in the capacity of butler?' said Mr Mac Carthy, with some surprise.

'Exactly so,' answered Leary, now for the first time looking up from the ground.

'Well, I believe you to be a good lad, and have no objection to give you a trial.'

'Long may your honour reign over us, and the Lord spare you to us!' ejaculated Leary, with another national bow, as his master rode off; and he continued for some time to gaze after him with a vacant stare, which slowly and gradually assumed a look of importance.

'Jack Leary,' said he, at length, 'Jack – is it Jack?' in a tone of wonder. 'Faith, 'tis not Jack now, but Mr John, the butler;' and with an air of becoming consequence he strode out of the stableyard towards the kitchen.

It is of little purport to my story, although it may afford an instructive lesson to the reader, to depict the sudden transition of nobody into somebody. Jack's former stable companion, a poor superannuated hound named Bran, who had been accustomed to receive many an affectionate pat on the head, was spurned from him with a kick and an 'Out of the way, sirrah.' Indeed, poor Jack's memory seemed sadly affected by this sudden change of situation. What established the point beyond all doubt was his almost forgetting the pretty face of Peggy, the kitchen wench, whose heart he had assailed but the preceding week by the offer of purchasing a gold ring for the fourth finger of her right hand, and a lusty imprint of good will upon her lips.

When Mr Mac Carthy returned from hunting, he sent for Jack Leary – so he still continued to call his new butler. 'Jack,' said he, 'I believe you are a trustworthy lad, and here are the keys of my cellar. I have asked the gentlemen with whom I hunted today to dine with me, and I hope they may be satisfied at the way in which you will wait on them at table; but, above all, let there be no want of wine after dinner.'

Mr John having a tolerably quick eye for such things, and being naturally a handy lad, spread his cloth accordingly, laid his plates and knives and forks in the same manner he had seen his predecessors in office perform these mysteries, and really, for the first time, got through attendance on dinner very well.

It must not be forgotten, however, that it was at the house of an Irish country squire, who was entertaining a company of booted and spurred fox-hunters, not very particular about what are considered matters of infinite importance under other circumstances and in other societies.

For instance, few of Mr Mac Carthy's guests (though all excellent and worthy men in their way) cared much whether the punch produced after soup was made of Jamaica or Antigua rum; some even would not have been inclined to question the correctness of good old Irish whiskey; and, with the exception of their liberal host himself, everyone in company preferred the port which Mr Mac Carthy put on his table to the less ardent flavour of claret – a choice rather at variance with modern sentiment.

It was waxing near midnight, when Mr Mac Carthy rung the bell three times. This was a signal for more wine; and Jack proceeded to the cellar to procure a fresh supply, but it must be confessed not without some little hesitation.

The luxury of ice was then unknown in the south of Ireland; but the superiority of cool wine had been acknowledged by all men of sound judgement and true taste.

The grandfather of Mr Mac Carthy, who had built the mansion of Ballinacarthy upon the site of an old castle which had belonged to his ancestors, was fully aware of this important fact; and in the construction of his magnificent wine cellar had availed himself of a deep vault, excavated out of the solid rock in former times as a place of retreat and security. The descent to this vault was by a flight of steep stone stairs, and here and there in the wall were narrow passages – I ought rather to call them crevices; and also certain projections, which cast deep shadows, and looked very frightful when anyone went down the cellar stairs with a single light: indeed, two lights did not much improve the matter, for though the breadth of the shadows became less, the narrow crevices remained as dark and darker than ever.

Summoning up all his resolution, down went the new butler, bearing in his right hand a lantern and the key of the cellar, and in his left a basket, which he considered sufficiently capacious to contain an adequate stock for the remainder of the evening: he arrived at the door without any interruption whatever; but when he put the key, which was of an ancient and clumsy kind – for it was before the days of Bramah's patent – and turned it in the lock, he thought he heard a strange kind of laughing within the cellar, to which some empty bottles that stood upon the floor outside vibrated so violently that they struck against each other: in this he could not be mistaken, although he may have been deceived in the laugh, for the bottles were just at his feet, and he saw them in motion.

Leary paused for a moment, and looked about him with becoming caution. He then boldly seized the handle of the key, and turned it with all his strength in the lock, as if he doubted his own power of doing so; and the door flew open with a most tremendous crash, that if the house had not been built upon the solid rock would have shook it from the foundation.

To recount what the poor fellow saw would be impossible, for he seems not to have known very clearly himself: but what he told the cook the next morning was, that he heard a roaring and bellowing like a mad bull, and that all the pipes and hogsheads and casks in the cellar went rocking backwards and forwards with so much force that he thought every one would have been staved in, and that he should have been drowned or smothered in wine.

When Leary recovered, he made his way back as well as he could to the dining room, where he found his master and the company very impatient for his return.

'What kept you?' said Mr Mac Carthy in an angry voice. 'And where is the wine? I rung for it half an hour since.'

'The wine is in the cellar, I hope, sir,' said Jack, trembling violently. 'I hope 'tis not all lost.'

What do you mean, fool?' exclaimed Mr Mac Carthy in a still more angry tone: 'why did you not fetch some with you?'

Jack looked wildly about him, and only uttered a deep groan.

'Gentlemen,' said Mr Mac Carthy to his guests, 'this is too much. When I next see you to dinner, I hope it will be in another house, for it is impossible I can remain longer in this, where a man has no command over his own wine cellar, and cannot get a butler to do his duty. I have long thought of moving from Ballinacarthy; and I am now determined, with the blessing of God, to leave it tomorrow. But wine shall you have were I to go myself to the cellar for it.' So saying, he rose from table, took the key and lantern from his half-stupefied servant, who regarded him with a look of vacancy, and descended the narrow stairs, already described, which led to his cellar.

When he arrived at the door, which he found open, he thought he heard a noise, as if of rats or mice scrambling over the casks, and on advancing perceived a little figure, about six inches in height, seated astride upon the pipe of the oldest port in the place, and bearing a spigot upon his shoulder. Raising the lantern, Mr Mac Carthy contemplated the little fellow with wonder: he wore a red nightcap on his head; before him was a short leather apron, which now, from his attitude, fell rather on one side; and he had stockings of a light blue colour, so long as nearly to cover the entire of his legs; with shoes, having huge silver buckles in them, and with high heels (perhaps out of vanity to make him appear taller). His face was like a withered winter apple; and his nose, which was of a bright crimson colour, about the tip wore a delicate purple bloom, like that of a plum; yet his eyes twinkled 'like those mites of candied dew in money nights – ' and his mouth twitched up at one side with an arch grin.

'Ha, scoundrel!' exclaimed Mr Mac Carthy. 'Have I found you at last? disturber of my cellar – what are you doing there?'

'Sure, and master,' returned the little fellow, looking up at him with one eye, and with the other throwing a sly glance towards the spigot on his shoulder, 'a'n't we going to move tomorrow? And sure you would not leave your own little Cluricaune Naggeneen behind you?'

'Oh!' thought Mr Mac Carthy. 'If you are to follow me, Master Naggeneen, I don't see much use in quitting Ballinacarthy.' So filling with wine the basket which young Leary in his fright had left behind him, and locking the cellar door, he rejoined his guests.

For some years after Mr Mac Carthy had always to fetch the wine for his table himself, as the little Cluricaune Naggeneen seemed to feel a personal respect towards him. Notwithstanding the labour of these journeys, the worthy lord of Ballinacarthy lived in his paternal mansion to a good round age, and was famous to the last for the excellence of his wine, and conviviality of his company; but at the time of his death, the same conviviality had nearly emptied his wine cellar; and as it was never so well filled again, nor so often visited, the revels of Master Naggeneen became less celebrated, and are now only spoken of among the legendary lore of the country. It is even said that the poor little fellow took the declension of the cellar so to heart, that he became negligent and careless of himself, and that he has been sometimes seen going about with hardly a *skreed* to cover him.

LEIXLIP CASTLE

CHARLES MATURIN

(1825)

*A terrific tale mixing history, politics and the devil ...
Easy bedfellows! The Collogue is a horridly familiar figure:
many of us grew up with the all too familiar verb 'collogin'
(to conspire or make mischief). For those of us who love
the Scottish play, what could be more evocative than 'the
bloodied dirk'? Except, perhaps, the music of 'Charlie is
my darling' echoing through time. We aired it in Ireland
much more recently. And mark the huge significance of 31
October — always a time to divine the future and usually
driven by the quest for knowledge of love. The latter can
prove our undoing.*

HE INCIDENTS OF THE following tale are not merely founded on fact, they are facts themselves, which occurred at no very distant period in my own family. The marriage of the parties, their sudden and mysterious separation, and their total alienation from each other until the last period of their mortal existence, are all facts. I cannot vouch for the truth of the supernatural solution given to all these mysteries; but I must still consider the story as a fine specimen of Gothic horrors, and can never forget the impression it made on me when I heard it related for the first time among many other thrilling traditions of the same description.

The tranquillity of the Catholics of Ireland during the disturbed periods of 1715 and 1745 was most commendable, and somewhat extraordinary; to enter into an analysis of their probable motives is not at all the object of the writer of this tale, as it is pleasanter to state the fact of their honour than at this distance of time to assign dubious and unsatisfactory reasons for it. Many of them, however, showed a kind of secret disgust at the existing state of affairs, by quitting their family residences and wandering about like persons who were uncertain of their homes, or possibly expecting better from some near and fortunate contingency.

Among the rest was a Jacobite Baronet, who, sick of his uncongenial situation in a Whig neighbourhood, in the north – where he heard of nothing but the heroic defence of Londonderry; the barbarities of the French generals; and the resistless exhortations of the godly Mr Walker, a Presbyterian clergyman, to whom the citizens gave the title of 'Evangelist' – quitted his paternal residence, and about the year 1720 hired the Castle of Leixlip for three years (it was then the property of the Connollys, who let it to triennial tenants); and removed thither with his family, which consisted of three daughters – their mother having long been dead.

The Castle of Leixlip, at that period, possessed a character of romantic beauty and feudal grandeur, such as few buildings in Ireland can claim, and which is now, alas, totally effaced by the destruction of its noble woods; on the destroyers of which the writer would wish 'a minstrel's malison were said'. Leixlip, though about seven miles from Dublin, has all the sequestered and picturesque character that imagination could ascribe to a landscape a hundred miles from, not only the metropolis but an inhabited town. After driving a dull mile (an Irish mile) in passing from Lucan to Leixlip, the road – hedged up on one side of the high wall that bounds the demesne of the Veseys, and on the other by low enclosures, over whose rugged tops you have no view at all – at once opens on Leixlip Bridge, at almost a right angle, and displays a luxury of landscape on which the eye that has seen it even in childhood dwells with delighted recollection. Leixlip Bridge, a rude but solid structure, projects from a high bank of the Liffey, and slopes rapidly to the opposite side, which there lies remarkably low. To the right the plantations of the Vesey's demesne – no longer obscured by walls – almost mingle their dark woods in its stream, with the opposite ones of Marshfield and St Catherine's. The river is scarcely visible, overshadowed as it is by the deep, rich and bending foliage of the trees. To the left it bursts out in all the brilliancy of light, washes the garden steps of the houses of Leixlip, wanders round the low walls of its churchyard, plays with the pleasure-boat moored under the arches on which the summer-house of the Castle is raised, and then loses itself among the rich woods that once skirted those grounds to its very brink. The contrast on the other side, with the luxuriant walks, scattered shrubberies, temples seated on pinnacles, and thickets that conceal from you the sight of the river until you are on its banks, that mark the character of the grounds which are now the property of Colonel Marly, is peculiarly striking.

Visible above the highest roofs of the town, though a quarter of a mile distant from them, are the ruins of Confy Castle, a right good old predatory tower of the stirring times when blood was shed like water; and as you pass the bridge you catch a glimpse of the waterfall (or salmon-leap, as it is called) on whose noon-day lustre, or moon-light beauty, probably the rough livers of that age when Confy Castle was 'a tower of strength' never glanced an eye or cast a thought, as they clattered in their harness over Leixlip Bridge, or waded through the stream before that convenience was in existence.

Whether the solitude in which he lived contributed to tranquil-lise Sir Redmond Blaney's feelings, or whether they had begun to rust from want of collision with those of others, it is impossible to say, but certain it is, that the good Baronet began gradually to lose his tenacity in political matters; and except when a Jacobite friend came to dine with him, and drink with many a significant 'nod and beck and smile', the King over the water – or the parish-priest (good man) spoke of the hopes of better times, and the final success of the right cause, and the old religion – or a Jacobite servant was heard in the solitude of the large mansion whistling 'Charlie is my darling', to which Sir Redmond involuntarily responded in a deep bass voice, somewhat the worse for wear, and marked with more emphasis than good discretion – except, as I have said, on such occasions, the Baronet's politics, like his life, seemed passing away without notice or effort. Domestic calamities, too, pressed sorely on the old gentleman: of his three daughters the youngest, Jane, had disappeared in so extraordinary a manner in her childhood, that though it is but a wild, remote family tradition, I cannot help relating it:

The girl was of uncommon beauty and intelligence, and was suffered to wander about the neighbourhood of the castle with the daughter of a servant, who was also called Jane, as a *nom de caresse*. One evening Jane Blaney and her young companion went far and deep into the woods; their absence created no uneasiness at the time, as these excursions were by no means unusual, till her playfellow returned home alone and weeping, at a very late hour. Her account was that, in passing through a lane at some distance from the castle, an old woman, in the Fingallian dress, (a red petticoat and a long green jacket), suddenly started out of a thicket, and took Jane Blaney by the arm: she had in her hand two rushes, one of which she threw over her shoulder, and giving the other to the child, motioned to her to do the same. Her young companion, terrified at what she saw, was running away, when Jane Blaney called after her – 'Good-bye, good-bye, it is a long time before you will see me again.' The girl said they then disappeared, and she found her way home as she could. An indefatigable search was immediately commenced

– woods were traversed, thickets were explored, ponds were drained – all in vain. The pursuit and the hope were at length given up. Ten years afterwards, the housekeeper of Sir Redmond, having remembered that she left the key of a closet where sweetmeats were kept, on the kitchen table, returned to fetch it. As she approached the door, she heard a childish voice murmuring – 'Cold – cold – cold how long it is since I have felt a fire!' She advanced, and saw, to her amazement, Jane Blaney, shrunk to half her usual size, and covered with rags, crouching over the embers of the fire. The housekeeper flew in terror from the spot, and roused the servants, but the vision had fled. The child was reported to have been seen several times afterwards, as diminutive in form as though she had not grown an inch since she was ten years of age, and always crouching over a fire, whether in the turret-room or kitchen, complaining of cold and hunger, and apparently covered with rags. Her existence is still said to be protracted under these dismal circumstances, so unlike those of Lucy Gray in Wordsworth's beautiful ballad:

> Yet some will say, that to this day
> She is a living child –
> That they have met sweet Lucy Gray
> Upon the lonely wild;
> O'er rough and smooth she trips along.
> And never looks behind;
> And hums a solitary song
> That whistles in the wind.

The fate of the eldest daughter was more melancholy, though less extraordinary; she was addressed by a gentleman of competent fortune and unexceptionable character: he was a Catholic, moreover;

and Sir Redmond Blaney signed the marriage articles, in full satisfaction of the security of his daughter's soul, as well as of her jointure. The marriage was celebrated at the Castle of Leixlip; and, after the bride and bridegroom had retired, the guests still remained drinking to their future happiness, when suddenly, to the great alarm of Sir Redmond and his friends, loud and piercing cries were heard to issue from the part of the castle in which the bridal chamber was situated.

Some of the more courageous hurried upstairs; it was too late – the wretched bridegroom had burst, on that fatal night, into a sudden and most horrible paroxysm of insanity. The mangled form of the unfortunate and expiring lady bore attestation to the mortal virulence with which the disease had operated on the wretched husband, who died a victim to it himself after the involuntary murder of his bride. The bodies were interred, as soon as decency would permit, and the story hushed up.

Sir Redmond's hopes of Jane's recovery were diminishing every day, though he still continued to listen to every wild tale told by the domestics; and all his care was supposed to be now directed towards his only surviving daughter. Anne, living in solitude, and partaking only of the very limited education of Irish females of that period, was left very much to the servants, among whom she increased her taste for superstitious and supernatural horrors, to a degree that had a most disastrous effect on her future life.

Among the numerous menials of the Castle, there was one withered crone, who had been nurse to the late Lady Blaney's mother, and whose memory was a complete *Thesaurus terrorum*. The mysterious fate of Jane first encouraged her sister to listen to the wild tales of this hag, who avouched that at one time she saw the fugitive standing before the portrait of her late mother in one of the apartments of the Castle, and muttering to herself – 'Woe's me, woe's me! how little

my mother thought her wee Jane would ever come to be what she is!'
But as Anne grew older she began more 'seriously to incline' to the
hag's promises that she could show her her future bridegroom, on the
performance of certain ceremonies, which she at first revolted from
as horrible and impious; but, finally, at the repeated instigation of the
old woman, consented to act a part in. The period fixed upon for the
performance of these unhallowed rites was now approaching – it was
near the 31st of October – the eventful night when such ceremonies
were, and still are, supposed, in the North of Ireland, to be most
potent in their effects. All day long the Crone took care to lower the
mind of the young lady to the proper key of submissive and trembling credulity, by every horrible story she could relate; and she told
them with frightful and supernatural energy. This woman was called
Collogue by the family, a name equivalent to Gossip in England, or
Cummer in Scotland (though her real name was Bridget Dease); and
she verified the name, by the exercise of an unwearied loquacity, an
indefatigable memory, and a rage for communicating and inflicting
terror, that spared no victim in the household, from the groom, whom
she sent shivering to his rug, to the Lady of the Castle, over whom
she felt she held unbounded sway.

The 31st of October arrived – the Castle was perfectly quiet
before eleven o'clock; half an hour afterwards, the Collogue and
Anne Blaney were seen gliding along a passage that led to what is
called King John's Tower, where it is said that monarch received the
homage of the Irish princes as Lord of Ireland and which was, at all
events, the most ancient part of the structure.

The Collogue opened a small door with a key which she had
secreted about her, and urged the young lady to hurry on. Anne
advanced to the postern, and stood there irresolute and trembling
like a timid swimmer on the bank of an unknown stream. It was a

dark autumnal evening; a heavy wind sighed among the woods of the Castle, and bowed the branches of the lower trees almost to the waves of the Liffey, which, swelled by recent rains, struggled and roared amid the stones that obstructed its channel. The steep descent from the Castle lay before her, with its dark avenue of elms; a few lights still burned in the little village of Leixlip – but from the lateness of the hour it was probable they would soon be extinguished.

The lady lingered – 'And must I go alone?' said she, foreseeing that the terrors of her fearful journey could be aggravated by her more fearful purpose.

'Ye must, or all will be spoiled,' said the hag, shading the miserable light, that did not extend its influence above six inches on the path of the victim. 'Ye must go alone – and I will watch for you here, dear, till you come back, and then see what will come to you at twelve o'clock.'

The unfortunate girl paused. 'Oh! Collogue, Collogue, if you would but come with me. Oh! Collogue, come with me, if it be but to the bottom of the castle hill.'

'If I went with you, dear, we should never reach the top of it alive again, for there are them near that would tear us both in pieces.'

'Oh! Collogue, Collogue – let me turn back then, and go to my own room – I have advanced too far, and I have done too much.'

'And that's what you have, dear, and so you must go further, and do more still, unless, when you return to your own room, you would see the likeness of someone instead of a handsome young bridegroom.'

The young lady looked about her for a moment, terror and wild hope trembling at her heart – then, with a sudden impulse of supernatural courage, she darted like a bird from the terrace of the Castle, the fluttering of her white garments was seen for a few moments, and then the hag, who had been shading the flickering light with her hand, bolted the postern, and, placing the candle before a glazed loophole, sat down on a stone seat in the recess of the tower, to watch the event of the spell. It was an hour before the young lady returned; when her face was as pale, and her eyes as fixed, as those of a dead body, but she held in her grasp a dripping garment, a proof that her errand had been performed. She flung it into her companion's hands, and then stood, panting and gazing wildly about her as if she knew not where she was. The hag herself grew terrified at the insane and breathless state of her victim, and hurried her to her chamber; but here the preparations for the terrible ceremonies of the night were the first objects that struck her, and, shivering at the sight, she covered her eyes with her hands, and stood immovably fixed in the middle of the room.

It needed all the hag's persuasions (aided even by mysterious menaces), combined with the returning faculties and reviving curiosity of the poor girl, to prevail on her to go through the remaining business of the night. At length she said, as if in desperation, 'I will go through with it: but be in the next room; and if what I dread should happen, I will ring my father's little silver bell which I have secured for the night – and as you have a soul to be saved, Collogue, come to me at its first sound.'

The hag promised, gave her last instructions with eager and jealous minuteness, and then retired to her own room, which was adjacent to that of the young lady. Her candle had burned out, but she stirred up the embers of her turf fire, and sat, nodding over them, and smoothing the pallet from time to time, but resolved not to lie down while there was a chance of a sound from the lady's room, for which she herself, withered as her feelings were, waited with a mingled feeling of anxiety and terror.

It was now long past midnight, and all was silent as the grave throughout the Castle. The hag dozed over the embers till her head touched her knees, then started up as the sound of the bell seemed to tinkle in her ears, then dozed again, and again started as the bell appeared to tinkle more distinctly – suddenly she was roused, not by the bell, but by the most piercing and horrible cries from the neighbouring chamber. The Collogue, aghast for the first time, at the possible consequences of the mischief she might have occasioned, hastened to the room. Anne was in convulsions, and the hag was compelled reluctantly to call up the housekeeper (removing meanwhile the implements of the ceremony), and assist in applying all the specifics known at that day, burnt feathers, etc., to restore her. When they had at length succeeded, the housekeeper was dismissed, the door was bolted, and the Collogue was left alone with Anne; the subject of their conference might have been guessed at, but was not known until many years afterwards; but Anne that night held in her hand, in the shape of a weapon with the use of which neither of them was acquainted, an evidence that her chamber had been visited by a being of no earthly form.

This evidence the hag importuned her to destroy, or to remove: but she persisted with fatal tenacity in keeping it. She locked it up, however, immediately, and seemed to think she had acquired a right, since she had grappled so fearfully with the mysteries of futurity, to know all the secrets of which that weapon might yet lead to the disclosure. But from that night it was observed that her character, her manner, and even her countenance, became altered. She grew stern and solitary, shrunk at the sight of her former associates, and imperatively forbade the slightest allusion to the circumstances which had occasioned this mysterious change.

It was a few days subsequent to this event that Anne, who after dinner had left the Chaplain reading the life of St Francis Xavier to Sir Redmond, and retired to her own room to work, and, perhaps, to muse, was surprised to hear the bell at the outer gate ring loudly and repeatedly – a sound she had never heard since her first residence in the Castle; for the few guests who resorted there came and departed as noiselessly as humble visitors at the house of a great man generally do. Straightway there rode up the avenue of elms, which we have already mentioned, a stately gentleman, followed by four servants, all mounted, the two former having pistols in their holsters, and the two latter carrying saddle-bags before them: though it was the first week in November, the dinner hour being one o'clock, Anne had light enough to notice all these circumstances. The arrival of the stranger seemed to cause much, though not unwelcome, tumult in the Castle; orders were loudly and hastily given for the accommodation of the servants and horses – steps were heard traversing the numerous passages for a full hour – then all was still; and it was said that Sir Redmond had locked with his own hand the door of the room where he and the stranger sat, and desired that no one should dare to approach it. About two hours afterwards, a female servant came with orders from her master, to have a plentiful supper ready by eight o'clock, at which he desired the presence of his daughter. The family establishment was on a handsome scale for an Irish house, and Anne had only to descend to the kitchen to order the roasted chickens to be well strewed with brown sugar according to the unrefined fashion of the day, to inspect the mixing of the bowl of sago with its allowance of a bottle of port wine and a large handful of the richest spices, and to order particularly that the pease pudding should have a huge lump of cold salt butter stuck in its centre; and then, her household cares

29

being over, to retire to her room and array herself in a robe of white damask for the occasion. At eight o'clock she was summoned to the supper-room. She came in, according to the fashion of the times, with the first dish; but as she passed through the ante-room, where the servants were holding lights and bearing the dishes, her sleeve was twitched, and the ghastly face of the Collogue pushed close to hers; while she muttered, 'Did not I say he would come for you, dear?' Anne's blood ran cold, but she advanced, saluted her father and the stranger with two low and distinct reverences, and then took her place at the table. Her feelings of awe and perhaps terror at the whisper of her associate were not diminished by the appearance of the stranger; there was a singular and mute solemnity in his manner during the meal. He ate nothing. Sir Redmond appeared constrained, gloomy and thoughtful. At length, starting, he said (without naming the stranger's name), 'You will drink my daughter's health?' The stranger intimated his willingness to have that honour, but absently filled his glass with water; Anne put a few drops of wine into hers, and bowed towards him. At that moment, for the first time since they had met, she beheld his face – it was pale as that of a corpse. The deadly whiteness of his cheeks and lips, the hollow and distant sound of his voice, and the strange lustre of his large dark moveless eyes, strongly fixed on her, made her pause and even tremble as she raised the glass to her lips; she set it down, and then with another silent reverence retired to her chamber.

There she found Bridget Dease, busy in collecting the turf that burned on the hearth, for there was no grate in the apartment. 'Why are you here?' she said, impatiently.

The hag turned on her, with a ghastly grin of congratulation. 'Did not I tell you that he would come for you?'

'I believe he has,' said the unfortunate girl, sinking into the huge wicker chair by her bedside, 'for never did I see mortal with such a look.'

'But is not he a fine stately gentleman?' pursued the hag.

'He looks as if he were not of this world,' said Anne.

'Of this world, or of the next,' said the hag, raising her bony forefinger, 'mark my words – so sure as the – (here she repeated some of the horrible formularies of the 31st of October) – so sure he will be your bridegroom.'

'Then I shall be the bride of a corpse,' said Anne, 'for he I saw tonight is no living man.'

A fortnight elapsed, and whether Anne became reconciled to the features she had thought so ghastly, by the discovery that they were the handsomest she had ever beheld – and that the voice, whose sound at first was so strange and unearthly, was subdued into a tone of plaintive softness when addressing her or whether it is impossible for two young persons with unoccupied hearts to meet in the country, and meet often, to gaze silently on the same stream, wander under the same trees, and listen together to the wind that waves the branches, without experiencing an assimilation of feeling rapidly succeeding an assimilation of taste; or whether it was from all these causes combined, but in less than a month Anne heard the declaration of the stranger's passion with many a blush, though without a sigh. He now avowed his name and rank. He stated himself to be a Scottish Baronet, of the name of Sir Richard Maxwell; family misfortunes had driven him from his country, and forever precluded the possibility of his return: he had transferred his property to Ireland, and purposed to fix his residence there for life. Such was his statement. The courtship of those days was brief and simple. Anne became the wife of Sir Richard, and, I believe, they resided with her father till his death, when they removed to their estate in the North. There they remained for several years, in tranquility and happiness, and had a numerous family. Sir Richard's conduct was marked by but two peculiarities: he not only shunned the intercourse, but the sight of any of his countrymen, and, if he happened to hear that a Scotsman had arrived in the neighbouring town, he shut himself up till assured of the stranger's departure. The other was his custom of retiring to his own chamber, and remaining invisible to his family, on the anniversary of the 31st of October. The lady, who had her own associations connected with that period, only questioned him once on the subject of this seclusion, and was then solemnly and even sternly enjoined never to repeat her inquiry. Matters stood thus, somewhat mysteriously, but not unhappily, when on a sudden, without any cause assigned or assignable, Sir Richard and Lady Maxwell parted, and never more met in this world, nor was she ever permitted to see one of her children to her dying hour. He continued to live at the family mansion and she fixed her residence with a distant relative in a remote part of the country. So total was the disunion that the name of either was never heard to pass the other's lips, from the moment of separation until that of dissolution.

Lady Maxwell survived Sir Richard forty years, living to the great age of ninety-six; and, according to a promise, previously given, disclosed to a descendent with whom she had lived, the following extraordinary circumstances.

She said that on the night of the 31st of October, about seventy-five years before, at the instigation of her ill-advising attendant, she had washed one of her garments in a place where four streams met, and performed other unhallowed ceremonies under the direction of the Collogue, in the expectation that her future husband would appear to her in her chamber at twelve o'clock that night. The critical moment arrived, but with it no lover-like form. A vision of indescribable horror approached her bed, and flinging at her an iron weapon of a shape and construction unknown to her, bade her 'recognise her future husband by that.' The terrors of this visit soon deprived her of her senses; but on her recovery, she persisted, as has been said, in keeping the fearful pledge of the reality of the vision, which, on examination, appeared to be incrusted with blood. It remained concealed in the inmost drawer of her cabinet till the morning of the separation. On that morning, Sir Richard Maxwell rose before daylight to join a hunting party – he wanted a knife for some accidental purpose, and, missing his own, called to Lady Maxwell, who was still in bed, to lend him one. The lady, who was half asleep, answered that in such a drawer of her cabinet he would find one. He went, however, to another, and the next moment she was fully awakened by seeing her husband present the terrible weapon to her throat, and threaten her with instant death unless she disclosed how she came by it. She supplicated for life, and then, in an agony of horror and contrition, told the tale of that eventful night. He gazed at her for a moment with a countenance which rage, hatred, and despair converted, as she avowed, into a living likeness of the demon-visage she had once beheld (so singularly was the fated resemblance fulfilled), and then exclaiming, 'You won me by the devil's aid, but you shall not keep me long,' left her – to meet no more in this world. Her husband's secret was not unknown to the lady, though the means by which she became possessed of it were wholly unwarrantable. Her curiosity had been strongly excited by her husband's aversion to his countrymen, and it was so – stimulated by the arrival of a Scottish gentleman in the neighbourhood some time before, who professed himself formerly acquainted with Sir Richard, and spoke mysteriously of the causes that drove him from his country

– that she contrived to procure an interview with him under a feigned name, and obtained from him the knowledge of circumstances which embittered her after-life to its latest hour. His story was this:

Sir Richard Maxwell was at deadly feud with a younger brother; a family feast was proposed to reconcile them, and as the use of knives and forks was then unknown in the Highlands, the company met armed with their dirks for the purpose of carving. They drank deeply; the feast, instead of harmonising, began to inflame their spirits; the topics of old strife were renewed; hands, that at first touched their weapons in defiance, drew them at last in fury, and in the fray, Sir Richard mortally wounded his brother. His life was with difficulty saved from the vengeance of the clan, and he was hurried towards the seacoast, near which the house stood, and concealed there till a vessel could be procured to convey him to Ireland. He embarked on the night of the 31st of October, and while he was traversing the deck in unutterable agony of spirit, his hand accidentally touched the dirk which he had unconsciously worn ever since the fatal night. He drew it, and, praying 'that the guilt of his brother's blood might be as far from his soul as he could fling that weapon from his body,' sent it with all his strength into the air. This instrument he found secreted in the lady's cabinet, and whether he really believed her to have become possessed of it by supernatural means, or whether he feared his wife was a secret witness of his crime, has not been ascertained, but the result was what I have stated.

The separation took place on the discovery: for the rest,

I know not how the truth may be.
I tell the Tale as 'twas told to me.

THE POT OF TULIPS

FITZ JAMES O'BRIEN

(1855)

A wonderfully atmospheric story with a haunting evil at its core. The canker of jealousy spreads its poison to steal life and happiness. Can good triumph and love overcome? The vivid detail and colour of the fine house and gardens contrast strikingly with the wickedness and malice that dwell there. Ghosts, hidden treasure, hate and love – this story is a favourite.

TWENTY-EIGHT YEARS AGO I went to spend the summer at an old Dutch villa which then lifted its head from the wild country that, in present days, has been tamed down into a site for a Crystal Palace. Madison Square was then a wilderness of fields and scrub oak, here and there diversified with tall and stately elms. Worthy citizens who could afford two establishments rusticated in the groves that then flourished where ranks of brownstone porticos now form the landscape; and the locality of 40th Street, where my summer palace stood, was justly looked upon as at an enterprising distance from the city.

I had had an imperious desire to live in this house ever since I could remember. I had often seen it when a boy, and its cool verandas and quaint garden seemed, whenever I passed, to attract me irresistibly. In after years, when I grew up to man's estate, I was not sorry, therefore, when one summer, fatigued with the labours of my business, I beheld a notice in the papers intimating that it was to be let furnished. I hastened to my dear friend Jasper Joye, painted the delights of this rural retreat in the most glowing colours, easily obtained his assent to share the enjoyments and the expense with me, and a month afterwards we were taking our ease in this new paradise.

Independent of early associations, other interests attached me to this house. It was somewhat historical, and had given shelter to George Washington on the occasion of one of his visits to the city. Furthermore, I knew the descendants of the family to whom it had originally belonged. Their history was strange and mournful, and it seemed to me as if their individuality was somehow shared by the edifice. It had been built by a Mr Van Koeren, a gentleman of Holland, the younger son of a rich mercantile firm at the Hague, who had emigrated to this country in order to establish a branch of his father's business in New York, which even then gave indications of the prosperity it has since reached with such marvellous rapidity. He had brought with him a fair young Belgian wife; a loving girl, if I may believe her portrait, with soft brown eyes, chestnut hair, and a deep, placid contentment spreading over her fresh and innocent features. Her son, Alain Van Koeren, had her picture – an old miniature in a red-gold frame – as well as that of his father, and in truth, when looking on the two, one could not conceive a greater contrast than must have existed between husband and wife. Mr Van Koeren must have been a man of terrible will and gloomy temperament. His face in the picture is dark and austere, his eyes deep-sunken, and burning as if with a slow, inward fire. The lips are thin and compressed, with much determination of purpose; and his chin, boldly salient, is brimful of power and resolution. When first I saw those two pictures I sighed inwardly and thought, 'Poor child! You must often have sighed for the sunny meadows of Brussels, in the long, gloomy nights spent in the company of that terrible man!'

I was not far wrong, as I afterwards discovered. Mr and Mrs Van Koeren were very unhappy. Jealousy was his monomania, and they had scarcely been married before his girl-wife began to feel the oppression of a gloomy and ceaseless tyranny. Every man under fifty, whose hair was not white and whose form was erect, was an object of suspicion to this Dutch Bluebeard. Not that he was vulgarly jealous. He did not frown at his wife before strangers, or attack her with reproaches in the midst of her festivities. He was too well-bred a man to bare his private woes to the world. But at night, when the guests had departed and the dull light of the quaint old Flemish lamps but half illuminated the nuptial chamber, then it was that with monotonous invective Mr Van Koeren crushed his wife. And Marie, weeping and silent, would sit on the edge of the bed listening to the cold, trenchant irony of her husband, who, pacing up and down the room, would now and then stop in his walk to gaze with his burning eyes upon the pallid face of his victim. Even the evidences that Marie gave of becoming a mother did not check him. He saw in that coming event, which most husbands anticipate with mingled joy and fear, only an approaching incarnation of his dishonour. He watched with a horrible refinement of suspicion for the arrival of that being in whose features he madly believed he should but too surely trace the evidences of his wife's crime.

Whether it was that these ceaseless attacks wore out her strength, or that Providence wished to add another chastening misery to her burden of woe, I dare not speculate; but it is certain that one luckless night Mr Van Koeren learned with fury that he had become a father two months before the allotted time.

During his first paroxysm of rage, on the receipt of intelligence which seemed to confirm all his previous suspicions, it was, I believe, with difficulty that he was prevented from slaying both the innocent causes of his resentment. The caution of his race and the presence of the physicians induced him, however, to put a curb upon his furious will until reflection suggested quite as criminal, if not as dangerous, a vengeance. As soon as his poor wife had recovered from her illness, unnaturally prolonged by the delicacy of constitution induced by previous mental suffering, she was astonished to find, instead of increasing his persecutions, that her husband had changed his tactics and treated her with studied neglect. He rarely spoke to her except on occasions when the decencies of society demanded that he should address her. He avoided her presence, and no longer inhabited the same apartments. He seemed, in short, to strive as much as possible to forget her existence. But if she did not suffer from personal ill-treatment it was because a punishment more acute was in store for her. If Mr Van Koeren had chosen to affect to consider her beneath his vengeance, it was because his hate had taken another direction, and seemed to have derived increased intensity from the alteration. It was upon the unhappy boy, the cause of all this misery, that the father lavished a terrible hatred.

Mr Van Koeren seemed determined that if this child sprang from other loins than his the mournful destiny which he forced upon him should amply avenge his own existence and the infidelity of his mother. While the child was an infant his plan seemed to have been formed. Ignorance and neglect were the two deadly influences with which he sought to assassinate the moral nature of this boy; and his terrible campaign against the virtue of his own son was, as he grew up, carried into execution with the most consummate generalship. He gave him money, but debarred him from education.

He allowed him liberty of action, but withheld advice. It was in vain that his mother, who foresaw the frightful consequences of such a training, sought in secret by every means in her power to nullify her husband's attempts. She strove in vain to seduce her son into an ambition to be educated. She beheld with horror all her agonised efforts frustrated, and saw her son and only child becoming, even in his youth, a drunkard and a libertine. In the end it proved too much for her strength; she sickened, and went home to her sunny Belgian plains. There she lingered for a few months in a calm but rapid decay, whose calmness was broken but by the one grief; until one autumn day, when the leaves were falling from the limes, she made a little prayer for her son to the good God, and died. Vain orison! Spendthrift, gamester, libertine and drunkard by turns, Alain Van Koeren's earthly destiny was unchangeable. The father, who should have been his guide, looked on each fresh depravity of his son's with a species of grim delight. Even the death of his wronged wife had no effect upon his fatal purpose. He still permitted the young man to run blindly to destruction by the course into which he himself had led him.

As years rolled by, and Mr Van Koeren himself approached to that time of life when he might soon expect to follow his persecuted wife, he relieved himself of the hateful presence of his son altogether. Even the link of a systematic vengeance, which had hitherto united them, was severed, and Alain was cast adrift without either money or principle. The occasion of this final separation between father and son was the marriage of the latter with a girl of humble, though honest extraction. This was a good excuse for the remorseless Van Koeren, so he availed himself of it by turning his son out of doors.

From that time forth they never met. Alain lived a life of meagre dissipation, and soon died, leaving behind him one child, a daughter.

By a coincidence natural enough, Mr Van Koeren's death followed his son's almost immediately. He died as he had lived, sternly. But those who were around his couch in his last moments mentioned some singular facts connected with the manner of his death. A few moments before he expired, he raised himself in the bed, and seemed as if conversing with some person invisible to the spectators. His lips moved as if in speech, and immediately afterwards he sank back, bathed in a flood of tears. 'Wrong! Wrong!' he was heard to mutter, feebly; then he implored passionately the forgiveness of someone who, he said, was present. The death struggle ensued almost immediately, and in the midst of his agony he seemed wrestling for speech. All that could be heard, however, were a few broken words. 'I was wrong. My unfounded … For God's sake look in … You will find … ' Having uttered these fragmentary sentences, he seemed to feel that the power of speech had passed away forever. He fixed his eyes piteously on those around him, and, with a great sigh of grief, expired. I gathered these facts from his granddaughter and Alain's daughter, Alice Van Koeren, who had been summoned by some friend to her grandfather's dying couch when it was too late. It was the first time she had seen him, and then she saw him die.

The results of Mr Van Koeren's death were a nine days' wonder to all the merchants in New York. Beyond a small sum in the bank, and the house in which he lived, which was mortgaged for its full value, Mr Van Koeren had died a pauper! To those who knew him and knew his affairs, this seemed inexplicable. Five or six years before his death he had retired from business with a fortune of several hundred thousand dollars. He had lived quietly since then, was known not to have speculated, and could not have gambled. The question then was where had his wealth vanished to? Search was made in every secretary, in every bureau, for some document which might throw a light on the mysterious disposition that he had made of his property. None was found. Neither will, nor certificates of stock, nor title deeds, nor bank accounts, were anywhere discernible. Enquiries were made at the offices of companies in which Mr Van Koeren was known to be largely interested; he had sold out his stock years ago. Real estate that had been believed to be his was found on investigation to have passed into other hands. There could be no doubt that for some years past Mr Van Koeren had been steadily converting all his property into money, and what he had done with that money no one knew. Alice Van Koeren and her mother, who at the old gentleman's death were at first looked on as millionaires, discovered, when all was over, that they were no better off than before. It was evident that the old man, determined that one whom, though bearing his name, he believed not to be of his blood, should never inherit his wealth or any share of it, had made away with his fortune before his death, a posthumous vengeance which was the only one by which the laws of the State of New York relative to inheritance could be successfully evaded. I took a peculiar interest in the case, and even helped to make some researches for the lost property, not so much, I confess, from a spirit of general philanthropy, as from certain feelings which I experienced toward Alice Van Koeren, the heir to this invisible estate. I had long known both her and her mother, when they were living in honest poverty and earning a scanty subsistence by their own labour; Mrs Van Koeren working as an embroideress, and Alice turning to account, as a preparatory governess, the education which her good mother, spite of her limited means, had bestowed on her.

In a few words, then, I loved Alice Van Koeren, and was determined to make her my wife as soon as my means would allow me to support a fitting establishment. My passion had never been declared.

I was content for the time with the secret consciousness of my own love, and the no less grateful certainty that Alice returned it, all unuttered as it was. I had, therefore, a double interest in passing the summer at the old Dutch villa, for I felt it to be connected somehow with Alice, and I could not forget the singular desire to inhabit it which I had so often experienced as a boy.

It was a lovely day in June when Jasper Joye and I took up our abode in our new residence; and as we smoked our cigars on the piazza in the evening we felt for the first time the unalloyed pleasure with which a townsman breathes the pure air of the country.

The house and grounds had a quaint sort of beauty that to me was eminently pleasing. Landscape gardening, in the modern acceptation of the term, was then almost unknown in this country, and the 'laying out' of the garden that surrounded our new home would doubtless have shocked Mr London, the late Mr Downing or Sir Thomas Dick Lauder. It was formal and artificial to the last degree. The beds were cut into long parallelograms, rigid and severe of aspect, and edged with prim rows of stiff dwarf box. The walks, of course, crossed always at right angles, and the laurel and cypress trees that grew here and there were clipped into cones and spheres and rhomboids. It is true that, at the time my friend and I hired the house, years of neglect had restored to this formal garden somewhat of the raggedness of nature. The box edgings were rank and wild. The clipped trees, forgetful of geometric propriety, flourished into unauthorised boughs and rebel offshoots. The walks were green with moss, and the beds of Dutch tulips, which had been planted in the shape of certain gorgeous birds, whose colours were represented by masses of blossoms, each of a single hue, had transgressed their limits, and the purple of a parrot's wings might have been seen running recklessly into the crimson of his head; while, as bulbs, however well-bred, will create other bulbs, the flower-birds of this queer old Dutch garden became in time abominably distorted in shape: flamingoes with humps, golden pheasants with legs preternaturally elongated, macaws afflicted with hydrocephalus, each species of deformity being proportioned to the rapidity with which the roots had spread in some particular direction. Still, this strange mixture of raggedness and formality, this conglomerate of nature and art, had its charms. It was pleasant to watch the struggle, as it were, between the opposing elements, and to see nature triumphing by degrees in every direction.

The house itself was pleasant and commodious. Rooms that, though not lofty, were spacious; wide windows, and cool piazzas extending over the four sides of the building; and a collection of antique carved furniture, some of which, from its elaborateness, might well have come from the chisel of Master Grinling Gibbons. There was a mantelpiece in the dining room with which I remember being very much struck when first I came to take possession. It was a singular and fantastical piece of carving – a perfect tropical garden, menagerie and aviary in one. Birds, beasts and flowers were sculptured on the wood with exquisite correctness of detail, and painted with the hues of nature. The Dutch taste for colour was here fully gratified. Parrots, lovebirds, scarlet lories, blue-faced baboons, crocodiles, passionflowers, tigers, Egyptian lilies and Brazilian butterflies were all mixed in gorgeous confusion. The artist, whoever he was, must have been an admirable naturalist, for the ease and freedom of his carving were only equalled by the wonderful accuracy with which the different animals were represented. Altogether it was one of those oddities of Dutch conception, whose strangeness was in this instance redeemed by the excellence of the execution.

Such was the establishment that Jasper Joye and myself were to inhabit for the summer months.

'What a strange thing it was,' said Jasper, as we lounged on the piazza together the night of our arrival, 'that old Van Koeren's property should never have turned up!'

'It is a question with some people whether he had any at his death,' I answered.

'Pshaw! Everyone knows that he did not or could not have lost that with which he retired from business.'

'It is strange,' said I, thoughtfully, 'yet every possible search has been made for documents that might throw light on the mystery. I have myself sought in every quarter for traces of this lost wealth, but in vain.'

'Perhaps he buried it,' suggested Jasper, laughing. 'If so, we may find it here in a hole one fine morning.'

'I think it much more likely that he destroyed it,' I replied. 'You know he never could be got to believe that Alain Van Koeren was his son, and I believe him quite capable of having flung all his money into the sea in order to prevent those whom he considered not of his blood inheriting it, which they must have done under our laws.'

'I am sorry that Alice did not become an heiress, both for your sake and hers. She is a charming girl.'

Jasper, from whom I concealed nothing, knew of my love. 'As to that,' I answered, 'it is little matter. I shall in a year or two be independent enough to marry, and can afford to let Mr Van Koeren's cherished gold sleep wherever he has concealed it.'

'Well, I'm off to bed,' said Jasper, yawning. 'This country air makes one sleepy early. Be on the lookout for trapdoors and all that sort of thing, old fellow. Who knows but the old chap's dollars will turn up. Good-night!'

'Good-night, Jasper!'

So we parted for the night. He to his room, which lay on the west side of the building; I to mine on the east, situated at the end of a long corridor and exactly opposite to Jasper's.

The night was very still and warm. The clearness with which I heard the song of the katydid and the croak of the bullfrog seemed to make the silence more distinct. The air was dense and breathless, and, although longing to throw wide my windows, I dared not; for, outside, the ominous trumpetings of an army of mosquitoes sounded threateningly.

I tossed on my bed oppressed with the heat; kicked the sheets into every spot where they ought not to be; turned my pillow every two minutes in the hope of finding a cool side; in short, did everything that a man does when he lies awake on a very hot night and cannot open his window.

Suddenly, in the midst of my miseries, and when I had made up my mind to fling open the casement in spite of the legion of mosquitoes that I knew were hungrily waiting outside, I felt a continuous stream of cold air blowing upon my face. Luxurious as the sensation was, I could not help starting as I felt it. Where could this draught come from? The door was closed; so were the windows. It did not come from the direction of the fireplace, and, even if it did, the air without was too still to produce so strong a current. I rose in my bed and gazed round the room, the whole of which, though only lit by a dim twilight, was still sufficiently visible. I thought at first it was a trick of Jasper's, who might have provided himself with a bellows or a long tube; but a careful investigation of the apartment convinced me that no one was present. Besides, I had locked the door, and it was not likely that anyone had been concealed in the room before I entered it. It was exceedingly strange; but still the draught of cool wind blew on my face and chest, every now and then changing its direction, sometimes on one side, sometimes on the other. I am not constitutionally nervous, and had been too long accustomed to reflect on philosophical subjects to become the prey of fear in the presence of mysterious phenomena. I had devoted much time to the investigation of what are popularly called supernatural matters by those who have not reflected or examined them sufficiently to discover that none of these apparent miracles are supernatural, but all, however singular, directly dependent on certain natural laws. I became speedily convinced, therefore, as I sat up in my bed peering into the dim recesses of my chamber, that this mysterious wind was the effect or forerunner of a supernatural visitation, and I mentally determined to investigate it, as it developed itself, with a philosophical calmness.

'Is anyone in this room?' I asked, as distinctly as I could. No reply; while the cool wind still swept over my cheek. I knew, in the case of Elizabeth Eslinger, who was visited by an apparition while in the Weinsberg jail, and whose singular and apparently authentic experiences were made the subject of a book by Dr Kerner, that the manifestation of the spirit was invariably accompanied by such a breezy sensation as I now experienced. I therefore gathered my will, as it were, into a focus, and endeavoured, as much as lay in my power, to put myself in accord with the disembodied spirit, if such there were, knowing that on such conditions alone would it be enabled to manifest itself to me.

Presently it seemed as if a luminous cloud was gathering in one corner of the room, a sort of dim phosphoric vapour, shadowy and ill-defined. It changed its position frequently, sometimes coming nearer and at others retreating to the farthest end of the room. As it grew intenser and more radiant, I observed a sickening and corpse-like odour diffuse itself through the chamber, and, despite my anxiety to witness this phenomenon undisturbed, I could with difficulty conquer a feeling of faintness which oppressed me.

The luminous cloud now began to grow brighter and brighter as I gazed. The horrible odour of which I have spoken did not cease to oppress me, and gradually I could discover certain lines making themselves visible in the midst of this lambent radiance. These lines took the form of a human figure, a tall man, clothed in a long dressing-robe, with a pale countenance, burning eyes, and a very bold and prominent chin. At a glance I recognised the original of the picture of old Van Koeren that I had seen with Alice. My interest was now aroused to the highest point; I felt that I stood face to face with a spirit, and doubted not that I should learn the fate of the old man's mysteriously concealed wealth.

The spirit presented a very strange appearance. He himself was not luminous, except some tongues of fire that seemed to proceed from the tips of his fingers, but was completely surrounded by a thin gauze of light, so to speak, through which his outlines were visible. His head was bare, and his white hair fell in huge masses around his stern, saturnine face. As he moved on the floor, I distinctly heard a strange crackling sound, such as one hears when a substance has been overcharged with electricity. But the circumstance that seemed to me most incomprehensible connected with the apparition was that Van Koeren held in both hands a curiously painted flowerpot, out of which sprang a number of the most beautiful tulips in full blossom. He seemed very uneasy and agitated, and moved about the room as if in pain, frequently bending over the pot of tulips as if to inhale their odour, then holding it out to me, seemingly in the hope of attracting my attention to it. I was, I confess, very much puzzled. I knew that Mr Van Koeren had in his lifetime devoted much of his leisure to the cultivation of flowers, importing from

Holland the most expensive and rarest bulbs; but how this innocent fancy could trouble him after death I could not imagine. I felt
assured, however, that some important reason lay at the bottom of
this spectral eccentricity, and determined to fathom it if I could.

'What brings you here?' I asked audibly; directing mentally, however, at the same time, the question to the spirit with all the power of
my will. He did not seem to hear me, but still kept moving uneasily
about, with the crackling noise I have mentioned, and holding the
pot of tulips towards me.

'It is evident,' I said to myself, 'that I am not sufficiently in accord
with this spirit for him to make himself understood by speech. He
has, therefore, recourse to symbols. The pot of tulips is a symbol.
But of what?'

Thus reflecting on these things, I continued to gaze upon the
spirit. While I was observing him attentively, he approached my
bedside by a rapid movement, and laid one hand on my arm. The
touch was icy cold, and pained me at the moment. Next morning
my arm was swollen, and marked with a round blue spot. Then,
passing to my bedroom door, the spirit opened it and went out,
shutting it behind him. Catching for a moment at the idea that I
was the dupe of a trick, I jumped out of bed and ran to the door. It
was locked with the key on the inside, and a brass safety-bolt, which
lay above the lock, shot safely home. All was as I had left it on going
to bed. Yet I declare most solemnly that, as the ghost made his exit,
I not only saw the door open, but I saw the corridor outside, and
distinctly observed a large picture of William of Orange that hung
just opposite to my room. This to me was the most curious portion
of the phenomena I had witnessed. Either the door had been opened
by the ghost, and the resistance of physical obstacles overcome in
some amazing manner, because in this case the bolts must have been

replaced when the ghost was outside the door, or he must have had a sufficient magnetic accord with my mind to impress upon it the belief that the door was opened, and also to conjure up in my brain the vision of the corridor and the picture, features that I should have seen if the door had been opened by any ordinary physical agency.

The next morning at breakfast I suppose my manner must have betrayed me, for Jasper said to me, after staring at me for some time, 'Why, Harry Escott, what's the matter with you? You look as if you had seen a ghost!'

'So I have, Jasper.'

Jasper, of course, burst into laughter, and said he'd shave my head and give me a shower-bath.

'Well, you may laugh,' I answered, 'but you shall see it tonight, Jasper.'

He became serious in a moment – I suppose there was something earnest in my manner that convinced him that my words were not idle – and asked me to explain. I described my interview as accurately as I could.

'How did you know that it was old Van Koeren?' he asked.

'Because I have seen his picture a hundred times with Alice,' I answered, 'and this apparition was as like it as it was possible for a ghost to be like a miniature.'

'You must not think I am laughing at you, Harry,' he continued, 'but I wish you would answer this. We have all heard of ghosts, ghosts of men, women, children, dogs, horses, in fact every living animal; but hang me if ever I heard of the ghost of a flowerpot before.'

'My dear Jasper, you would have heard of such things if you had studied such branches of learning. All the phenomena I witnessed last night are supportable by well-authenticated facts. The cool wind has attended the appearance of more than one ghost, and Baron Reichenbach asserts that his patients, who you know are for the most part sensitive to apparitions, invariably feel this wind when a magnet is brought close to their bodies. With regard to the flowerpot about which you make so merry, it is to me the least wonderful portion of the apparition. When a ghost is unable to find a person of sufficient receptivity, in order to communicate with him by speech it is obliged to have recourse to symbols to express its wishes. These it either creates by some mysterious power out of the surrounding atmosphere, or it impresses, by magnetic force on the mind of the person it visits, the form of the symbol it is anxious to have represented. There is an instance mentioned by Jung Stilling of a student at Brunswick who appeared to a professor of his college with a picture in his hands, which picture had a hole in it that the ghost thrust his head through. For a long time this symbol was a mystery, but the student was persevering, and appeared every night with his head through the picture, until at last it was discovered that, before he died, he had got some painted slides for a magic lantern from a shopkeeper in the town, which had not been paid for at his death; and when the debt had been discharged, he and his picture vanished forevermore. Now here was a symbol distinctly bearing on the question at issue. This poor student could find no better way of expressing his uneasiness at the debt for the painted slides than by thrusting his head through a picture. How he conjured up the picture I cannot pretend to explain, but that it was used as a symbol is evident.'

'Then you think the flowerpot of old Van Koeren is a symbol?'

'Most assuredly; the pot of tulips he held was intended to express that which he could not speak. I think it must have had some reference to his missing property, and it is our business to discover in what manner.'

'Let us go and dig up all the tulip beds,' said Jasper. 'Who knows but he may have buried his money in one of them.'

I grieve to say that I assented to Jasper's proposition, and on that eventful day every tulip in that quaint old garden was ruthlessly uprooted. The gorgeous macaws, and ragged parrots, and long-legged pheasants, so cunningly formed by those brilliant flowers, were that day exterminated. Jasper and I had a regular battle amidst this floral preserve, and many a splendid bird fell before our unerring spades. We, however, dug in vain. No secret coffer turned up out of the deep mould of the flowerbeds. We evidently were not on the right scent. Our researches for that day terminated, and Jasper and I waited impatiently for the night.

It was arranged that Jasper should sleep in my room. I had a bed rigged up for him near my own, and I was to have the additional assistance of his senses in the investigation of the phenomena that we so confidently expected to appear.

The night came. We retired to our respective couches, after carefully bolting the doors, and subjecting the entire apartment to the strictest scrutiny, rendering it totally impossible that a secret entrance should exist unknown to us. We then put out the lights, and awaited the apparition.

We did not remain in suspense long. About twenty minutes after we retired to bed, Jasper called out, 'Harry, I feel the cool wind!'

'So do I,' I answered, for at that moment a light breeze seemed to play across my temples.

'Look, look, Harry!' continued Jasper in a tone of painful eagerness, 'I see a light there in the comer!'

It was the phantom. As before, the luminous cloud appeared to gather in the room, growing more and more intense each minute. Presently the dark lines mapped themselves out, as it were, in the midst of this pale, radiant vapour, and there stood Mr Van Koeren, ghastly and mournful as ever, with the pot of tulips in his hands.

'Do you see it?' I asked Jasper.

'My God! Yes,' said Jasper, in a low voice. 'How terrible he looks!'

'Can you speak to me, tonight?' I said, addressing the apparition, and again concentrating my will upon my question. 'If so, unburden yourself. We will assist you, if we can.'

There was no reply. The ghost preserved the same sad, impassive countenance; he had heard me not. He seemed in great distress on this occasion, moving up and down, and holding out the pot of tulips imploringly towards me, each motion of his being accompanied by the crackling noise and the corpse-like odour. I felt sorely troubled myself to see this poor spirit torn by an endless grief, so anxious to communicate to me what lay on his soul, and yet debarred by some occult power from the privilege.

'Why, Harry,' cried Jasper after a silence, during which we both watched the motions of the ghost intently, 'why, Harry, my boy, there are two of them!'

Astonished by his words, I looked around, and became immediately aware of the presence of a second luminous cloud, in the midst of which I could distinctly trace the figure of a pale but lovely woman. I needed no second glance to assure me that it was the unfortunate wife of Van Koeren.

'It is his wife, Jasper,' I replied. 'I recognise her, as I have recognised her husband, by the portrait.'

'How sad she looks!' exclaimed Jasper in a low voice.

She did indeed look sad. Her face, pale and mournful, did not, however, seem convulsed with sorrow, as was her husband's. She seemed to be oppressed with a calm grief, and gazed with a look of interest that was painful in its intensity on Van Koeren. It struck me, from his air, that though she saw him he did not see her. His whole attention was concentrated on the pot of tulips, while Mrs Van Koeren, who floated at an elevation of about three feet from the floor, and thus over-topped her husband, seemed equally absorbed in the contemplation of his slightest movement. Occasionally she would turn her eyes on me, as if to call my attention to her companion, and then, returning, gaze on him with a sad, womanly, half-eager smile, that to me was inexpressibly mournful.

There was something exceedingly touching in this strange sight; these two spirits so near, yet so distant. The sinful husband torn with grief and weighed down with some terrible secret, and so blinded by the grossness of his being as to be unable to see the wife-angel who was watching over him; while she, forgetting all her wrongs, and attracted to earth by perhaps the same human sympathies, watched from a greater spiritual height, and with a tender interest, the struggles of her suffering spouse.

'By Jove!' exclaimed Jasper, jumping from his bed, 'I know what it means now.'

'What does it mean?' I asked, as eager to know as he was to communicate.

'Well, that flowerpot that the old chap is holding – ' Jasper, I grieve to say, was rather profane.

'Well, what of that flowerpot?'

'Observe the pattern. It has two handles made of red snakes, whose tails twist round the top and form a rim. It contains tulips of three colours, yellow, red, and purple.'

'I see all that as well as you do. Let us have the solution.'

'Well, Harry, my boy! Don't you remember that there is just such a flowerpot, tulips, snakes and all, carved on the queer old painted mantelpiece in the dining room?'

'So there is!' and a gleam of hope shot across my brain, and my heart beat quicker.

'Now, as sure as you are alive, Harry, the old fellow has concealed something important behind that mantelpiece.'

'Jasper, if ever I am Emperor of France, I will make you chief of police; your inductive reasoning is magnificent.'

Actuated by the same impulse, and without another word, we both sprang out of bed and lit a candle. The apparitions, if they remained, were no longer visible in the light. Hastily throwing on some clothes, we rushed downstairs to the dining room, determined to have the old mantelpiece down without loss of time. We had scarce entered the room when we felt the cool wind blowing on our faces.

'Jasper,' said I, 'they are here!'

'Well,' answered Jasper, 'that only confirms my suspicions that we are on the right track this time. Let us go to work. See! here's the pot of tulips.'

This pot of tulips occupied the centre of the mantelpiece, and served as a nucleus round which all the fantastic animals sculptured elsewhere might be said to gather. It was carved on a species of raised shield, or boss, of wood, that projected some inches beyond the plane of the remainder of the mantelpiece. The pot itself was painted a brick colour. The snakes were of bronze colour, gilt, and the tulips, yellow, red and purple, were painted after nature with the most exquisite accuracy.

For some time Jasper and I tugged away at this projection without any avail. We were convinced that it was a movable panel of some kind, but yet were totally unable to move it. Suddenly it struck me that we had not yet twisted it. I immediately proceeded to apply all my strength, and after a few seconds of vigorous exertion I had the satisfaction of finding it move slowly round. After I had given it half a dozen turns, to my astonishment the long upper panel of the mantelpiece fell out towards us, apparently on concealed hinges, after the manner of the portion of escritoires that is used as a writing-table. Within were several square cavities sunk in the wall, and lined with wood. In one of these was a bundle of papers.

We seized these papers with avidity, and hastily glanced over them. They proved to be documents vouching for property to the amount of several hundred thousand dollars, invested in the name of Mr Van Koeren in a certain firm at Bremen, who, no doubt, thought by this time that the money would remain unclaimed forever. The desires of these poor troubled spirits were accomplished.

Justice to the child had been given through the instrumentality of the erring father.

The formalities necessary to prove Alice and her mother sole heirs to Mr Van Koeren's estate were briefly gone through, and the poor governess passed suddenly from the task of teaching stupid children to the envied position of a great heiress. I had ample reason afterwards for thinking that her heart did not change with her fortunes.

That Mr Van Koeren became aware of his wife's innocence, just before he died, I have no doubt. How this was manifested I cannot of course say, but I think it highly probable that his poor wife herself was enabled at the critical moment of dissolution, when the link that binds body and soul together is attenuated to the last thread, to put herself in accord with her unhappy husband. Hence his sudden starting up in his bed, his apparent conversation with some invisible being, and his fragmentary disclosures, too broken, however, to be comprehended.

The question of apparitions has been so often discussed that I feel no inclination to enter here upon the truth or fallacy of the ghostly theory. I myself believe in ghosts. Alice my wife believes in them firmly; and if it suited me to do so I could overwhelm you with a scientific theory of my own on the subject, reconciling ghosts and natural phenomena.

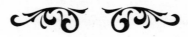

THE GHOST OF A HAND

SHERIDAN LE FANU

(1863)

I have always disliked plump white hands. I never had them, but a least favourite relative did. More charitably, I can blame this prejudice on reading Le Fanu's story as a child and being scared witless. Nightmares ensued that could easily have been attributed to water on the brain. The slow descent of the Prosser family from annoyance into terror was petrifying to a child. But even more terrifying was the fact that only the hand was visible to everyone except the child. The thought of the ghost entire caused many sleepless nights!

ISS REBECCA CHATTESWORTH, in a letter dated late in the autumn of 1753, gives a minute and curious relation of occurrences in the Tiled House, which, it is plain, although at starting she protests against all such fooleries, she has heard with a peculiar sort of particularity.

I was for printing the entire letter, which is really very singular, as well as characteristic. But my publisher meets me with his veto; and I believe he is right. The worthy old lady's letter is, perhaps, too long; and I must rest content with a few hungry notes of its tenor.

That year, and somewhere about the 24th October, there broke out a strange dispute between Mr Alderman Harper, of High Street, Dublin, and my Lord Castlemallard, who, in virtue of his cousinship to the young heir's mother, had undertaken for him the management of the tiny estate on which the Tiled or Tyled House – for I find it spelt both ways – stood.

This Alderman Harper had agreed for a lease of the house for his daughter, who was married to a gentleman named Prosser. He furnished it and put up hangings, and otherwise went to considerable expense. Mr and Mrs Prosser came there some time in June, and after having parted with a good many servants in the interval, she made up her mind that she could not live in the house, and her father waited on Lord Castlemallard, and told him plainly that he would not take out the lease because the house was subjected to annoyances which he could not explain. In plain terms, he said it was haunted, and that no servants would live there more than a few weeks, and that after what his son-in-law's family had suffered there, not only should he be excused from taking a lease of it, but that the house itself ought to be pulled down as a nuisance and the habitual haunt of something worse than human malefactors.

Lord Castlemallard filed a bill in the Equity side of the Exchequer to compel Mr Alderman Harper to perform his contract, by taking out the lease. But the Alderman drew an answer, supported by no less than seven long affidavits, copies of all of which were furnished to his lordship, and with the desired effect; for rather than compel him to place them upon the file of the court, his lordship struck, and consented to release him.

I am sorry the case did not proceed at least far enough to place upon the files of the court the very authentic and unaccountable story which Miss Rebecca relates.

The annoyances described did not begin till the end of August, when, one evening, Mrs Prosser, quite alone, was sitting in the twilight at the back parlour window, which was open, looking out into the orchard, and plainly saw a hand stealthily placed upon the stone windowsill outside, as if by someone beneath the window, at her right side, intending to climb up. There was nothing but the hand, which was rather short, but handsomely formed, and white and plump, laid on the edge of the windowsill; and it was not a very young hand, but one aged somewhere about forty, as she conjectured. It was only a few weeks before that the horrible robbery at Clondalkin had taken place, and the lady fancied that the hand was that of one of the miscreants who was now about to scale the windows of the Tiled House. She uttered a loud scream and an ejaculation of terror, and at the same moment the hand was quietly withdrawn.

Search was made in the orchard, but there were no indications of any person's having been under the window, beneath which, ranged along the wall, stood a great column of flowerpots, which it seemed must have prevented anyone's coming within reach of it.

The same night there came a hasty tapping, every now and then, at the window of the kitchen. The women grew frightened, and the servant-man, taking firearms with him, opened the back door, but discovered nothing. As he shut it, however, he said, 'a thump came on it', and a pressure as of somebody striving to force his way in, which frightened *him*; and though the tapping went on upon the kitchen window panes, he made no further explorations.

About six o'clock on the Saturday evening following, the cook, 'an honest, sober woman, now aged nigh sixty years', being alone in the kitchen, saw, on looking up, it is supposed the same fat but aristocratic-looking hand, laid with its palm against the glass, as if feeling carefully for some inequality in its surface. She cried out, and said something like a prayer on seeing it. But it was not withdrawn for several seconds after.

After this, for a great many nights, there came at first a low, and afterwards an angry rapping, as it seemed with a set of clenched knuckles at the back door. And the servant-man would not open it, but called to know who was there; and there came no answer, only a sound as if the palm of the hand was placed against it, and drawn slowly from side to side with a sort of soft, groping motion.

All this time, sitting in the back parlour, which, for the time, they used as a drawing room, Mr and Mrs Prosser were disturbed by rappings at the window, sometimes very low and furtive, like a clandestine signal, and at others sudden, and so loud as to threaten the breaking of the pane.

This was all at the back of the house, which looked upon the orchard, as you know. But on a Tuesday night, at about half past nine, there came precisely the same rappings at the hall door, and went on, to the great annoyance of the master and terror of his wife, at intervals, for nearly two hours.

After this, for several days and nights, they had no annoyance whatsoever, and began to think that the nuisance had expended itself. But on the night of the 13th September, Jane Easterbrook, an English maid, having gone into the pantry for the small silver bowl in which her mistress's posset was served, happening to look up at the little window of only four panes, observed, through an auger-hole which was drilled through the window frame, for the admission of a bolt to secure the shutter, a white pudgy finger – first the tip, and then the two first joints introduced, and turned about this way and that, crooked against the inside, as if in search of a fastening which its owner designed to push aside. When the maid got back into the kitchen, we are told 'she fell into "a swounde", and was all the next day very weak.'

Mr Prosser, being, I've heard, a hard-headed and conceited sort of fellow, scouted the ghost, and sneered at the fears of his family. He was privately of opinion that the whole affair was a practical joke or a fraud, and waited an opportunity of catching the rogue *flagrante delicto*. He did not long keep this theory to himself, but let it out by degrees with no stint of oaths, and threats, believing that some domestic traitor held the thread of the conspiracy.

Indeed it was time something were done; for not only his servants, but good Mrs Prosser herself, had grown to look unhappy and anxious. They kept at home from the hour of sunset, and would not venture about the house after nightfall, except in couples.

The knocking had ceased for about a week; when one night, Mrs Prosser being in the nursery, her husband, who was in the parlour, heard it begin very softly at the hall door. The air was quite still, which favoured his hearing distinctly. This was the first time there had been any disturbance at that side of the house, and the character of the summons was changed.

Mr Prosser, leaving the parlour door open, it seems, went quietly into the hall. The sound was that of beating on the outside of the stout door, softly and regularly, 'with the flat of the hand'. He was going to open it suddenly but changed his mind; and went back very quietly, and on to the head of the kitchen stair, where was a 'strong closet' over the pantry, in which he kept his firearms, swords, and canes.

Here he called his manservant, whom he believed to be honest, and, with a pair of loaded pistols in his own coat pockets, and giving another pair to him, he went as lightly as he could, followed by the man, and with a stout walking cane in his hand, forward to the door.

Everything went as Mr Prosser wished. The besieger of his house, so far from taking fright at their approach, grew more impatient; and the sort of patting which had aroused his attention at first assumed the rhythm and emphasis of a series of double knocks.

Mr Prosser, angry, opened the door with his right arm across, cane in hand. Looking, he saw nothing; but his arm was jerked up oddly, as it might be with the hollow of a hand, and something passed under it, with a kind of gentle squeeze. The servant neither saw nor felt anything, and did not know why his master looked back so hastily, cutting with his cane, and shutting the door with so sudden a slam.

From that time Mr Prosser discontinued his angry talk and swearing about it, and seemed nearly as averse from the subject as the rest of his family. He grew, in fact, very uncomfortable, feeling an inward persuasion that when, in answer to the summons, he had opened the hall door, he had actually given admission to the besieger.

He said nothing to Mrs Prosser, but went up earlier to his bedroom, 'where he read a while in his Bible, and said his prayers'. I hope the particular relation of this circumstance does not indicate its singularity. He lay awake for a good while, it appears; and, as he supposed, about a quarter past twelve he heard the soft palm of a hand patting on the outside of the bedroom door, and then brushed slowly along it.

Up bounced Mr Prosser, very much frightened, and locked the door, crying, 'Who's there?' but receiving no answer, but the same brushing sound of a soft hand drawn over the panels which he knew only too well.

In the morning the housemaid was terrified by the impression of a hand in the dust of the 'little parlour' table, where they had been unpacking delft and other things the day before. The print of the naked foot in the sea sand did not frighten Robinson Crusoe half so much. They were by this time all nervous, and some of them half-crazed, about the hand.

Mr Prosser went to examine the mark, and made light of it, but, as he swore afterwards, rather to quiet his servants than from any comfortable feeling about it in his own mind; however, he had them all, one by one, into the room, and made each place his or her hand, palm downward, on the same table, thus taking a similar impression from every person in the house, including himself and his wife; and his 'affidavit' deposed that the formation of the hand so impressed differed altogether from those of the living inhabitants of the house, and corresponded with that of the hand seen by Mrs Prosser and by the cook.

Whoever or whatever the owner of that hand might be, they all felt this subtle demonstration to mean that it was declared he was no longer out of doors, but had established himself in the house.

And now Mrs Prosser began to be troubled with strange and horrible dreams, some of which as set out in detail, in Aunt Rebecca's long letter, are really very appalling nightmares. But one night, as Mr Prosser closed his bedchamber door, he was struck somewhat by the utter silence of the room, there being no sound of breathing, which seemed unaccountable to him, as he knew his wife was in bed, and his ears were particularly sharp.

There was a candle burning on a small table at the foot of the bed, besides the one he held in one hand, a heavy ledger, connected with his father-in-law's business, being under his arm. He drew the curtain at the side of the bed, and saw Mrs Prosser lying, as for a few seconds he mortally feared, dead, her face being motionless, white, and covered with a cold dew; and on the pillow, close beside her head, and just within the curtains, was as he first thought, a toad – but really the same fattish hand, the wrist resting on the pillow, and the fingers extended towards her temple.

Mr Prosser, with a horrified jerk, pitched the ledger right at the curtains, behind which the owner of the hand might be supposed to stand. The hand was instantaneously and smoothly snatched away, the curtains made a great wave, and Mr Prosser got round the bed in time to see the closet door, which was at the other side, pulled to by the same white, puffy hand, as he believed.

He drew the door open with a fling, and stared in: but the closet was empty, except for the clothes hanging from the pegs on the wall, and the dressing table and looking-glass facing the windows. He shut it sharply, and locked it, and felt for a minute, he says, 'as if he were like to lose his wits'; then, ringing at the bell, he brought the servants, and with much ado they recovered Mrs Prosser from a sort of 'trance', in which, he says, from her looks, she seemed to have suffered 'the pains of death'; and Aunt Rebecca adds, 'from what she told me of her visions, with her own lips, he might have added, "and of hell also".'

But the occurrence which seems to have determined the crisis was the strange sickness of their eldest child, a little boy aged between two and three years. He lay awake, seemingly in paroxysms of terror, and the doctors, who were called in, set down the symptoms to incipient water on the brain. Mrs Prosser used to sit up with the nurse, by the nursery fire, much troubled in mind about the condition of her child.

His bed was placed sideways along the wall, with its head against the door of a press or cupboard, which, however, did not shut quite close. There was a little valance, about a foot deep, round the top of the child's bed, and this descended within some ten or twelve inches of the pillow on which it lay.

They observed that the little creature was quieter whenever they took it up and held it on their laps. They had just replaced him, as he seemed to have grown quite sleepy and tranquil, but he was not five minutes in his bed when he began to scream in one of his frenzies of terror; at the same moment the nurse, for the first time, detected, and Mrs Prosser equally plainly saw, following the direction of *her* eyes, the real cause of the child's sufferings.

Protruding through the aperture of the press, and shrouded in the shade of the valance, they plainly saw the white fat hand, palm downwards, presented towards the head of the child. The mother uttered a scream, and snatched the child from its little bed, and she and the nurse ran down to the lady's sleeping room, where Mr Prosser was in bed, shutting the door as they entered; and they had hardly done so, when a gentle tap came to it from the outside.

There is a great deal more, but this will suffice. The singularity of the narrative seems to me to be this, that it describes the ghost of a hand, and no more. The person to whom that hand belonged never once appeared; nor was it a hand separated from a body, but only a hand so manifested and introduced that its owner was always, by some crafty accident, hidden from view.

In the year 1819, at a college breakfast, I met a Mr Prosser – a thin, grave, but rather chatty old gentleman, with very white hair drawn back into a pigtail – and he told us all, with a concise particularity, a story of his cousin, James Prosser, who, when an infant, had slept for some time in what his mother said was a haunted nursery in an old house near Chapelizod, and who, whenever he was ill, over-fatigued, or in any wise feverish, suffered all through his life as he had done from a time he could scarcely remember, from a vision of a certain gentleman, fat and pale, every curl of whose wig, every button and fold of whose laced clothes, and every feature and line of whose sensual, benignant, and unwholesome face, was as minutely engraven upon his memory as the dress and lineaments of his own grandfather's portrait, which hung before him every day at breakfast, dinner, and supper.

Mr Prosser mentioned this as an instance of a curiously monotonous, individualised, and persistent nightmare, and hinted the extreme horror and anxiety with which his cousin, of whom he spoke in the past tense as 'poor Jemmie', was at any time induced to mention it.

THE BANSHEE'S WARNING

CHARLOTTE RIDDELL

(1867)

The Banshee, or the Bow, as she is known in my home county of Wexford, was an accepted part of life and death when I was growing up. Tales of her origin and appearance varied but never the belief that she was a harbinger of death. I remember meeting a Wexford man in a Manhattan pub, his local tavern since he emigrated at seventeen, and we talked of the Bow as the world rushed past. He told me that we were related … and we were! Fear of seeing her combing her long silver hair caused many a rush past a graveyard, or even past a low wall on a wide street in Manhattan. As for the version in which a motorcyclist looked around to find her riding pillion, that nearly put me off motorbikes!

ANY A YEAR AGO, before chloroform was thought of, there lived in an old rambling house, in Gerrard Street, Soho, a clever Irishman called Hertford O'Donnell.

After Hertford O'Donnell he was entitled to write, M.R.C.S., for he had studied hard to gain this distinction, and the older surgeons at Guy's (his hospital) considered him one of the most rising operators of the day.

Having said chloroform was unknown at the time this story opens, it will strike my readers that, if Hertford O'Donnell were a rising and successful operator in those days, of necessity he combined within himself a larger number of striking qualities than are by any means necessary to form a successful operator in these.

There was more than mere hand skill, more than even thorough knowledge of his profession, then needful for the man, who, dealing with conscious subjects, essayed to rid them of some of the diseases to which flesh is heir. There was greater courage required in the manipulator of old than is altogether essential at present. Then, as now, a thorough mastery of his instruments, a steady hand, a keen eye, a quick dexterity were indispensable to a good operator; but, added to all these things, there formerly required a pulse which knew no quickening, a mental strength which never faltered, a ready power of adaptation in unexpected circumstances, fertility of resource in difficult cases, and a brave front under all emergencies.

If I refrain from adding that a hard as well as a courageous heart was an important item in the programme, it is only out of deference to general opinion, which, amongst other strange delusions, clings to the belief that courage and hardness are antagonistic qualities.

Hertford O'Donnell, however, was hard as steel. He understood his work, and he did it thoroughly; but he cared no more for quivering nerves and shrinking muscles, for screams of agony, for faces white with pain, and teeth clenched in the extremity of anguish, than he did for the stony countenances of the dead, which so often in the dissecting room appalled younger and less experienced men.

He had no sentiment, and he had no sympathy. The human body was to him, merely an ingenious piece of mechanism, which it was at once a pleasure and a profit to understand. Precisely as Brunel loved the Thames Tunnel, or any other singular engineering feat, so O'Donnell loved a patient on whom he had operated successfully, more especially if the ailment possessed by the patient were of a rare and difficult character.

And for this reason he was much liked by all who came under his hands, since patients are apt to mistake a surgeon's interest in their cases for interest in themselves; and it was gratifying to John Dicks, plasterer, and Timothy Regan, labourer, to be the happy possessors of remarkable diseases, which produced a cordial understanding between them and the handsome Irishman.

If he had been hard and cool at the moment of hacking them to pieces, that was all forgotten or remembered only as a virtue, when, after being discharged from hospital like soldiers who have served in a severe campaign, they met Mr O'Donnell in the street, and were accosted by that rising individual just as though he considered himself nobody.

He had a royal memory, this stranger in a strange land, both for faces and cases; and like the rest of his countrymen, he never felt it beneath his dignity to talk cordially to corduroy and fustian.

In London, as at Calgillan, he never held back his tongue from speaking a cheery or a kindly word. His manners were pliable enough, if his heart were not; and the porters, and the patients, and the nurses, and the students at Guy's were all pleased to see Hertford O'Donnell.

Rain, hail, sunshine, it was all the same; there was a life and a brightness about the man which communicated itself to those with whom he came in contact. Let the mud in the Borough be a foot deep or the London fog as thick as pea-soup, Mr O'Donnell never lost his temper, never muttered a surly reply to the gatekeeper's salutation, but spoke out blithely and cheerfully to his pupils and his patients, to the sick and to the well, to those below and to those above him.

And yet, spite of all these good qualities, spite of his handsome face, his fine figure, his easy address, and his unquestionable skill as an operator, the dons, who acknowledged his talent, shook their heads gravely when two or three of them in private and solemn conclave, talked confidentially of their younger brother.

If there were many things in his favour, there were more in his disfavour. He was Irish – not merely by the accident of birth, which might have been forgiven, since a man cannot be held accountable for such caprices of Nature, but by every other accident and design which is objectionable to the orthodox and respectable and representative English mind.

In speech, appearance, manner, taste, modes of expression, habits of life, Hertford O'Donnell was Irish. To the core of his heart he loved the island which he declared he never meant to revisit; and amongst the English he moved to all intents and purposes a foreigner, who was resolved, so said the great prophets at Guy's, to rush to destruction as fast as he could, and let no man hinder him.

'He means to go the whole length of his tether,' observed one of the ancient wiseacres to another; which speech implied a conviction that Hertford O'Donnell having sold himself to the Evil One, had determined to dive the full length of his rope into wickedness before being pulled to that shore where even wickedness is negative – where there are no mad carouses, no wild, sinful excitements, nothing but impotent wailing and gnashing of teeth.

A reckless, graceless, clever, wicked devil – going to his natural home as fast as in London anyone possibly speed thither; this was the opinion his superiors held of the man who lived all alone with a housekeeper and her husband (who acted as butler) in his big house near Soho.

Gerrard Street – made famous by De Quincey, was not then an utterly shady and forgotten locality; carriage-patients found their way to the rising young surgeon – some great personages thought it not beneath them to fee an individual whose consulting rooms were situated on what was even then considered the wrong side of Regent Street. He was making money, and he was spending it; he was over head and ears in debt – useless, vulgar debt – senselessly contracted, never bravely faced. He had lived at an awful pace ever since he came to London, a pace which only a man who hopes and expects to die young can ever travel.

Life, what good was it? Death, was he a child, or a woman, or a coward, to be afraid of that hereafter? God knew all about the trifle which had upset his coach, better than the dons at Guy's.

Hertford O'Donnell understood the world pretty thoroughly, and the ways thereof were to him as roads often traversed; therefore, when he said that at the Day of Judgment he felt certain he should come off as well as many of those who censured him, it may be assumed, that, although his views of post-mortem punishment were vague, unsatisfactory and infidel, still his information as to the peccadilloes of his neighbours was such as consoled himself.

And yet, living all alone in the old house near Soho Square, grave thoughts would intrude into the surgeon's mind – thoughts which were, so to say, italicised by peremptory letters, and still more peremptory visits from people who wanted money.

Although he had many acquaintances he had no single friend, and accordingly these thoughts were received and brooded over in solitude – in those hours when, after returning from dinner, or supper, or congenial carouse, he sat in his dreary rooms, smoking his pipe and considering means and ways, chances and certainties.

In good truth he had started in London with some vague idea that as his life in it would not be of long continuance, the pace at which he elected to travel could be of little consequence; but the years since his first entry into the Metropolis were now piled one on the top of another, his youth was behind him, his chances of longevity, spite of the way he had striven to injure his constitution, quite as good as ever. He had come to that period in existence, to that narrow strip of tableland, whence the ascent of youth and the descent of age are equally discernible – when, simply because he has lived for so many years, it strikes a man as possible he may have to live for just as many more, with the ability for hard work gone, with the boon companions scattered, with the capacity for enjoying convivial meetings a mere memory, with small means perhaps, with no bright hopes, with the pomp and the circumstance and the fairy carriages, and the glamour which youth flings over earthly objects, faded away like the pageant of yesterday, while the dreary ceremony of living has to be gone through today and tomorrow and the morrow after, as though the gay cavalcade and the martial music, and the glittering helmets and the prancing steeds were still accompanying the wayfarer to his journey's end.

Ah! my friends, there comes a moment when we must all leave the coach, with its four bright bays, its pleasant outside freight, its cheery company, its guard who blows the horn so merrily through villages and along lonely country roads.

Long before we reach that final stage, where the black business claims us for its own special property, we have to bid goodbye to all easy, thoughtless journeying, and betake ourselves, with what zest we may, to traversing the common of reality. There is no royal road across it that ever I heard of. From the king on his throne to the labourer who vaguely imagines what manner of being a king is, we have all to tramp across that desert at one period of our lives, at all events; and that period usually is when, as I have said, a man starts to find the hopes, and the strength, and the buoyancy of youth left behind, while years and years of life lie stretching out before him.

The coach he has travelled by drops him here. There is no appeal, there is no help; therefore, let him take off his hat and wish the new passengers good speed, without either envy or repining.

Behold, he has had his turn, and let whosoever will, mount on the box-seat of life again, and tip the coachman and handle the ribbons – he shall take that pleasant journey no more, no more for ever.

Even supposing a man's springtime to have been a cold and ungenial one, with bitter easterly winds and nipping frosts, biting the buds and retarding the blossoms, still it was spring for all that – spring with the young green leaves sprouting forth, with the flowers unfolding tenderly, with the songs of the birds and the rush of waters, with the summer before and the autumn afar off, and winter remote as death and eternity, but when once the trees have donned their summer foliage, when the pure white blossoms have disappeared, and the gorgeous red and orange and purple blaze of many-coloured flowers fills the gardens, then if there come a wet, dreary day, the idea of autumn and winter is not so difficult to realise. When once twelve o'clock is reached, the evening and night become facts, not possibilities; and it was of the afternoon, and the evening, and the night, Hertford O'Donnell sat thinking on the Christmas Eve, when I crave permission to introduce him to my readers.

A good-looking man ladies considered him. A tall, dark-complexioned, black-haired, straight-limbed, deeply divinely blue-eyed fellow, with a soft voice, with a pleasant brogue, who had ridden like a centaur over the loose stone walls in Connemara, who had danced all night at the Dublin balls, who had walked across the Bennebeola Mountains, gun in hand, day after day, without weariness, who had fished in every one of the hundred lakes you can behold from the top of that mountain near the Recess Hotel, who had led a mad, wild life in Trinity College, and a wilder, perhaps, while 'studying for a doctor' – as the Irish phrase goes – in Edinburgh, and who, after the death of his eldest brother left him free to return to Calgillan, and pursue the usual utterly useless, utterly purposeless, utterly pleasant life of an Irish gentleman possessed of health, birth, and expectations, suddenly kicked over the paternal traces, bade adieu to Calgillan Castle and the blandishments of a certain beautiful Miss Clifden, beloved of his mother, and laid out to be his wife, walked down the avenue without even so much company as a Gossoon to carry his carpet bag, shook the dust from his feet at the lodge gates, and took his seat on the coach, never once looking back at Calgillan, where his favourite mare was standing in the stable, his greyhounds chasing one another round the home paddock, his gun at half-cock in his dressing-room and his fishing-tackle all in order and ready for use.

He had not kissed his mother, or asked for his father's blessing; he left Miss Clifden, arrayed in her brand-new riding habit, without a word of affection or regret; he had spoken no syllable of farewell to any servant about the place; only when the old woman at the lodge bade him good morning and God-blessed his handsome face, he recommended her bitterly to look at it well for she would never see it more.

Twelve years and a half had passed since then, without either Miss Clifden or any other one of the Calgillan people having set eyes on Master Hertford's handsome face.

He had kept his vow to himself; he had not written home; he had not been indebted to mother or father for even a tenpenny piece during the whole of that time; he had lived without friends; and he had lived without God – so far as God ever lets a man live without him.

One thing only he felt to be needful – money; money to keep him when the evil days of sickness, or age, or loss of practice came upon him. Though a spendthrift, he was not a simpleton; around him he saw men, who, having started with fairer prospects than his own, were, nevertheless, reduced to indigence; and he knew that what had happened to others might happen to himself.

An unlucky cut, slipping on a piece of orange peel in the street, the merest accident imaginable, is sufficient to change opulence to beggary in the life's programme of an individual, whose income depends on eye, on nerve, on hand; and, besides the consciousness of this fact, Hertford O'Donnell knew that beyond a certain point in his profession, progress was not easy.

It did not depend quite on the strength of his own bow and shield whether he counted his earnings by hundreds or thousands. Work may achieve competence; but mere work cannot, in a profession, at all events, compass fortune.

He looked around him, and he perceived that the majority of great men – great and wealthy – had been indebted for their elevation, more to the accident of birth, patronage, connection, or marriage, than to personal ability.

Personal ability, no doubt, they possessed; but then, little Jones, who lived in Frith Street, and who could barely keep himself and his wife and family, had ability, too, only he lacked the concomitants of success.

He wanted something or someone to puff him into notoriety – a brother at Court – a lord's leg to mend – a rich wife to give him prestige in Society; and in the absence of this something or someone, he had grown grey-haired and faint-hearted while labouring for a world which utterly despises its most obsequious servants.

'Clatter along the streets with a pair of fine horses, snub the middle classes, and drive over the commonalty – that is the way to compass wealth and popularity in England,' said Hertford O'Donnell, bitterly; and as the man desired wealth and popularity, he sat before his fire, with a foot on each hob, and a short pipe in his mouth, considering how he might best obtain the means to clatter along the streets in his carriage, and splash plebeians with mud from his wheels like the best.

In Dublin he could, by means of his name and connection, have done well; but then he was not in Dublin, neither did he want to be. The bitterest memories of his life were inseparable from the very name of the Green Island, and he had no desire to return to it.

Besides, in Dublin, heiresses are not quite so plentiful as in London; and an heiress, Hertford O'Donnell had decided, would do more for him than years of steady work.

A rich wife could clear him of debt, introduce him to fashionable practice, afford him that measure of social respectability which a medical bachelor invariably lacks, deliver him from the loneliness of Gerrard Street, and the domination of Mr and Mrs Coles.

To most men, deliberately bartering away their independence for money seems so prosaic a business that they strive to gloss it over even to themselves, and to assign every reason for their choice, save that which is really the influencing one.

Not so, however, with Hertford O'Donnell. He sat beside the fire scoffing over his proposed bargain – thinking of the lady's age, her money bags, her desirable house in town, her seat in the country, her snobbishness, her folly.

'It would be a fitting ending,' he sneered, 'and why I did not settle the matter tonight passes my comprehension. I am not a fool, to be frightened with old women's tales; and yet I must have turned white. I felt I did, and she asked me whether I were ill. And then to think of my being such an idiot as to ask her if she had heard anything like a cry, as though she would be likely to hear *that*, she with her poor parvenu blood, which I often imagine must have been mixed with some of her father's strong pickling vinegar. What the deuce could I have been dreaming about? I wonder what it really was.' And Hertford O'Donnell pushed his hair back off his forehead, and took another draught from the too familiar tumbler, which was placed conveniently on the chimney-piece.

'After expressly making up my mind to propose, too!' he mentally continued. 'Could it have been conscience – that myth, which somebody, who knew nothing about the matter, said, "Makes cowards of us all"? I don't believe in conscience; and even if there be such a thing capable of being developed by sentiment and cultivation, why should it trouble me? I have no intention of wronging Miss Janet Price Ingot, not the least. Honestly and fairly I shall marry her; honestly and fairly I shall act by her. An old wife is not exactly an ornamental article of furniture in a man's house; and I do not know that the fact of her being well gilded makes her look any handsomer. But she shall have no cause for complaint; and I will go and dine with her tomorrow, and settle the matter.'

Having arrived at which resolution, Mr O'Donnell arose, kicked down the fire – burning hollow – with the heel of his boot, knocked the ashes out of his pipe, emptied his tumbler, and bethought him it was time to go to bed. He was not in the habit of taking his rest so early as a quarter to twelve o'clock; but he felt unusually weary – tired mentally and bodily – and lonely beyond all power of expression.

'The fair Janet would be better than this,' he said, half aloud; and then, with a start and a shiver, and a blanched face, he turned sharply round, whilst a low, sobbing, wailing cry echoed mournfully through the room. No form of words could give an idea of the sound. The plaintiveness of the Æolian harp – that plaintiveness which so soon affects and lowers the highest spirits – would have seemed wildly gay in comparison with the sadness of the cry which seemed floating in the air. As the summer wind comes and goes amongst the trees, so that mournful wail came and went – came and went. It came in a rush of sound, like a gradual crescendo managed by a skilful musician, and died away in a lingering note, so gently that the listener could scarcely tell the exact moment when it faded into utter silence.

I say faded, for it disappeared as the coastline disappears in the twilight, and there was total stillness in the apartment.

Then, for the first time, Hertford O'Donnell looked at his dog, and beholding the creature crouched into a corner beside the fireplace, called upon him to come out.

His voice sounded strange even to himself, and apparently the dog thought so too, for he made no effort to obey the summons.

'Come here, sir,' his master repeated, and then the animal came crawling reluctantly forward with his hair on end, his eyes almost starting from his head, trembling violently, as the surgeon, who caressed him, felt.

'So you heard it, Brian?' he said to the dog. 'And so your ears are sharper than Miss Ingot's, old fellow. It's a mighty queer thing to think of, being favoured with a visit from a Banshee in Gerrard Street; and as the lady has travelled so far, I only wish I knew whether there is any sort of refreshment she would like to take after her long journey.'

He spoke loudly, and with a certain mocking defiance, seeming to think the phantom he addressed would reply; but when he stopped at the end of his sentence, no sound came through the stillness. There was a dead silence in the room – a silence broken only by the falling of the cinders on the hearth and the breathing of his dog.

'If my visitor would tell me,' he proceeded, 'for whom this lamentation is being made, whether for myself, or for some member of my illustrious family, I should feel immensely obliged. It seems too much honour for a poor surgeon to have such attention paid him. Good Heavens! What is that?' he exclaimed, as a ring, loud and peremptory, woke all the echoes in the house, and brought his housekeeper, in a state of distressing *dishabille*, 'out of her warm bed', as she subsequently stated, to the head of the staircase.

Across the hall Hertford O'Donnell strode, relieved at the prospect of speaking to any living being. He took no precaution of putting up the chain, but flung the door wide. A dozen burglars would have proved welcome in comparison with that ghostly intruder he had been interviewing; therefore, as has been said, he threw the door wide, admitting a rush of wet, cold air, which made poor Mrs Coles' few remaining teeth chatter in her head.

'Who is there? What do you want?' asked the surgeon, seeing no person, and hearing no voice. 'Who is there? Why the devil can't you speak?'

When even this polite exhortation failed to elicit an answer, he passed out into the night and looked up the street and down the street, to see nothing but the driving rain and the blinking lights.

'If this goes on much longer I shall soon think I must be either mad or drunk,' he muttered, as he re-entered the house and locked and bolted the door once more.

'Lord's sake! What is the matter, sir?' asked Mrs Coles, from the upper flight, careful only to reveal the borders of her nightcap to Mr O'Donnell's admiring gaze. 'Is anybody killed? Have you to go out, sir?'

'It was only a runaway ring,' he answered, trying to reassure himself with an explanation he did not in his heart believe.

'Runaway – I'd run away them!' murmured Mrs Coles, as she retired to the conjugal couch, where Coles was, to quote her own expression, 'snoring like a pig through it all'.

Almost immediately afterwards she heard her master ascend the stairs and close his bedroom door.

'Madam will surely be too much of a gentlewoman to intrude here,' thought the surgeon, scoffing even at his own fears; but when he lay down he did not put out his light, and made Brian leap up and crouch on the coverlet beside him.

The man was fairly frightened, and would have thought it no discredit to his manhood to acknowledge as much. He was not afraid of death, he was not afraid of trouble, he was not afraid of danger; but he was afraid of the Banshee; and as he laid with his hand on the dog's head, he recalled the many stories he had been told concerning this family retainer in the days of his youth.

He had not thought about her for years and years. Never before had he heard her voice himself. When his brother died she had not thought it necessary to travel up to Dublin and give him notice of the impending catastrophe. 'If she had, I would have gone down to Calgillan, and perhaps saved his life,' considered the surgeon. 'I wonder who this is for? If for me, that will settle my debts and my marriage. If I could be quite certain it was either of the old people, I would start tomorrow.'

Then vaguely his mind wandered on to think of every Banshee story he had ever heard in his life. About the beautiful lady with the wreath of flowers, who sat on the rocks below Red Castle, in the County Antrim, crying till one of the sons died for love of her; about the Round Chamber at Dunluce, which was swept clean by the Banshee every night; about the bed in a certain great house in Ireland, which was slept in constantly, although no human being ever passed in or out after dark; about that General Officer who, the night before Waterloo, said to a friend, 'I have heard the Banshee, and shall not come off the field alive tomorrow; break the news gently to poor Carry; and who, nevertheless, coming safe off the field, had subsequently news about poor Carry broken tenderly and pitifully to him; about the lad, who, aloft in the rigging, hearing through the night a sobbing and wailing coming over the waters, went down to the captain and told him he was afraid they were somehow out of their reckoning, just in time to save the ship, which, when morning broke, they found but for his warning would have been on the rocks. It was blowing great guns, and the sea was all in a fret and turmoil, and they could sometimes see in the trough of the waves, as down a valley, the cruel black reefs they had escaped.

On deck the captain stood speaking to the boy who had saved them, and asking how he knew of their danger; and when the lad told him, the captain laughed, and said her ladyship had been out-witted that time.

But the boy answered, with a grave shake of his head, that the warning was either for him or his, and that if he got safe to port there would be bad tidings waiting for him from home; whereupon the captain bade him go below, and get some brandy and lie down.

He got the brandy, and he lay down, but he never rose again; and when the storm abated – when a great calm succeeded to the previous tempest – there was a very solemn funeral at sea; and on their arrival at Liverpool the captain took a journey to Ireland to tell a widowed mother how her only son died, and to bear his few effects to the poor desolate soul.

And Hertford O'Donnell thought again about his own father riding full-chase across country, and hearing, as he galloped by a clump of plantation, something like a sobbing and wailing. The hounds were in full cry, but he still felt, as he afterwards expressed it, that there was something among those trees he could not pass; and so he jumped off his horse, and hung the reins over the branch of a Scotch fir, and beat the cover well, but not a thing could he find in it.

Then, for the first time in his life, Miles O'Donnell turned his horse's head *from* the hunt, and, within a mile of Calgillan, met a man running to tell him his brother's gun had burst, and injured him mortally.

And he remembered the story also, of how Mary O'Donnell, his great-aunt, being married to a young Englishman, heard the Banshee as she sat one evening waiting for his return; and of how she, thinking the bridge by which he often came home unsafe for horse and man, went out in a great panic, to meet and entreat him to go round by the main road for her sake. Sir Everard was riding along in the moonlight, making straight for the bridge, when he beheld a figure dressed all in white crossing it. Then there was a crash, and the figure disappeared.

The lady was rescued and brought back to the hall; but next morning there were two dead bodies within its walls – those of Lady Eyreton and her stillborn son.

Quicker than I write them, these memories chased one another through Hertford O'Donnell's brain; and there was one more terrible memory than any, which would recur to him, concerning an Irish nobleman who, seated alone in his great townhouse in London, heard the Banshee, and rushed out to get rid of the phantom, which wailed in his ear, nevertheless, as he strode down Piccadilly. And then the surgeon remembered how that nobleman went with a friend to the Opera, feeling sure that there no Banshee, unless she had a box, could find admittance, until suddenly he heard her singing up amongst the highest part of the scenery, with a terrible mournfulness, and a pathos which made the prima donna's tenderest notes seem harsh by comparison.

As he came out, some quarrel arose between him and a famous fire-eater, against whom he stumbled; and the result was that the next afternoon there was a new Lord – vice Lord –, killed in a duel with Captain Bravo.

Memories like these are not the most enlivening possible; they are apt to make a man fanciful, and nervous, and wakeful; but as time ran on, Hertford O'Donnell fell asleep, with his candle still burning, and Brian's cold nose pressed against his hand.

He dreamt of his mother's family – the Hertfords of Artingbury, Yorkshire, far-off relatives of Lord Hertford – so far off that even Mrs O'Donnell held no clue to the genealogical maze.

He thought he was at Artingbury, fishing; that it was a misty summer morning, and the fish rising beautifully. In his dreams he hooked one after another, and the boy who was with him threw them into the basket.

At last there was one more difficult to land than the others; and the boy, in his eagerness to watch the sport, drew nearer and nearer to the brink, while the fisher, intent on his prey, failed to notice his companion's danger.

Suddenly there was a cry, a splash, and the boy disappeared from sight.

Next instant he rose again, however, and then, for the first time, Hertford O'Donnell saw his face.

It was one he knew well.

In a moment he plunged into the water, and struck out for the lad. He had him by the hair, he was turning to bring him back to land, when the stream suddenly changed into a wide, wild, shoreless sea, where the billows were chasing one another with a mad demoniac mirth.

For a while O'Donnell kept the lad and himself afloat. They were swept under the waves, and came up again, only to see larger waves rushing towards them; but through all, the surgeon never loosened his hold, until a tremendous billow, engulfing them both, tore the boy from his grasp.

With the horror of his dream upon him he awoke, to hear a voice quite distinctly:

'Go to the hospital – go at once!'

The surgeon started up in bed, rubbed his eyes, and looked around. The candle was flickering faintly in its socket. Brian, with his ears pricked forward, had raised his head at his master's sudden movement.

Everything was quiet, but still those words were ringing in his ear:

'Go to the hospital – go at once!'

The tremendous peal of the bell overnight, and this sentence, seemed to be simultaneous.

That he was wanted at Guy's – wanted imperatively – came to O'Donnell like an inspiration. Neither sense nor reason had anything to do with the conviction that roused him out of bed, and made him dress as speedily as possible, and grope his way down the staircase, Brian following.

He opened the front door, and passed out into the darkness. The rain was over, and the stars were shining as he pursued his way down Newport Market, and thence, winding in and out in a south-easterly direction, through Lincoln's Inn Fields and Old Square to Chancery Lane, whence he proceeded to St Paul's.

Along the deserted streets he resolutely continued his walk. He did not know what he was going to Guy's for. Some instinct was urging him on, and he neither strove to combat nor control it. Only once did the thought of turning back cross his mind, and that was at the archway leading into Old Square. There he had paused for a moment, asking himself whether he were not gone stark, staring mad; but Guy's seemed preferable to the haunted house in Gerrard Street; and he walked resolutely on, determined to say, if any surprise were expressed at his appearance, that he had been sent for.

Sent for? – Yea, truly; but by whom?

On through Cannon Street; on over London Bridge, where the lights flickered in the river, and the sullen splash of the water flowing beneath the arches, washing the stone piers, could be heard, now the human din was hushed and lulled to sleep. On, thinking of many things: of the days of his youth; of his dead brother; of his father's heavily-encumbered estate; of the fortune his mother had vowed she would leave to some charity rather than to him, if he refused to marry according to her choice; of his wild life in London; of the terrible cry he had heard overnight – that unearthly wail which he could not drive from his memory even when he entered Guy's, and confronted the porter, who said:

'You have been sent for, sir; did you meet the messenger?'

Like one in a dream, Hertford O'Donnell heard him; like one in a dream, also, he asked what was the matter.

'Bad accident, sir; fire; fell off a balcony – unsafe – old building. Mother and child – a son; child with compound fracture of thigh.'

This, the joint information of porter and house surgeon, mingled together, and made a boom in Mr O'Donnell's ears like the sound of the sea breaking on a shingly shore.

Only one sentence he understood properly – 'Immediate amputation necessary.' At this point he grew cool; he was the careful, cautious, successful surgeon, in a moment.

'The child you say?' he answered. 'Let me see him.'

The Guy's Hospital of today may be different to the Guy's Hertford O'Donnell knew so well. Railways have, I believe, swept away the old operating room; railways may have changed the position of the former accident ward, to reach which, in the days of which I am writing, the two surgeons had to pass a staircase leading to the upper stories.

On the lower step of this staircase, partially in shadow, Hertford O'Donnell beheld, as he came forward, an old woman seated.

An old woman with streaming grey hair, with attenuated arms, with head bowed forward, with scanty clothing, with bare feet; who never looked up at their approach, but sat unnoticing, shaking her head and wringing her hands in an extremity of despair.

'Who is that?' asked Mr O'Donnell, almost involuntarily.

'Who is what?' demanded his companion.

'That – that woman,' was the reply.

'What woman?'

'There – are you blind? – seated on the bottom step of the staircase. What is she doing?' persisted Mr O'Donnell.

'There is no woman near us,' his companion answered, looking at the rising surgeon very much as though he suspected him of seeing double.

'No woman!' scoffed Hertford. 'Do you expect me to disbelieve the evidence of my own eyes?' and he walked up to the figure, meaning to touch it.

But as he essayed to do so, the woman seemed to rise in the air and float away, with her arms stretched high up over her head, uttering such a wail of pain, and agony, and distress, as caused the Irishman's blood to curdle.

'My God! Did you hear that?' he said to his companion.

'What?' was the reply.

Then, although he knew the sound had fallen on deaf ears, he answered:

'The wail of the Banshee! Some of my people are doomed!'

'I trust not,' answered the house surgeon, who had an idea, nevertheless, that Hertford O'Donnell's Banshee lived in a whiskey bottle, and would at some not remote day make an end of the rising and clever operator.

With nerves utterly shaken, Mr O'Donnell walked forward to the accident ward. There with his face shaded from the light, lay his patient – a young boy, with a compound fracture of the thigh.

In that ward, in the face of actual danger or pain capable of relief the surgeon had never known faltering or fear; and now he carefully examined the injury, felt the pulse, inquired as to the treatment pursued, and ordered the sufferer to be carried to the operating room.

While he was looking out his instruments he heard the boy lying on the table murmur faintly:

'Tell her not to cry so – tell her not to cry.'

'What is he talking about?' Hertford O'Donnell inquired.

'The nurse says he has been speaking about some woman crying ever since he came in – his mother, most likely,' answered one of the attendants.

'He is delirious then?' observed the surgeon.

'No, sir,' pleaded the boy, excitedly, 'no; it is that woman – that woman with the grey hair. I saw her looking from the upper window before the balcony gave way. She has never left me since, and she won't be quiet, wringing her hands and crying.'

'Can you see her now?' Hertford O'Donnell inquired, stepping to the side of the table. 'Point out where she is.'

Then the lad stretched forth a feeble finger in the direction of the door, where clearly, as he had seen her seated on the stairs, the surgeon saw a woman standing – a woman with grey hair and scanty clothing, and upstretched arms and bare feet.

'A word with you, sir,' O'Donnell said to the house surgeon, drawing him back from the table. 'I cannot perform this operation: send for some other person. I am ill; I am incapable.'

'But,' pleaded the other, 'there is no time to get anyone else. We sent for Mr West, before we troubled you, but he was out of town, and all the rest of the surgeons live so far away. Mortification may set in at any moment, and –'

'Do you think you require to teach me my business?' was the reply. 'I know the boy's life hangs on a thread, and that is the very reason I cannot operate. I am not fit for it. I tell you I have seen tonight that which unnerves me utterly. My hand is not steady. Send for someone else without delay. Say I am ill – dead! – what you please. Heavens! There she is again, right over the boy! Do you hear her?' and Hertford O'Donnell fell fainting on the floor.

How long he lay in that deathlike swoon I cannot say; but when he returned to consciousness, the principal physician of Guy's was standing beside him in the cold grey light of the Christmas morning.

'The boy?' murmured O'Donnell, faintly.

'Now, my dear fellow, keep yourself quiet,' was the reply.

'The boy?' he repeated, irritably. 'Who operated?'

'No one,' Dr Lanson answered. 'It would have been useless cruelty. Mortification had set in, and –'

Hertford O'Donnell turned his face to the wall, and his friend could not see it.

'Do not distress yourself,' went on the physician, kindly. 'Allington says he could not have survived the operation in any case. He was quite delirious from the first, raving about a woman with grey hair and –'

'I know,' Hertford O'Donnell interrupted, 'and the boy had a mother, they told me, or I dreamt it.'

'Yes, she was bruised and shaken, but not seriously injured.'

'Has she blue eyes and fair hair – fair hair all rippling and wavy? Is she white as a lily, with just a faint flush of colour in her cheek? Is she young and trusting and innocent? No; I am wandering. She must be nearly thirty now. Go, for God's sake, and tell me if you can find a woman you could imagine having once been as a girl such as I describe.'

'Irish?' asked the doctor; and O'Donnell made a gesture of assent.

'It is she then,' was the reply, 'a woman with the face of an angel.'

'A woman who should have been my wife,' the surgeon answered, 'whose child was my son'.

'Lord help you!' ejaculated the doctor. Then Hertford O'Donnell raised himself from the sofa where they had laid him, and told his companion the story of his life – how there had been bitter feud between his people and her people – how they were divided by old animosities and by difference of religion – how they had met by stealth, and exchanged rings and vows, all for naught – how his family had insulted hers, so that her father, wishful for her to marry a kinsman of his own, bore her off to a far-away land, and made her write him a letter of eternal farewell – how his own parents had kept all knowledge of the quarrel from him till she was utterly beyond his reach – how they had vowed to discard him unless he agreed to marry according to their wishes – how he left his home, and came to London, and sought his fortune. All this Hertford O'Donnell repeated; and when he had finished, the bells were ringing for morning service – ringing loudly, ringing joyfully, 'Peace on earth, goodwill towards men'.

But there was little peace that morning for Hertford O'Donnell. He had to look on the face of his dead son, wherein he beheld, as though reflected, the face of the boy in his dream.

Afterwards, stealthily he followed his friend, and beheld, with her eyes closed, her cheeks pale and pinched, her hair thinner but still falling like a veil over her, the love of his youth, the only woman he had ever loved devotedly and unselfishly.

There is little space left here to tell of how the two met at last – of how the stone of the years seemed suddenly rolled away from the tomb of their past, and their youth arose and returned to them, even amid their tears.

She had been true to him, through persecution, through contumely, through kindness, which was more trying; through shame, and grief, and poverty, she had been loyal to the lover of her youth; and before the New Year dawned there came a letter from Calgillan, saying that the Banshee's wail had been heard there, and praying Hertford, if he were still alive, to let bygones be bygones, in consideration of the long years of estrangement – the anguish and remorse of his afflicted parents.

More than that. Hertford O'Donnell, if a reckless man, was honourable; and so, on the Christmas Day when he was to have proposed for Miss Ingot, he went to that lady, and told her how he had wooed and won, in the years of his youth, one who after many days was miraculously restored to him; and from the hour in which he took her into his confidence, he never thought her either vulgar or foolish, but rather he paid homage to the woman who, when she had heard the whole tale repeated, said, simply, 'Ask her to come to me till you can claim her – and God bless you both!'

THE CANTERVILLE GHOST

OSCAR WILDE

(1887)

An all-time favourite. Just the tonic needed when the shivers are setting in. A simple question: can ghost stories be fun? For sure, when the family is that of Hiram B. Otis and the ghost is the long-suffering spirit, Sir Simon de Canterville. A ghost with elegantly described graveclothes, meticulously documented armour and an acerbic tongue. Take this tonic regularly, whether or not your hair is standing on end.

HEN MR HIRAM B. OTIS, the American Minister, bought Canterville Chase, everyone told him he was doing a very foolish thing, as there was no doubt at all that the place was haunted. Indeed, Lord Canterville himself, who was a man of the most punctilious honour, had felt it his duty to mention the fact to Mr Otis when they came to discuss terms.

'We have not cared to live in the place ourselves,' said Lord Canterville, 'since my grandaunt, the Dowager Duchess of Bolton, was frightened into a fit, from which she never really recovered, by two skeleton hands being placed on her shoulders as she was dressing for dinner, and I feel bound to tell you, Mr Otis, that the ghost has been seen by several living members of my family, as well as by the rector of the parish, the Reverend Augustus Dampier, who is a Fellow of King's College, Cambridge. After the unfortunate accident to the Duchess, none of our younger servants would stay with us, and Lady Canterville often got very little sleep at night, in consequence of the mysterious noises that came from the corridor and the library.'

'My Lord,' answered the minister, 'I will take the furniture and the ghost at a valuation. I come from a modern country, where we have everything that money can buy; and with all our spry young fellows painting the Old World red, and carrying off your best actresses and prima donnas, I reckon that if there were such a thing as a ghost in Europe, we'd have it at home in a very short time in one of our public museums, or on the road as a show.'

'I fear that the ghost exists,' said Lord Canterville, smiling, 'though it may have resisted the overtures of your enterprising impresarios. It has been well known for three centuries, since 1584 in fact, and always makes its appearance before the death of any member of our family.'

'Well, so does the family doctor for that matter, Lord Canterville. But there is no such thing, sir, as a ghost, and I guess the laws of nature are not going to be suspended for the British aristocracy.'

'You are certainly very natural in America,' answered Lord Canterville, who did not quite understand Mr Otis's last observation, 'and if you don't mind a ghost in the house, it is all right. Only you must remember I warned you.'

A few weeks after this, the purchase was completed, and at the close of the season the minister and his family went down to Canterville Chase. Mrs Otis, who, as Miss Lucretia R. Tappan, of West 53rd Street, had been a celebrated New York belle, was now a very handsome, middle-aged woman, with fine eyes and a superb profile. Many American ladies on leaving their native land adopt an appearance of chronic ill health, under the impression that it is a form of European refinement, but Mrs Otis had never fallen into this error. She had a magnificent constitution, and a really wonderful amount of animal spirits. Indeed, in many respects, she was quite English, and was an excellent example of the fact that we have really everything in common with America nowadays, except, of course, language. Her eldest son, christened Washington by his parents in a moment of patriotism, which he never ceased to regret, was a fair-haired, rather good-looking young man, who had qualified himself for American diplomacy by leading the German at the Newport Casino for three successive seasons, and even in London was well known as an excellent dancer. Gardenias and the peerage were his only weaknesses. Otherwise he was extremely sensible. Miss Virginia E. Otis was a little girl of fifteen, lithe and lovely as a fawn, and with a fine freedom in her large blue eyes. She was a wonderful amazon, and had once raced old Lord Bilton on her pony twice round the park, winning by a length and a half, just in front of the Achilles statue, to the huge delight of the young Duke of Cheshire, who proposed for her on the spot, and was sent back to Eton that very night by his guardians, in floods of tears. After Virginia came the twins, who were usually called 'the Stars and Stripes', as they were always getting swished. They were delightful boys, and with the exception of the worthy minister, the only true republicans of the family.

As Canterville Chase is seven miles from Ascot, the nearest railway station, Mr Otis had telegraphed for a waggonette to meet them, and they started on their drive in high spirits. It was a lovely July evening, and the air was delicate with the scent of the pine woods. Now and then they heard a woodpigeon brooding over its own sweet voice, or saw, deep in the rustling fern, the burnished breast of the pheasant. Little squirrels peered at them from the beech trees as they went by, and the rabbits scudded away through the brushwood and over the mossy knolls, with their white tails in the air. As they entered the avenue of Canterville Chase, however, the sky became suddenly overcast with clouds, a curious stillness seemed to hold the atmosphere, a great flight of rooks passed silently over their heads, and, before they reached the house, some big drops of rain had fallen.

Standing on the steps to receive them was an old woman, neatly dressed in black silk, with a white cap and apron. This was Mrs Umney, the housekeeper, whom Mrs Otis, at Lady Canterville's earnest request, had consented to keep on in her former position. She made them each a low curtsey as they alighted and said, in a quaint, old-fashioned manner, 'I bid you welcome to Canterville Chase.' Following her, they passed through the fine Tudor hall into the library, a long, low room, panelled in black oak, at the end of which was a large stained-glass window. Here they found tea laid out for them, and, after taking off their wraps, they sat down and began to look round, while Mrs Umney waited on them.

Suddenly Mrs Otis caught sight of a dull red stain on the floor just by the fireplace and, quite unconscious of what it really signified, said to Mrs Umney, 'I am afraid something has been spilt there.'

'Yes, madam,' replied the old housekeeper in a low voice, 'blood has been spilt on that spot.'

'How horrid,' cried Mrs Otis. 'I don't at all care for bloodstains in a sitting room. It must be removed at once.'

The old woman smiled, and answered in the same low, mysterious voice, 'It is the blood of Lady Eleanore de Canterville, who was murdered on that very spot by her own husband, Sir Simon de Canterville, in 1575. Sir Simon survived her nine years, and disappeared suddenly under very mysterious circumstances. His body has never been discovered, but his guilty spirit still haunts the Chase. The bloodstain has been much admired by tourists and others, and cannot be removed.'

'That is all nonsense,' cried Washington Otis. 'Pinkerton's Champion Stain Remover and Paragon Detergent will clean it up in no time,' and before the terrified housekeeper could interfere he had fallen upon his knees, and was rapidly scouring the floor with a small stick of what looked like a black cosmetic. In a few moments no trace of the bloodstain could be seen.

'I knew Pinkerton would do it,' he exclaimed triumphantly, as he looked round at his admiring family; but no sooner had he said these words than a terrible flash of lightning lit up the sombre room, a fearful peal of thunder made them all start to their feet, and Mrs Umney fainted.

'What a monstrous climate!' said the American Minister calmly, as he lit a long cheroot. 'I guess the old country is so overpopulated that they have not enough decent weather for everybody. I have always been of opinion that emigration is the only thing for England.'

'My dear Hiram,' cried Mrs Otis, 'what can we do with a woman who faints?'

'Charge it to her like breakages,' answered the minister; 'she won't faint after that,' and in a few moments Mrs Umney certainly came to. There was no doubt, however, that she was extremely upset, and she sternly warned Mr Otis to beware of some trouble coming to the house.

'I have seen things with my own eyes, sir,' she said, 'that would make any Christian's hair stand on end, and many and many a night I have not closed my eyes in sleep for the awful things that are done here.' Mr Otis, however, and his wife warmly assured the honest soul that they were not afraid of ghosts, and, after invoking the blessings of Providence on her new master and mistress, and making arrangements for an increase of salary, the old housekeeper tottered off to her own room.

2

The storm raged fiercely all that night, but nothing of particular note occurred. The next morning, however, when they came down to breakfast, they found the terrible stain of blood once again on the floor. 'I don't think it can be the fault of the Paragon Detergent,' said Washington, 'for I have tried it with everything. It must be the ghost.' He accordingly rubbed out the stain a second time, but the second morning it appeared again. The third morning also it was there, though the library had been locked up at night by Mr Otis himself, and the key carried upstairs. The whole family were now quite interested; Mr Otis began to suspect that he had been too dogmatic in his denial of the existence of ghosts, Mrs Otis expressed her intention of joining the Psychical Society, and Washington prepared a long letter to Messrs Myers and Podmore on the subject of the Permanence of Sanguineous Stains when connected with Crime. That night all doubts about the objective existence of phantasmata were removed forever.

The day had been warm and sunny; and, in the cool of the evening, the whole family went out for a drive. They did not return home till nine o'clock, when they had a light supper. The conversation in no way turned upon ghosts, so there were not even those primary conditions of receptive expectation which so often precede the presentation of psychical phenomena. The subjects discussed, as I have since learned from Mr Otis, were merely such as form the ordinary conversation of cultured Americans of the better class, such as the immense superiority of Miss Fanny Davenport over Sarah Bernhardt as an actress; the difficulty of obtaining green corn, buckwheat cakes and hominy, even in the best English houses; the importance of Boston in the development of the world-soul; the advantages of the baggage-check system in railway travelling; and the sweetness of the New York accent as compared to the London drawl. No mention at all was made of the supernatural, nor was Sir Simon de Canterville alluded to in any way. At eleven o'clock the family retired, and by half-past all the lights were out. Some time after, Mr Otis was awakened by a curious noise in the corridor, out-side his room. It sounded like the clank of metal, and seemed to be coming nearer every moment. He got up at once, struck a match, and looked at the time. It was exactly one o'clock. He was quite calm, and felt his pulse, which was not at all feverish. The strange noise still continued, and with it he heard distinctly the sound of footsteps. He put on his slippers, took a small oblong phial out of his dressing case, and opened the door. Right in front of him he saw, in the wan moonlight, an old man of terrible aspect. His eyes were as red burning coals; long grey hair fell over his shoulders in matted coils; his garments, which were of antique cut, were soiled and ragged, and from his wrists and ankles hung heavy manacles and rusty gyves.

'My dear sir,' said Mr Otis, 'I really must insist on your oiling those chains, and have brought you for that purpose a small bottle of the Tammany Rising Sun Lubricator. It is said to be completely efficacious upon one application, and there are several testimonials to that effect on the wrapper from some of our most eminent native divines. I shall leave it here for you by the bedroom candles, and will be happy to supply you with more should you require it.' With these words the United States Minister laid the bottle down on a marble table, and, closing his door, retired to rest.

For a moment the Canterville ghost stood quite motionless in natural indignation; then, dashing the bottle violently upon the polished floor, he fled down the corridor, uttering hollow groans, and emitting a ghastly green light. Just, however, as he reached the top of the great oak staircase, a door was flung open, two little white-robed figures appeared, and a large pillow whizzed past his head! There was evidently no time to be lost, so, hastily adopting the Fourth Dimension of Space as a means of escape, he vanished through the wainscoting, and the house became quite quiet.

On reaching a small secret chamber in the left wing, he leaned up against a moonbeam to recover his breath, and began to try and realise his position. Never, in a brilliant and uninterrupted career of three hundred years, had he been so grossly insulted. He thought of the Dowager Duchess, whom he had frightened into a fit as she stood before the glass in her lace and diamonds; of the four house-maids, who had gone off into hysterics when he merely grinned at them through the curtains of one of the spare bedrooms; of the rector of the parish, whose candle he had blown out as he was coming late one night from the library, and who had been under the care of Sir William Gull ever since, a perfect martyr to nervous disorders; and of old Madame de Tremouillac, who, having wakened up one morning early and seen a skeleton seated in an armchair by the fire reading her diary, had been confined to her bed for six weeks with an attack of brain fever, and, on her recovery, had become reconciled to the church, and broken off her connection with that notorious sceptic Monsieur de Voltaire. He remembered the ter-rible night when the wicked Lord Canterville was found choking in his dressing room, with the knave of diamonds halfway down his throat, and confessed, just before he died, that he had cheated Charles James Fox out of £50,000 at Crockford's by means of that very card, and swore that the ghost had made him swallow it. All his great achievements came back to him again, from the butler who had shot himself in the pantry because he had seen a green hand tapping at the window pane, to the beautiful Lady Stutfield, who was always obliged to wear a black velvet band round her throat to hide the mark of five fingers burnt upon her white skin, and who drowned herself at last in the carp pond at the end of the King's Walk. With the enthusiastic egotism of the true artist he went over his most celebrated performances, and smiled bitterly to himself as he recalled to mind his last appearance as 'Red Ruben, or the Strangled Babe', his début as 'Gaunt Gibeon, the Bloodsucker of Bexley Moor', and the furore he had excited one lovely June evening by merely playing ninepins with his own bones upon the lawn-tennis ground. And after all this, some wretched modern Americans were to come and offer him the Rising Sun Lubricator, and throw pillows at his head! It was quite unbearable. Besides, no ghosts in history had ever been treated in this manner. Accordingly, he determined to have vengeance, and remained till daylight in an attitude of deep thought.

3

The next morning when the Otis family met at breakfast, they discussed the ghost at some length. The United States Minister was naturally a little annoyed to find that his present had not been accepted. 'I have no wish,' he said, 'to do the ghost any personal injury, and I must say that, considering the length of time he has been in the house, I don't think it is at all polite to throw pillows at him' – a very just remark, at which, I am sorry to say, the twins burst into shouts of laughter. 'Upon the other hand,' he continued, 'if he really declines to use the Rising Sun Lubricator, we shall have to take his chains from him. It would be quite impossible to sleep, with such a noise going on outside the bedrooms.'

For the rest of the week, however, they were undisturbed, the only thing that excited any attention being the continual renewal of the bloodstain on the library floor. This certainly was very strange, as the door was always locked at night by Mr Otis, and the windows kept closely barred. The chameleon-like colour, also, of the stain excited a good deal of comment. Some mornings it was a dull (almost Indian) red, then it would be vermilion, then a rich purple, and once when they came down for family prayers, according to the simple rites of the Free American Reformed Episcopalian Church, they found it a bright emerald green. These kaleidoscopic changes naturally amused the party very much, and bets on the subject were freely made every evening. The only person who did not enter into the joke was little Virginia, who, for some unexplained reason, was always a good deal distressed at the sight of the bloodstain, and very nearly cried the morning it was emerald green.

The second appearance of the ghost was on Sunday night. Shortly after they had gone to bed they were suddenly alarmed by a fearful crash in the hall. Rushing downstairs, they found that a large suit of old armour had become detached from its stand, and had fallen on the stone floor, while, seated in a high-backed chair, was the Canterville ghost, rubbing his knees with an expression of acute agony on his face. The twins, having brought their peashooters with them, at once discharged two pellets on him, with that accuracy of aim which can only be attained by long and careful practice on a writing master, while the United States Minister covered him with his revolver, and called upon him, in accordance with Californian etiquette, to hold up his hands! The ghost started up with a wild shriek of rage, and swept through them like a mist, extinguishing Washington Otis's candle as he passed, and so leaving them all in total darkness. On reaching the top of the staircase he recovered himself, and determined to give his celebrated peal of demoniac laughter. This he had on more than one occasion found extremely useful. It was said to have turned Lord Raker's wig grey in a single night, and had certainly made three of Lady Canterville's French governesses give warning before their month was up. He accordingly laughed his most horrible laugh, till the old vaulted roof rang and rang again, but hardly had the fearful echo died away when a door opened, and Mrs Otis came out in a light blue dressing gown. 'I am afraid you are far from well,' she said, 'and have brought you a bottle of Dr Dobell's tincture. If it is indigestion, you will find it a most excellent remedy.' The ghost glared at her in fury, and began at once to make preparations for turning himself into a large black dog, an accomplishment for which he was justly renowned, and to which the family doctor always attributed the permanent idiocy of Lord Canterville's uncle, the Hon. Thomas Horton. The sound of approaching footsteps, however, made him hesitate in his fell purpose, so he contented himself with becoming faintly phosphorescent, and vanished with a deep churchyard groan, just as the twins had come up to him.

On reaching his room he entirely broke down, and became a prey to the most violent agitation. The vulgarity of the twins, and the gross materialism of Mrs Otis, were naturally extremely annoying, but what really distressed him most was that he had been unable to wear the suit of mail. He had hoped that even modern Americans would be thrilled by the sight of a Spectre In Armour, if for no more sensible reason, at least out of respect for their national poet Longfellow, over whose graceful and attractive poetry he himself had whiled away many a weary hour when the Cantervilles were up in town. Besides, it was his own suit. He had worn it with great success at the Kenilworth tournament, and had been highly complimented on it by no less a person than the Virgin Queen herself. Yet when he had put it on, he had been completely overpowered by the weight of the huge breastplate and steel casque, and had fallen heavily on the stone pavement, barking both his knees severely, and bruising the knuckles of his right hand.

For some days after this he was extremely ill, and hardly stirred out of his room at all, except to keep the bloodstain in proper repair. However, by taking great care of himself, he recovered, and resolved to make a third attempt to frighten the United States Minister and his family. He selected Friday, the 17th of August, for his appearance, and spent most of that day in looking over his wardrobe, ultimately deciding in favour of a large slouched hat with a red feather, a winding-sheet frilled at the wrists and neck, and a rusty dagger. Towards evening a violent storm of rain came on, and the wind was so high that all the windows and doors in the old house shook and rattled. In fact, it was just such weather as he loved. His plan of action was this. He was to make his way quietly to Washington Otis's room, gibber at him from the foot of the bed, and stab himself three times in the throat to the sound of slow music. He bore Washington a special grudge, being quite aware that it was he who was in the habit of removing the famous Canterville bloodstain, by means of Pinkerton's Paragon Detergent. Having reduced the reckless and foolhardy youth to a condition of abject terror, he was then to proceed to the room occupied by the United States Minister and his wife, and there to place a clammy hand on Mrs Otis's forehead, while he hissed into her trembling husband's ear the awful secrets of the charnel house. With regard to little Virginia, he had not quite made up his mind. She had never insulted him in any way, and was pretty and gentle. A few hollow groans from the wardrobe, he thought, would be more than sufficient, or, if that failed to wake her, he might grabble at the counterpane with palsy-twitching fingers. As for the twins, he was quite determined to teach them a lesson. The first thing to be done was, of course, to sit upon their chests, so as to produce the stifling sensation of nightmare. Then, as their beds were quite close to each other, to stand between them in the form of a green, icy-cold corpse, till they became paralysed with fear, and, finally, to throw off the winding-sheet, and crawl round the room, with white bleached bones and one rolling eyeball, in the character of 'Dumb Daniel, or the Suicide's Skeleton', a role in which he had on more than one occasion produced a great effect, and which he considered quite equal to his famous part of 'Martin the Maniac, or the Masked Mystery'.

At half-past ten he heard the family going to bed. For some time he was disturbed by wild shrieks of laughter from the twins, who, with the light-hearted gaiety of schoolboys, were evidently amusing themselves before they retired to rest, but at a quarter past eleven all was still, and, as midnight sounded, he sallied forth. The owl beat against the window panes, the raven croaked from the old yew tree, and the wind wandered moaning round the house like a lost soul; but the Otis family slept unconscious of their doom, and high above the rain and storm he could hear the steady snoring of the Minister for the United States. He stepped stealthily out of the wainscoting, with an evil smile on his cruel, wrinkled mouth, and the moon hid her face in a cloud as he stole past the great oriel window, where his own arms and those of his murdered wife were blazoned in azure and gold. On and on he glided, like an evil shadow, the very darkness seeming to loathe him as he passed. Once he thought he heard something call, and stopped; but it was only the baying of a dog from the Red Farm, and he went on, muttering strange sixteenth-century curses, and ever and anon brandishing the rusty dagger in the midnight air. Finally he reached the corner of the passage that led to luckless Washington's room. For a moment he paused there, the wind blowing his long grey locks about his head, and twisting into grotesque and fantastic folds the nameless horror of the dead man's shroud. Then the clock struck the quarter, and he felt the time was come. He chuckled to himself, and turned the corner; but no sooner had he done so, than, with a piteous wail of terror, he fell back, and hid his blanched face in his long, bony hands. Right in front of him was standing a horrible spectre, motionless as a carven image, and monstrous as a madman's dream! Its head was bald and burnished; its face round, and fat, and white; and hideous laughter seemed to have writhed its features into an eternal grin. From the eyes streamed rays of scarlet light, the mouth was a wide well of fire, and a hideous garment, like to his own, swathed with its silent snows the Titan form. On its breast was a placard with strange writing in antique characters, some scroll of shame it seemed, some record of wild sins, some awful calendar of crime, and, with its right hand, it bore aloft a falchion of gleaming steel.

Never having seen a ghost before, he naturally was terribly frightened, and, after a second hasty glance at the awful phantom, he fled back to his room, tripping up in his long winding-sheet as he sped down the corridor, and finally dropping the rusty dagger into the minister's jackboots, where it was found in the morning by the butler. Once in the privacy of his own apartment, he flung himself down on a small pallet bed, and hid his face under the clothes. After a time, however, the brave old Canterville spirit asserted itself, and he determined to go and speak to the other ghost as soon as it was daylight. Accordingly, just as the dawn was touching the hills with silver, he returned towards the spot where he had first laid eyes on the grisly phantom, feeling that, after all, two ghosts were better than one, and that, by the aid of his new friend, he might safely grapple with the twins. On reaching the spot, however, a terrible sight met his gaze. Something had evidently happened to the spectre, for the light had entirely faded from its hollow eyes, the gleaming falchion had fallen from its hand, and it was leaning up against the wall in a strained and uncomfortable attitude. He rushed forward and seized it in his arms, when, to his horror, the head slipped off and rolled on the floor, the body assumed a recumbent posture, and he found himself clasping a white dimity bed curtain, with a sweeping brush, a kitchen cleaver, and a hollow turnip lying at his feet! Unable to understand this curious transformation, he clutched the placard with feverish haste, and there, in the grey morning light, he read these fearful words:

The Otis Ghoste
Ye Onlie True and Originale Spook
Beware of Ye Imitations
All others are Counterfeite

The whole thing flashed across him. He had been tricked, foiled and outwitted! The old Canterville look came into his eyes; he ground his toothless gums together; and, raising his withered hands high above his head, swore, according to the picturesque phraseology of the antique school, that when Chanticleer had sounded twice his merry horn, deeds of blood would be wrought, and Murder walk abroad with silent feet.

Hardly had he finished this awful oath when, from the red-tiled roof of a distant homestead, a cock crew. He laughed a long, low, bitter laugh, and waited. Hour after hour he waited, but the cock, for some strange reason, did not crow again. Finally, at half-past seven, the arrival of the housemaids made him give up his fearful vigil, and he stalked back to his room, thinking of his vain hope and baffled purpose. There he consulted several books of ancient chivalry, of which he was exceedingly fond, and found that, on every occasion on which his oath had been used, Chanticleer had always crowed a second time. 'Perdition seize the naughty fowl,' he muttered. 'I have seen the day when, with my stout spear, I would have run him through the gorge, and made him crow for me as 'twere in death!' He then retired to a comfortable lead coffin, and stayed there till evening.

4

The next day the ghost was very weak and tired. The terrible excitement of the last four weeks was beginning to have its effect. His nerves were completely shattered, and he started at the slightest noise. For five days he kept his room, and at last made up his mind to give up the point of the bloodstain on the library floor. If the Otis family did not want it, they clearly did not deserve it. They were evidently people on a low, material plane of existence, and quite incapable of appreciating the symbolic value of sensuous phenomena. The question of phantasmic apparitions, and the development of astral bodies, was of course quite a different matter, and really not under his control. It was his solemn duty to appear in the corridor once a week, and to gibber from the large oriel window on the first and third Wednesday in every month, and he did not see how he could honourably escape from his obligations. It is quite true that his life had been very evil, but, upon the other hand, he was most conscientious in all things connected with the supernatural. For the next three Saturdays, accordingly, he traversed the corridor as usual between midnight and three o'clock, taking every possible precaution against being either heard or seen. He removed his boots, trod as lightly as possible on the old worm-eaten boards, wore a large black velvet cloak, and was careful to use the Rising Sun Lubricator for oiling his chains. I am bound to acknowledge that it was with a good deal of difficulty that he brought himself to adopt this last mode of protection. However, one night, while the family were at dinner, he slipped into Mr Otis's bedroom and carried off the bottle. He felt a little humiliated at first, but afterwards was sensible enough to see that there was a great deal to be said for the invention, and, to a certain degree, it served his purpose. Still, in spite of everything, he was not left unmolested. Strings were continually being stretched across the corridor, over which he tripped in the dark, and on one occasion, while dressed for the part of 'Black Isaac, or the Huntsman of Hogley Woods', he met with a severe fall, through treading on a butter slide, which the twins had constructed from the entrance of the Tapestry Chamber to the top of the oak staircase. This last insult so enraged him, that he resolved to make one final effort to assert his dignity and social position, and determined to visit the insolent young Etonians the next night in his celebrated character of 'Reckless Rupert, or the Headless Earl'.

He had not appeared in this disguise for more than seventy years; in fact, not since he had so frightened pretty Lady Barbara Modish by means of it, that she suddenly broke off her engagement with the present Lord Canterville's grandfather, and ran away to Gretna Green with handsome Jack Castleton, declaring that nothing in the world would induce her to marry into a family that allowed such a horrible phantom to walk up and down the terrace at twilight. Poor Jack was afterwards shot in a duel by Lord Canterville on

Wandsworth Common, and Lady Barbara died of a broken heart at Tunbridge Wells before the year was out, so, in every way, it had been a great success. It was, however, an extremely difficult 'make-up', if I may use such a theatrical expression in connection with one of the greatest mysteries of the supernatural, or, to employ a more scientific term, the higher-natural world, and it took him fully three hours to make his preparations. At last everything was ready, and he was very pleased with his appearance. The big leather riding boots that went with the dress were just a little too large for him, and he could only find one of the two horse pistols, but, on the whole, he was quite satisfied, and at a quarter past one he glided out of the wainscoting and crept down the corridor. On reaching the room occupied by the twins, which I should mention was called the Blue Bedchamber, on account of the colour of its hangings, he found the door just ajar. Wishing to make an effective entrance, he flung it wide open, when a heavy jug of water fell right down on him, wetting him to the skin, and just missing his left shoulder by a couple of inches. At the same moment he heard stifled shrieks of laughter proceeding from the four-post bed. The shock to his nervous system was so great that he fled back to his room as hard as he could go, and the next day he was laid up with a severe cold. The only thing that at all consoled him in the whole affair was the fact that he had not brought his head with him, for, had he done so, the consequences might have been very serious.

He now gave up all hope of ever frightening this rude American family, and contented himself, as a rule, with creeping about the passages in list slippers, with a thick red muffler round his throat for fear of draughts, and a small arquebuse, in case he should be attacked by the twins. The final blow he received occurred on the 19th of September. He had gone downstairs to the great entrance hall, feeling sure that there, at any rate, he would be quite unmolested, and was amusing himself by making satirical remarks on the large Saroni photographs of the United States Minister and his wife, which had now taken the place of the Canterville family pictures. He was simply but neatly clad in a long shroud, spotted with churchyard mould, had tied up his jaw with a strip of yellow linen, and carried a small lantern and a sexton's spade. In fact, he was dressed for the character of 'Jonas the Graveless, or the Corpse-Snatcher of Chertsey Barn', one of his most remarkable impersonations, and one which the Cantervilles had every reason to remember, as it was the real origin of their quarrel with their neighbour, Lord Rufford. It was about a quarter past two o'clock in the morning, and, as far as he could ascertain, no one was stirring. As he was strolling towards the library, however, to see if there were any traces left of the bloodstain, suddenly there leaped out on him from a dark corner two figures, who waved their arms wildly above their heads, and shrieked out 'boo!' in his ear.

Seized with a panic, which, under the circumstances, was only natural, he rushed for the staircase, but found Washington Otis waiting for him there with the big garden syringe; and being thus hemmed in by his enemies on every side, and driven almost to bay, he vanished into the great iron stove which, fortunately for him, was not lit, and had to make his way home through the flues and chimneys, arriving at his own room in a terrible state of dirt, disorder and despair.

After this he was not seen again on any nocturnal expedition. The twins lay in wait for him on several occasions, and strewed the passages with nutshells every night to the great annoyance of their parents and the servants, but it was of no avail. It was quite evident that his feelings were so wounded that he would not appear. Mr Otis consequently resumed his great work on the history of the Democratic Party, on which he had been engaged for some years; Mrs Otis organised a wonderful clam bake, which amazed the whole county; the boys took to lacrosse, euchre, poker, and other American national games; and Virginia rode about the lanes on her pony, accompanied by the young Duke of Cheshire, who had come to spend the last week of his holidays at Canterville Chase. It was generally assumed that the ghost had gone away, and, in fact, Mr Otis wrote a letter to that effect to Lord Canterville, who, in reply, expressed his great pleasure at the news, and sent his best congratulations to the minister's worthy wife.

The Otises, however, were deceived, for the ghost was still in the house, and though now almost an invalid, was by no means ready to let matters rest, particularly as he heard that among the guests was the young Duke of Cheshire, whose granduncle, Lord Francis Stilton, had once bet a hundred guineas with Colonel Carbury that he would play dice with the Canterville ghost, and was found the next morning lying on the floor of the cardroom in such a helpless paralytic state, that though he lived on to a great age, he was never able to say anything again but 'Double Sixes'. The story was well known at the time, though, of course, out of respect for the feelings of the two noble families, every attempt was made to hush it up; and a full account of all the circumstances connected with it will be found in the third volume of Lord Tattle's *Recollections of the Prince Regent and his Friends*. The ghost, then, was naturally very anxious to show that he had not lost his influence over the Stiltons, with whom, indeed, he was distantly connected, his own first cousin having been married *en secondes noces* to the Sieur de Bulkeley, from whom, as everyone knows, the Dukes of Cheshire are lineally descended. Accordingly, he made arrangements for appearing to Virginia's little lover in his celebrated impersonation of 'The Vampire Monk, or the Bloodless Benedictine', a performance so horrible that when old Lady Startup saw it, which she did on one fatal New Year's Eve, in the year 1764, she went off into the most piercing shrieks, which culminated in violent apoplexy, and died in three days, after disinheriting the Cantervilles, who were her nearest relations, and leaving all her money to her London apothecary. At the last moment, however, his terror of the twins prevented his leaving his room, and the little Duke slept in peace under the great feathered canopy in the Royal Bedchamber, and dreamed of Virginia.

5

A few days after this, Virginia and her curly-haired cavalier went out riding on Brockley meadows, where she tore her habit so badly in getting through a hedge, that, on her return home, she made up her mind to go up by the back staircase so as not to be seen. As she was running past the Tapestry Chamber, the door of which happened to be open, she fancied she saw someone inside, and thinking it was her mother's maid, who sometimes used to bring her work there, looked in to ask her to mend her habit. To her immense surprise, however, it was the Canterville Ghost himself! He was sitting by the window, watching the ruined gold of the yellowing trees fly through the air, and the red leaves dancing madly down the long avenue. His head was leaning on his hand, and his whole attitude was one of extreme depression. Indeed, so forlorn, and so much out of repair did he look, that little Virginia, whose first idea had been to run away and lock herself in her room, was filled with pity, and determined to try and comfort him. So light was her footfall, and so deep his melancholy, that he was not aware of her presence till she spoke to him.

'I am so sorry for you,' she said, 'but my brothers are going back to Eton tomorrow, and then, if you behave yourself, no one will annoy you.'

'It is absurd asking me to behave myself,' he answered, looking round in astonishment at the pretty little girl who had ventured to address him, 'quite absurd. I must rattle my chains, and groan through keyholes, and walk about at night, if that is what you mean. It is my only reason for existing.'

'It is no reason at all for existing, and you know you have been very wicked. Mrs Umney told us, the first day we arrived here, that you had killed your wife.'

'Well, I quite admit it,' said the Ghost petulantly, 'but it was a purely family matter, and concerned no one else.'

'It is very wrong to kill anyone,' said Virginia, who at times had a sweet Puritan gravity, caught from some old New England ancestor.

'Oh, I hate the cheap severity of abstract ethics! My wife was very plain, never had my ruffs properly starched, and knew nothing about cookery. Why, there was a buck I had shot in Hogley Woods, a magnificent pricket, and do you know how she had it sent up to table? However, it is no matter now, for it is all over, and I don't think it was very nice of her brothers to starve me to death, though I did kill her.'

'Starve you to death? Oh, Mr Ghost, I mean Sir Simon, are you hungry? I have a sandwich in my case. Would you like it?'

'No, thank you, I never eat anything now; but it is very kind of you, all the same, and you are much nicer than the rest of your horrid, rude, vulgar, dishonest family.'

Stop!' cried Virginia, stamping her foot, 'it is you who are rude, and horrid, and vulgar, and as for dishonesty, you know you stole the paints out of my box to try and furbish up that ridiculous bloodstain in the library. First you took all my reds, including the vermilion, and I couldn't do any more sunsets, then you took the emerald green and the chrome yellow, and finally I had nothing left but indigo and Chinese white, and could only do moonlight scenes, which are always depressing to look at, and not at all easy to paint. I never told on you, though I was very much annoyed, and it was most ridiculous, the whole thing; for who ever heard of emerald-green blood?'

'Well, really,' said the Ghost, rather meekly, 'what was I to do? It is a very difficult thing to get real blood nowadays, and as your brother began it all with his Paragon Detergent, I certainly saw no reason why I should not have your paints. As for colour, that is always a matter of taste: the Cantervilles have blue blood, for instance, the very bluest in England; but I know you Americans don't care for things of this kind.'

'You know nothing about it, and the best thing you can do is to emigrate and improve your mind. My father will be only too happy to give you a free passage, and though there is a heavy duty on spirits of every kind, there will be no difficulty about the Custom House, as the officers are all Democrats. Once in New York, you are sure to be a great success. I know lots of people there who would give a hundred thousand dollars to have a grandfather, and much more than that to have a family Ghost.'

'I don't think I should like America.'

'I suppose because we have no ruins and no curiosities,' said Virginia satirically.

'No ruins! No curiosities!' answered the Ghost; 'you have your navy and your manners.'

'Good evening; I will go and ask papa to get the twins an extra week's holiday.'

'Please don't go, Miss Virginia,' he cried. 'I am so lonely and so unhappy, and I really don't know what to do. I want to go to sleep and I cannot.'

'That's quite absurd! You have merely to go to bed and blow out the candle. It is very difficult sometimes to keep awake, especially at church, but there is no difficulty at all about sleeping. Why, even babies know how to do that, and they are not very clever.'

'I have not slept for three hundred years,' he said sadly, and Virginia's beautiful blue eyes opened in wonder. 'For three hundred years I have not slept, and I am so tired.'

Virginia grew quite grave, and her little lips trembled like rose-leaves. She came towards him, and kneeling down at his side, looked up into his old withered face.

'Poor, poor Ghost', she murmured, 'have you no place where you can sleep?'

'Far away beyond the pine woods,' he answered, in a low dreamy voice, 'there is a little garden. There the grass grows long and deep, there are the great white stars of the hemlock flower, there the night-ingale sings all night long. All night long he sings, and the cold, crystal moon looks down, and the yew tree spreads out its giant arms over the sleepers.'

Virginia's eyes grew dim with tears, and she hid her face in her hands.

'You mean the Garden of Death,' she whispered.

'Yes, Death. Death must be so beautiful. To lie in the soft brown earth, with the grasses waving above one's head, and listen to silence. To have no yesterday, and no tomorrow. To forget time, to forgive life, to be at peace. You can help me. You can open for me the portals of Death's house, for Love is always with you, and Love is stronger than Death is.'

Virginia trembled, a cold shudder ran through her, and for a few moments there was silence. She felt as if she was in a terrible dream.

Then the Ghost spoke again, and his voice sounded like the sighing of the wind.

'Have you ever read the old prophecy on the library window?'

'Oh, often,' cried the little girl, looking up. 'I know it quite well. It is painted in curious black letters, and it is difficult to read. There are only six lines:

When a golden girl can win
Prayer from out the lips of sin,
When the barren almond bears,
And a little child gives away its tears,
Then shall all the house be still
And peace come to Canterville.

But I don't know what they mean.'

'They mean,' he said sadly, 'that you must weep for me for my sins, because I have no tears, and pray with me for my soul, because I have no faith, and then, if you have always been sweet, and good, and gentle, the Angel of Death will have mercy on me. You will see fearful shapes in darkness, and wicked voices will whisper in your ear, but they will not harm you, for against the purity of a little child the powers of hell cannot prevail.'

Virginia made no answer, and the Ghost wrung his hands in wild despair as he looked down at her bowed golden head. Suddenly she stood up, very pale, and with a strange light in her eyes. 'I am not afraid,' she said firmly, 'and I will ask the Angel to have mercy on you.'

He rose from his seat with a faint cry of joy, and taking her hand bent over it with old-fashioned grace and kissed it. His fingers were as cold as ice, and his lips burned like fire, but Virginia did not falter, as he led her across the dusky room. On the faded green tapestry were broidered little huntsmen. They blew their tasselled horns and with their tiny hands waved to her to go back. 'Go back! Little Virginia,' they cried, 'go back!' but the Ghost clutched her hand more tightly, and she shut her eyes against them. Horrible animals with lizard tails, and goggle eyes, blinked at her from the carven chimneypiece, and murmured 'Beware! Little Virginia, beware! We may never see you again,' but the Ghost glided on more swiftly, and Virginia did not listen. When they reached the end of the room he stopped, and muttered some words she could not understand. She opened her eyes, and saw the wall slowly fading away like a mist, and a great black cavern in front of her. A bitter cold wind swept round them, and she felt something pulling at her dress. 'Quick, quick,' cried the Ghost, 'or it will be too late,' and, in a moment, the wainscoting had closed behind them, and the Tapestry Chamber was empty.

6

About ten minutes later, the bell rang for tea, and, as Virginia did not come down, Mrs Otis sent up one of the footmen to tell her. After a little time he returned and said that he could not find Miss Virginia anywhere. As she was in the habit of going out to the garden every evening to get flowers for the dinner table, Mrs Otis was not at all alarmed at first, but when six o'clock struck, and Virginia did not appear, she became really agitated, and sent the boys out to look for her, while she herself and Mr Otis searched every room in the house. At half-past six the boys came back and said that they could find no trace of their sister anywhere. They were all now in the greatest state of excitement, and did not know what to do, when Mr Otis suddenly remembered that, some few days before, he had given a band of gypsies permission to camp in the park. He accordingly at once set off for Blackfell Hollow, where he knew they were, accompanied by his eldest son and two of the farm servants. The little Duke of Cheshire, who was perfectly frantic with anxiety, begged hard to be allowed to go too, but Mr Otis would not allow him, as he was afraid there might be a scuffle. On arriving at the spot, however, he found that the gypsies had gone, and it was evident that their departure had been rather sudden, as the fire was still burning, and some plates were lying on the grass. Having sent off Washington and the two men to scour the district, he ran home, and despatched telegrams to all the police inspectors in the county, telling them to look out for a little girl who had been kidnapped by tramps or gypsies. He then ordered his horse to be brought round, and, after insisting on his wife and the three boys sitting down to dinner, rode off down the Ascot Road with a groom. He had hardly, however, gone a couple of miles when he heard somebody galloping after him, and, looking round, saw the little Duke coming up on his pony, with his face very flushed and no hat. 'I'm awfully sorry, Mr Otis,' gasped out the boy, 'but I can't eat any dinner as long as Virginia is lost. Please, don't be angry with me; if you had let us be engaged last year, there would never have been all this trouble. You won't send me back, will you? I can't go! I won't go!'

The minister could not help smiling at the handsome young scapegrace, and was a good deal touched at his devotion to Virginia, so leaning down from his horse, he patted him kindly on the shoulders, and said, 'Well, Cecil, if you won't go back I suppose you must come with me, but I must get you a hat at Ascot.'

'Oh, bother my hat! I want Virginia!' cried the little Duke, laughing, and they galloped on to the railway station. There Mr Otis enquired of the station master if anyone answering the description of Virginia had been seen on the platform, but could get no news of her. The station master, however, wired up and down the line, and assured him that a strict watch would be kept for her, and, after having bought a hat for the little Duke from a linen draper, who was just putting up his shutters, Mr Otis rode off to Bexley, a village about four miles away, which he was told was a well-known haunt of the gypsies, as there was a large common next to it. Here they roused up the rural policeman, but could get no information from him, and, after riding all over the common, they turned their horses' heads homewards and reached the Chase about eleven o'clock, dead tired and almost heartbroken. They found Washington and the twins waiting for them at the gatehouse with lanterns, as the avenue was very dark. Not the slightest trace of Virginia had been discovered. The gypsies had been caught on Brockley meadows, but she was not with them, and they had explained their sudden departure by saying that they had mistaken the date of Chorton Fair, and had gone off in a hurry for fear they might be late. Indeed, they had been quite distressed at hearing of Virginia's disappearance, as they were very grateful to Mr Otis for having allowed them to camp in his park, and four of their number had stayed behind to help in the search. The carp pond had been dragged, and the whole Chase thoroughly gone over, but without any result. It was evident that, for that night at any rate, Virginia was lost to them; and it was in a state of the deepest depression that Mr Otis and the boys walked up to the house, the groom following behind with the two horses and the pony. In the hall they found a group of frightened servants, and lying on a sofa in the library was poor Mrs Otis, almost out of her mind with terror and anxiety, and having her forehead bathed with eau de Cologne by the old housekeeper. Mr Otis at once insisted on her having something to eat, and ordered up supper for the whole party. It was a melancholy meal, as hardly anyone spoke, and even the twins were awestruck and subdued, as they were very fond of their sister. When they had finished, Mr Otis, in spite of the entreaties of the little Duke, ordered them all to bed, saying that nothing more could be done that night, and that he would telegraph in the morning to Scotland Yard for some detectives to be sent down immediately. Just as they were passing out of the dining room, midnight began to boom from the clock tower, and when the last stroke sounded they heard a crash and a sudden shrill cry; a dreadful peal of thunder shook the house, a strain of unearthly music floated through the air, a panel at the top of the staircase flew back with a loud noise, and out on the landing, looking very pale and white, with a little casket in her hand, stepped Virginia. In a moment they had all rushed up to her. Mrs Otis clasped her passionately in her arms, the Duke smothered her with violent kisses, and the twins executed a wild war-dance round the group.

'Good heavens! Child, where have you been?' said Mr Otis, rather angrily, thinking that she had been playing some foolish trick on them. 'Cecil and I have been riding all over the country looking for you, and your mother has been frightened to death. You must never play these practical jokes any more.'

'Except on the Ghost! Except on the Ghost!' shrieked the twins, as they capered about.

'My own darling, thank God you are found; you must never leave my side again,' murmured Mrs Otis, as she kissed the trembling child, and smoothed the tangled gold of her hair.

'Papa,' said Virginia quietly, 'I have been with the Ghost. He is dead, and you must come and see him. He had been very wicked, but he was really sorry for all that he had done, and he gave me this box of beautiful jewels before he died.'

The whole family gazed at her in mute amazement, but she was quite grave and serious; and, turning round, she led them through the opening in the wainscoting down a narrow secret corridor, Washington following with a lighted candle, which he had caught up from the table. Finally, they came to a great oak door, studded with rusty nails. When Virginia touched it, it swung back on its heavy hinges, and they found themselves in a little low room, with a vaulted ceiling, and one tiny grated window. Imbedded in the wall was a huge iron ring, and chained to it was a gaunt skeleton, that was stretched out at full length on the stone floor, and seemed to be trying to grasp with its long fleshless fingers an old-fashioned trencher and ewer, that were placed just out of its reach. The jug had evidently been once filled with water, as it was covered inside with green mould. There was nothing on the trencher but a pile of dust. Virginia knelt down beside the skeleton, and, folding her little hands together, began to pray silently, while the rest of the party looked on in wonder at the terrible tragedy whose secret was now disclosed to them.

'Hallo!' suddenly exclaimed one of the twins, who had been looking out of the window to try and discover in what wing of the house the room was situated. 'Hallo! The old withered almond tree has blossomed. I can see the flowers quite plainly in the moonlight.'

'God has forgiven him,' said Virginia gravely, as she rose to her feet, and a beautiful light seemed to illumine her face.

'What an angel you are!' cried the young Duke, and he put his arm round her neck and kissed her.

7

Four days after these curious incidents a funeral started from Canterville Chase at about eleven o'clock at night. The hearse was drawn by eight black horses, each of which carried on its head a great tuft of nodding ostrich plumes, and the leaden coffin was covered by a rich purple pall, on which was embroidered in gold the Canterville coat of arms. By the side of the hearse and the coaches walked the servants with lighted torches, and the whole procession was wonderfully impressive. Lord Canterville was the chief mourner, having come up specially from Wales to attend the funeral, and sat in the first carriage along with little Virginia. Then came the United States Minister and his wife, then Washington and the three boys, and in the last carriage was Mrs Umney. It was generally felt that, as she had been frightened by the ghost for more than fifty years of her life, she had the right to see the last of him. A deep grave had been dug in the corner of the churchyard, just under the old yew tree, and the service was read in the most impressive manner by the Reverend Augustus Dampier. When the ceremony was over, the servants, according to an old custom observed in the Canterville family, extinguished their torches, and, as the coffin was being lowered into the grave, Virginia stepped forward and laid on it a large cross made of white and pink almond blossoms. As she did so, the moon came out from behind a cloud, and flooded with its silent silver the little churchyard, and from a distant copse a nightingale began to sing. She thought of the ghost's description of the Garden of Death, her eyes became dim with tears, and she hardly spoke a word during the drive home.

The next morning, before Lord Canterville went up to town, Mr Otis had an interview with him on the subject of the jewels the ghost had given to Virginia. They were perfectly magnificent, especially a certain ruby necklace with old Venetian setting, which was really a superb specimen of sixteenth-century work, and their value was so great that Mr Otis felt considerable scruples about allowing his daughter to accept them.

'My lord,' he said, 'I know that in this country mortmain is held to apply to trinkets as well as to land; and it is quite clear to me that these jewels are, or should be, heirlooms in your family. I must beg you, accordingly, to take them to London with you, and to regard them simply as a portion of your property which has been restored to you under certain strange conditions. As for my daughter, she is merely a child, and has as yet, I am glad to say, but little interest in such appurtenances of idle luxury. I am also informed by Mrs Otis, who, I may say, is no mean authority upon art – having had the privilege of spending several winters in Boston when she was a girl – that these gems are of great monetary worth, and if offered for sale would fetch a tall price. Under these circumstances, Lord Canterville, I feel sure that you will recognise how impossible it would be for me to allow them to remain in the possession of any member of my family; and, indeed, all such vain gauds and toys, however suitable or necessary to the dignity of the British aristoc-racy, would be completely out of place among those who have been brought up on the severe, and I believe immortal, principles of republican simplicity. Perhaps I should mention that Virginia is very anxious that you should allow her to retain the box as a memento of your unfortunate but misguided ancestor. As it is extremely old, and consequently a good deal out of repair, you may perhaps think fit to comply with her request. For my own part, I confess I am a good deal surprised to find a child of mine expressing sympathy with medievalism in any form, and can only account for it by the fact that Virginia was born in one of your London suburbs shortly after Mrs Otis had returned from a trip to Athens.'

Lord Canterville listened very gravely to the worthy minister's speech, pulling his grey moustache now and then to hide an involuntary smile, and when Mr Otis had ended, he shook him cordially by the hand, and said, 'My dear sir, your charming little daughter rendered my unlucky ancestor, Sir Simon, a very important service, and I and my family are much indebted to her for her marvellous courage and pluck. The jewels are clearly hers, and, egad, I believe that if I were heartless enough to take them from her, the wicked old fellow would be out of his grave in a fortnight, leading me the devil of a life. As for their being heirlooms, nothing is an heirloom that is not so mentioned in a will or legal document, and the existence of these jewels has been quite unknown. I assure you I have no more claim on them than your butler, and when Miss Virginia grows up I dare say she will be pleased to have pretty things to wear. Besides, you forget, Mr Otis, that you took the furniture and the ghost at a valuation, and anything that belonged to the ghost passed at once into your possession, as, whatever activity Sir Simon may have shown in the corridor at night, in point of law he was really dead, and you acquired his property by purchase.'

Mr Otis was a good deal distressed at Lord Canterville's refusal, and begged him to reconsider his decision, but the good-natured peer was quite firm, and finally induced the minister to allow his daughter to retain the present the ghost had given her, and when, in the spring of 1890, the young Duchess of Cheshire was presented at the Queen's first drawing room on the occasion of her marriage, her jewels were the universal theme of admiration. For Virginia received the coronet, which is the reward of all good little American girls, and was married to her boy-lover as soon as he came of age. They were both so charming, and they loved each other so much, that everyone was delighted at the match, except the old Marchioness of Dumbleton, who had tried to catch the Duke for one of her seven unmarried daughters, and had given no less than three expensive dinner parties for that purpose, and, strange to say, Mr Otis himself. Mr Otis was extremely fond of the young Duke personally, but, theoretically, he objected to titles, and, to use his own words, 'was not without apprehension lest, amid the enervating influences of a pleasure-loving aristocracy, the true principles of republican simplicity should be forgotten'. His objections, however, were completely overruled, and I believe that when he walked up the aisle of St George's, Hanover Square, with his daughter leaning on his arm, there was not a prouder man in the whole length and breadth of England.

The Duke and Duchess, after the honeymoon was over, went down to Canterville Chase, and on the day after their arrival they walked over in the afternoon to the lonely churchyard by the pine woods. There had been a great deal of difficulty at first about the inscription on Sir Simon's tombstone, but finally it had been decided to engrave on it simply the initials of the old gentleman's name, and the verse from the library window. The Duchess had brought with her some lovely roses, which she strewed upon the grave, and after they had stood by it for some time they strolled into the ruined chancel of the old abbey. There the Duchess sat down on a fallen pillar, while her husband lay at her feet smoking a cigarette and looking up at her beautiful eyes. Suddenly he threw his cigarette away, took hold of her hand, and said to her, 'Virginia, a wife should have no secrets from her husband.'

'Dear Cecil! I have no secrets from you.'

'Yes, you have,' he answered, smiling, 'you have never told me what happened to you when you were locked up with the ghost.'

'I have never told anyone, Cecil,' said Virginia gravely.

'I know that, but you might tell me.'

'Please don't ask me, Cecil, I cannot tell you. Poor Sir Simon! I owe him a great deal. Yes, don't laugh, Cecil, I really do. He made me see what Life is, and what Death signifies, and why Love is stronger than both.'

The Duke rose and kissed his wife lovingly.

'You can have your secret as long as I have your heart,' he murmured.

'You have always had that, Cecil.'

'And you will tell our children someday, won't you?'

Virginia blushed.

THE CURSE OF THE FIRES
AND OF THE SHADOWS

W. B. YEATS

(1914)

What wouldn't be haunting about Yeats, so often in the shadow of another world? It's always interesting when a story of the supernatural weaves its narrative through history. The historical fact of the burning of Sligo Abbey leads us into the ambivalent mindsets of the new converts. But then their mixed feelings are cast aside by the fairy woman, washing a corpse whose face, in each case, is theirs. I love stories where you are confronted by your own face — the fetch, the gravely ill person seen walking abroad when bedridden, the living ghost.

NE SUMMER NIGHT, WHEN there was peace, a score of Puritan troopers, under the pious Sir Frederick Hamilton, broke through the door of the Abbey of the White Friars which stood over the Gara Lough at Sligo. As the door fell with a crash they saw a little knot of friars, gathered about the altar, their white habits glimmering in the steady light of the holy candles. All the monks were kneeling except the abbot, who stood upon the altar steps with a great brazen crucifix in his hand. 'Shoot them!' cried Sir Frederick Hamilton, but none stirred, for all were new converts and feared the crucifix and the holy candles. The white lights from the altar threw the shadows of the troopers up on to roof and wall. As the troopers moved about, the shadows began a fantastic dance among the corbels and the memorial tablets. For a little while all was silent, and then five troopers who were the bodyguard of Sir Frederick Hamilton lifted their muskets and shot down five of the friars. The noise and the smoke drove away the mystery of the pale altar lights and the other troopers took courage

and began to strike. In a moment the friars lay about the altar steps, their white habits stained with blood. 'Set fire to the house!' cried Sir Frederick Hamilton, and at his word one went out and came in again carrying a heap of dry straw and piled it against the western wall, and, having done this, fell back, for the fear of the crucifix and of the holy candles was still in his heart. Seeing this, the five troopers who were Sir Frederick Hamilton's bodyguard darted forward, and taking each a holy candle set the straw in a blaze. The red tongues of fire rushed up and flickered from corbel to corbel and from tablet to tablet, and crept along the floor, setting in a blaze the seats and benches. The dance of the shadows passed away, and the dance of the fires began. The troopers fell back towards the door in the southern wall, and watched those yellow dancers springing hither and thither.

For a time the altar stood safe and apart in the midst of its white light; the eyes of the troopers turned upon it. The abbot whom they had thought dead had risen to his feet and now stood before it with the crucifix lifted in both hands high above his head. Suddenly he cried with a loud voice, 'Woe unto all who smite those who dwell within the Light of the Lord, for they shall wander among the ungovernable shadows, and follow the ungovernable fires!' And having so cried he fell on his face dead, and the brazen crucifix rolled down the steps of the altar. The smoke had now grown very thick, so that it drove the troopers out into the open air. Before them were burning houses. Behind them shone the painted windows of the abbey filled with saints and martyrs, awakened, as from a sacred trance, into an angry and animated life. The eyes of the troopers were dazzled, and for a while could see nothing but the flaming faces of saints and martyrs. Presently, however, they saw a man covered with dust who came running towards them. 'Two messengers,' he cried, 'have been sent by the defeated Irish to raise against you the whole country about Manor Hamilton, and if you do not stop them you will be overpowered in the woods before you reach home again! They ride north-east between Ben Bulben and Cashel na Gael.'

Sir Frederick Hamilton called to him the five troopers who had first fired upon the monks and said, 'Mount quickly, and ride through the woods towards the mountain, and get before these men, and kill them.'

In a moment the troopers were gone, and before many moments they had splashed across the river at what is now called Buckley's Ford, and plunged into the woods. They followed a beaten track that wound along the northern bank of the river. The boughs of the birch and quicken trees mingled above, and hid the cloudy moonlight, leaving the pathway in almost complete darkness. They rode at a rapid trot, now chatting together, now watching some stray weasel or rabbit scuttling away in the darkness. Gradually, as the gloom and silence of the woods oppressed them, they drew closer together, and began to talk rapidly; they were old comrades and knew each other's lives. One was married, and told how glad his wife would be to see him return safe from this hare-brained expedition against the White Friars, and to hear how fortune had made amends for rashness. The oldest of the five, whose wife was dead, spoke of a flagon of wine which awaited him upon an upper shelf; while the third, who was the youngest, had a sweetheart watching for his return, and he rode a little way before the others not talking at all. Suddenly the young man stopped, and they saw that his horse was trembling. 'I saw something,' he said, 'and yet I do not know but it may have been one of the shadows. It looked like a great worm with a silver crown upon his head.' One of the five put his hand up to his forehead as if about to cross himself, but remembering that he had changed his religion he put it down, and said: 'I am certain it was but a shadow,

for there are a great many about us, and of very strange kinds.' Then
they rode on in silence. It had been raining in the earlier part of the
day, and the drops fell from the branches, wetting their hair and
their shoulders. In a little they began to talk again. They had been
in many battles against many a rebel together, and now told each
other over again the story of their wounds, and so awakened in their
hearts the strongest of all fellowships, the fellowship of the sword,
and half forgot the terrible solitude of the woods.

Suddenly the first two horses neighed, and then stood still, and
would go no farther. Before them was a glint of water, and they knew
by the rushing sound that it was a river. They dismounted, and after
much tugging and coaxing brought the horses to the riverside. In
the midst of the water stood a tall old woman with grey hair flowing
over a grey dress. She stood up to her knees in the water, and stooped
from time to time as though washing. Presently they could see that
she was washing something that half floated. The moon cast a flickering light upon it, and they saw that it was the dead body of a man,
and, while they were looking at it, an eddy of the river turned the
face towards them, and each of the five troopers recognised at the
same moment his own face. While they stood dumb and motionless
with horror, the woman began to speak, saying slowly and loudly:
'Did you see my son? He has a crown of silver on his head, and there
are rubies in the crown.' Then the oldest of the troopers, he who had
been most often wounded, drew his sword and cried: 'I have fought
for the truth of my God, and need not fear the shadows of Satan,'
and with that rushed into the water. In a moment he returned. The
woman had vanished, and though he had thrust his sword into air
and water he had found nothing.

The five troopers remounted, and set their horses at the ford, but
all to no purpose. They tried again and again, and went plunging

hither and thither, the horses foaming and rearing. 'Let us,' said
the old trooper, 'ride back a little into the wood, and strike the
river higher up.' They rode in under the boughs, the ground-ivy
crackling under the hoofs, and the branches striking against their
steel caps. After about twenty minutes' riding they came out again
upon the river, and after another ten minutes found a place where
it was possible to cross without sinking below the stirrups. The
wood upon the other side was very thin, and broke the moonlight
into long streams. The wind had arisen and had begun to drive the
clouds rapidly across the face of the moon, so that thin streams of
light seemed to be dancing a grotesque dance among the scattered
bushes and small fir trees. The tops of the trees began also to moan,
and the sound of it was like the voice of the dead in the wind; and
the troopers remembered the belief that tells how the dead in pur-
gatory are spitted upon the points of the trees and upon the points
of the rocks. They turned a little to the south, in the hope that they
might strike the beaten path again, but they could find no trace of it.

Meanwhile, the moaning grew louder and louder, and the dance
of the white moon-fires more and more rapid. Gradually they began
to be aware of a sound of distant music. It was the sound of a
bagpipe, and they rode towards it with great joy. It came from the
bottom of a deep, cuplike hollow. In the midst of the hollow was
an old man with a red cap and withered face. He sat beside a fire
of sticks, and had a burning torch thrust into the earth at his feet,
and played an old bagpipe furiously. His red hair dripped over his
face like the iron rust upon a rock. 'Did you see my wife?' he cried,
looking up a moment. 'She was washing! She was washing!' 'I am
afraid of him,' said the young trooper, 'I fear he is one of the Sidhe.'
'No,' said the old trooper, 'he is a man, for I can see the sun-freckles
upon his face. We will compel him to be our guide,' and at that

he drew his sword, and the others did the same. They stood in a ring round the piper, and pointed their swords at him, and the old trooper then told him that they must kill two rebels, who had taken the road between Ben Bulben and the great mountain spur that is called Cashel na Gael, and that he must get up before one of them and be their guide, for they had lost their way. The piper turned, and pointed to a neighbouring tree, and they saw an old white horse ready bitted, bridled and saddled. He slung the pipe across his back, and, taking the torch in his hand, got upon the horse, and started off before them, as hard as he could go.

The wood grew thinner and thinner, and the ground began to slope up toward the mountain. The moon had already set, and the little white flames of the stars had come out everywhere. The ground sloped more and more until at last they rode far above the woods upon the wide top of the mountain. The woods lay spread out mile after mile below, and away to the south shot up the red glare of the burning town. But before and above them were the little white flames. The guide drew rein suddenly, and pointing upwards with the hand that did not hold the torch, shrieked out: 'Look; look at the holy candles!' and then plunged forward at a gallop, waving the torch hither and thither. 'Do you hear the hoofs of the messengers?' cried the guide. 'Quick, quick! Or they will be gone out of your hands!' and he laughed as with delight of the chase. The troopers thought they could hear far off, and as if below them, rattle of hoofs; but now the ground began to slope more and more, and the speed grew more headlong moment by moment. They tried to pull up, but in vain, for the horses seemed to have gone mad. The guide had thrown the reins onto the neck of the old white horse, and was waving his arms and singing a wild Gaelic song. Suddenly they saw the thin gleam of a river, at an immense distance below, and knew that they were upon the brink of the abyss that is now called Lug-na-Gael, or in English the Stranger's Leap. The six horses sprang forward, and five screams went up in the air, a moment later five men and horses fell with a dull crash upon the green slopes at the foot of the rocks.

WHERE THE TIDES EBB AND FLOW

LORD DUNSANY

(1910)

I love this story — the dreamy quality, the fantasy, the insidious terror. A peace descends, only to be snatched away in a world that is hypnotic in its horror. And then a redemption as nature triumphs. Is it a metaphor for our times, or an omen?

DREAMT THAT I HAD done a horrible thing, so that burial was to be denied me either in soil or sea, neither could there be any hell for me.

I waited for some hours, knowing this. Then my friends came for me, and slew me secretly and with ancient rite, and lit great tapers, and carried me away.

It was all in London that the thing was done, and they went furtively at dead of night along grey streets and among mean houses until they came to the river. And the river and the tide of the sea were grappling with one another between the mudbanks, and both of them were black and full of lights. A sudden wonder came into the eyes of each, as my friends came near to them with their glaring tapers. All these things I saw as they carried me dead and stiffening, for my soul was still among my bones, because there was no hell for it, and because Christian burial was denied me.

They took me down a stairway that was green with slimy things, and so came slowly to the terrible mud. There, in the territory of forsaken things, they dug a shallow grave. When they had finished they laid me in the grave, and suddenly they cast their tapers to the river. And when the water had quenched the flaring lights the tapers looked pale and small as they bobbed upon the tide, and at once the glamour of the calamity was gone, and I noticed then the approach of the huge dawn; my friends cast their cloaks over their faces, and the solemn procession was turned into many fugitives that furtively stole away.

Then the mud came back wearily and covered all but my face. There I lay alone with quite forgotten things, with drifting things that the tides will take no farther, with useless things and lost things, and with the horrible unnatural bricks that are neither stone nor soil. I was rid of feeling, because I had been killed, but perception and thought were in my unhappy soul. The dawn widened, and I saw the desolate houses that crowded the marge of the river, and their dead windows peered into my dead eyes, windows with bales behind them instead of human souls. I grew so weary looking at these forlorn things that I wanted to cry out, but could not, because I was dead. Then I knew, as I had never known before, that for all the years that herd of desolate houses had wanted to cry out too, but, being dead, were dumb. And I knew then that it had yet been well with the forgotten drifting things if they had wept, but they were eyeless and without life. And I, too, tried to weep, but there were no tears in my dead eyes. And I knew then that the river might have cared for us, might have caressed us, might have sung to us, but he swept broadly onwards, thinking of nothing but the princely ships.

At last the tide did what the river would not, and came and covered me over, and my soul had rest in the green water, and rejoiced and believed that it had the Burial of the Sea. But with the ebb the water fell again, and left me alone again with the callous mud among the forgotten things that drift no more, and with the sight of all those desolate houses, and with the knowledge among all of us that each was dead.

In the mournful wall behind me, hung with green weeds, forsaken of the sea, dark tunnels appeared, and secret narrow passages that were clamped and barred. From these at last the stealthy rats came down to nibble me away, and my soul rejoiced thereat and believed that he would be free perforce from the accursed bones to which burial was refused. Very soon the rats ran away a little space and whispered among themselves. They never came any more. When I found that I was accursed even among the rats I tried to weep again.

Then the tide came swinging back and covered the dreadful mud, and hid the desolate houses, and soothed the forgotten things, and my soul had ease for a while in the sepulture of the sea. And then the tide forsook me again.

To and fro it came about me for many years. Then the County Council found me, and gave me decent burial. It was the first grave that I had ever slept in. That very night my friends came for me. They dug me up and put me back again in the shallow hole in the mud.

Again and again through the years my bones found burial, but always behind the funeral lurked one of those terrible men who, as soon as night fell, came and dug them up and carried them back again to the hole in the mud.

And then one day the last of those men died who once had done to me this terrible thing. I heard his soul go over the river at sunset.

And again I hoped.

A few weeks afterwards I was found once more, and once more taken out of that restless place and given deep burial in sacred ground, where my soul hoped that it should rest.

Almost at once men came with cloaks and tapers to give me back to the mud, for the thing had become a tradition and a rite. And all the forsaken things mocked me in their dumb hearts when they saw me carried back, for they were jealous of me because I had left the mud. It must be remembered that I could not weep.

And the years went by seawards where the black barges go, and the great derelict centuries became lost at sea, and still I lay there without any cause to hope, and daring not to hope without a cause, because of the terrible envy and the anger of the things that could drift no more.

Once a great storm rode up, even as far as London, out of the sea from the South; and he came curving into the river with the fierce East wind. And he was mightier than the dreary tides, and went with great leaps over the listless mud. And all the sad forgotten things rejoiced, and mingled with things that were haughtier than they, and rode once more amongst the lordly shipping that was driven up and down. And out of their hideous home he took my bones, never again, I hoped, to be vexed with the ebb and flow. And with the fall of the tide he went riding down the river and turned to the south-wards, and so went to his home. And my bones he scattered among many isles and along the shores of happy alien mainlands. And for a moment, while they were far asunder, my soul was almost free.

Then there arose, at the will of the moon, the assiduous flow of the tide, and it undid at once the work of the ebb, and gathered my bones from the marge of sunny isles, and gleaned them all along the mainland's shores, and went rocking northwards till it came to the mouth of the Thames, and there turned westwards its relentless face, and so went up the river and came to the hole in the mud, and into it dropped my bones; and partly the mud covered them and partly it left them white, for the mud cares not for its forsaken things.

Then the ebb came, and I saw the dead eyes of the houses and the jealousy of the other forgotten things that the storm had not carried thence.

And some more centuries passed over the ebb and flow and over the loneliness of things forgotten. And I lay there all the while in the careless grip of the mud, never wholly covered, yet never able to go free, and I longed for the great caress of the warm Earth or the comfortable lap of the Sea.

Sometimes men found my bones and buried them, but the tradition never died, and my friends' successors always brought them back. At last the barges went no more, and there were fewer lights; shaped timbers no longer floated down the fairway, and there came instead old wind-uprooted trees in all their natural simplicity.

At last I was aware that somewhere near me a blade of grass was growing, and the moss began to appear all over the dead houses. One day some thistledown went drifting over the river.

For some years I watched these signs attentively, until I became certain that London was passing away. Then I hoped once more, and all along both banks of the river there was anger among the lost things that anything should dare to hope upon the forsaken mud. Gradually the horrible houses crumbled, until the poor dead things that never had had life got decent burial among the weeds and moss. At last the may appeared and the convolvulus. Finally, the wild rose stood up over mounds that had been wharves and warehouses. Then I knew that the cause of Nature had triumphed, and London had passed away.

The last man in London came to the wall by the river, in an ancient cloak that was one of those that once my friends had worn, and peered over the edge to see that I still was there. Then he went, and I never saw men again: they had passed away with London.

A few days after the last man had gone the birds came into London, all the birds that sing. When they first saw me they all looked sideways at me, then they went away a little and spoke among themselves.

'He only sinned against Man,' they said. 'It is not our quarrel.'

'Let us be kind to him,' they said.

Then they hopped nearer me and began to sing. It was the time of the rising of the dawn, and from both banks of the river, and from the sky, and from the thickets that were once the streets, hundreds of birds were singing. As the light increased the birds sang more and more; they grew thicker and thicker in the air above my head, till there were thousands of them singing there, and then millions, and at last I could see nothing but a host of flickering wings with the sunlight on them, and little gaps of sky. Then when there was nothing to be heard in London but the myriad notes of that exultant song, my soul rose up from the bones in the hole in the mud and began to climb up the song heavenwards. And it seemed that a laneway opened amongst the wings of the birds, and it went up and up, and one of the smaller gates of Paradise stood ajar at the end of it. And then I knew by a sign that the mud should receive me no more, for suddenly I found that I could weep.

At this moment I opened my eyes in bed in a house in London, and outside some sparrows were twittering in a tree in the light of the radiant morning; and there were tears still wet upon my face, for one's restraint is feeble while one sleeps. But I arose and opened the window wide, and, stretching my hands out over the little garden, I blessed the birds whose song had woken me up from the troubled and terrible centuries of my dream.

THE JUDGE'S HOUSE

BRAM STOKER

(1914)

I never quite recovered from Dracula, *and I still wouldn't dream of watching a vampire film. But never mind the Transylvanian terrors, the Hanging Judge can pack a serious punch. And I didn't have to read it with a brown-paper cover, like I did with* Dracula. *(Did I peek under that cover? Oh yes, that's the allure of fear.) This is a story for bright lights and a roaring fire and absolutely no excessive tea-drinking! It comes with a salutary lesson: don't ignore the warnings of sensible people!*

HEN THE TIME FOR his examination drew near Malcolm Malcolmson made up his mind to go somewhere to read by himself. He feared the attractions of the seaside, and also he feared completely rural isolation, for of old he knew its charms, and so he determined to find some unpretentious little town where there would be nothing to distract him. He refrained from asking suggestions from any of his friends, for he argued that each would recommend some place of which he had knowledge, and where he had already acquaintances. As Malcolmson wished to avoid friends he had no wish to encumber himself with the attention of friends' friends, and so he determined to look out for a place for himself. He packed a portmanteau with some clothes and all the books he required, and then took ticket for the first name on the local timetable which he did not know.

When at the end of three hours' journey he alighted at Benchurch, he felt satisfied that he had so far obliterated his tracks as to be sure of having a peaceful opportunity of pursuing his studies. He went straight to the one inn which the sleepy little place contained, and put up for the night. Benchurch was a market town, and once in three weeks was crowded to excess, but for the remainder of the twenty-one days it was as attractive as a desert. Malcolmson looked around the day after his arrival to try to find quarters more isolated than even so quiet an inn as the Good Traveller afforded. There was only one place which took his fancy, and it certainly satisfied his wildest ideas regarding quiet; in fact, quiet was not the proper word to apply to it – desolation was the only term conveying any suitable idea of its isolation. It was an old rambling, heavy-built house of the Jacobean style, with heavy gables and windows, unusually small, and set higher than was customary in such houses, and was surrounded with a high brick wall massively built. Indeed, on examination, it looked more like a fortified house than an ordinary dwelling. But all these things pleased Malcolmson. 'Here,' he thought, 'is the very spot I have been looking for, and if I can only get opportunity of using it I shall be happy.' His joy was increased when he realised beyond doubt that it was not at present inhabited.

From the post office he got the name of the agent, who was rarely surprised at the application to rent a part of the old house. Mr Carnford, the local lawyer and agent, was a genial old gentleman, and frankly confessed his delight at anyone being willing to live in the house.

'To tell you the truth,' said he, 'I should be only too happy, on behalf of the owners, to let anyone have the house rent free for a term of years if only to accustom the people here to see it inhabited. It has been so long empty that some kind of absurd prejudice has grown up about it, and this can be best put down by its occupation –

if only,' he added with a sly glance at Malcolmson, 'by a scholar like yourself, who wants its quiet for a time.'

Malcolmson thought it needless to ask the agent about the 'absurd prejudice'; he knew he would get more information, if he should require it, on that subject from other quarters. He paid his three months' rent, got a receipt, and the name of an old woman who would probably undertake to 'do' for him, and came away with the keys in his pocket. He then went to the landlady of the inn, who was a cheerful and most kindly person, and asked her advice as to such stores and provisions as he would be likely to require. She threw up her hands in amazement when he told her where he was going to settle himself.

'Not in the Judge's House!' she said and grew pale as she spoke. He explained the locality of the house, saying that he did not know its name. When he had finished, she answered: 'Aye, sure enough – sure enough the very place. It is the Judge's House sure enough.' He asked her to tell him about the place, why so called, and what there was against it. She told him that it was so called locally because it had been many years before – how long she could not say, as she was herself from another part of the country, but she thought it must have been a hundred years or more – the abode of a judge who was held in great terror on account of his harsh sentences and his hostility to prisoners at Assizes. As to what there was against the house itself she could not tell. She had often asked, but no one could inform her; but there was a general feeling that there was *something*, and for her own part she would not take all the money in Drinkwater's Bank and stay in the house an hour by herself. Then she apologised to Malcolmson for her disturbing talk.

'It is too bad of me, sir, and you – and a young gentleman, too – if you will pardon me saying it, going to live there all alone. If you were my boy – and you'll excuse me for saying it – you wouldn't sleep there a night, not if I had to go there myself and pull the big alarm bell that's on the roof.' The good creature was so manifestly in earnest, and was so kindly in her intentions, that Malcolmson, although amused, was touched. He told her kindly how much he appreciated her interest in him, and added: 'But, my dear Mrs Witham, indeed you need not be concerned about me! A man who is reading for the Mathematical Tripos has too much to think of to be disturbed by any of these mysterious "somethings", and his work is of too exact and prosaic a kind to allow of his having any corner in his mind for mysteries of any kind. Harmonical Progression, Permutations and Combinations, and Elliptic Functions have sufficient mysteries for me!' Mrs Witham kindly undertook to see after his commissions, and he went himself to look for the old woman who had been recommended to him. When he returned to the Judge's House with her, after an interval of a couple of hours, he found Mrs Witham herself waiting with several men and boys carrying parcels, and an upholsterer's man with a bed in a cart, for she said, though tables and chairs might be all very well, a bed that hadn't been aired for maybe fifty years was not proper for young ones to lie on. She was evidently curious to see the inside of the house; and though manifestly so afraid of the 'somethings' that at the slightest sound she clutched on to Malcolmson, whom she never left for a moment, went over the whole place.

After his examination of the house, Malcolmson decided to take up his abode in the great dining room, which was big enough to serve for all his requirements; and Mrs Witham, with the aid of the charwoman, Mrs Dempster, proceeded to arrange matters. When the hampers were brought in and unpacked, Malcolmson saw that with much kind forethought she had sent from her own kitchen sufficient provisions to last for a few days. Before going she expressed all sorts of kind wishes; and at the door turned and said: 'And perhaps, sir, as the room is big and drafty it might be well to have one of those big screens put round your bed at night – though, truth to tell, I would die myself if I were to be so shut in with all kinds of – of "things" that put their heads round the sides, or over the top, and look on me!' The image which she had called up was too much for her nerves, and she fled incontinently.

Mrs Dempster sniffed in a superior manner as the landlady disappeared, and remarked that for her own part she wasn't afraid of all the bogies in the kingdom.

'I'll tell you what it is, sir,' she said, 'bogies is all kinds and sorts of things – except bogies! Rats and mice, and beetles; and creaky doors, and loose slates, and broken panes, and stiff drawer handles, that stay out when you pull them and then fall down in the middle of the night. Look at the wainscot of the room! It is old – hundreds of years old! Do you think there's no rats and beetles there! And do you imagine, sir, that you won't see none of them? Rats is bogies, I tell you, and bogies is rats; and don't you get to think anything else!'

'Mrs Dempster,' said Malcolmson gravely, making her a polite bow, 'you know more than a Senior Wrangler! And let me say, that, as a mark of esteem for your indubitable soundness of head and heart, I shall, when I go, give you possession of this house, and let you stay here by yourself for the last two months of my tenancy, for four weeks will serve my purpose.'

'Thank you kindly, sir!' she answered, 'but I couldn't sleep away from home a night. I am in Greenhow's Charity, and if I slept a night away from my rooms I should lose all I have got to live on. The rules is very strict; and there's too many watching for a vacancy for me to run any risks in the matter. Only for that, sir, I'd gladly come here and attend on you altogether during your stay.'

'My good woman,' said Malcolmson hastily, 'I have come here on a purpose to obtain solitude; and believe me that I am grateful to the late Greenhow for having organised his admirable charity – whatever it is – that I am perforce denied the opportunity of suffering from such a form of temptation! St Anthony himself could not be more rigid on the point!'

The old woman laughed harshly. 'Ah, you young gentlemen,' she said, 'you don't fear for naught; and belike you'll get all the solitude you want here.' She set to work with her cleaning; and by nightfall, when Malcolmson returned from his walk – he always had one of his books to study as he walked – he found the room swept and tidied, a fire burning on the old hearth, the lamp lit, and the table spread for supper with Mrs Witham's excellent fare. 'This is comfort, indeed,' he said, as he rubbed his hands.

When he had finished his supper, and lifted the tray to the other end of the great oak dining table, he got out his books again, put fresh wood on the fire, trimmed his lamp, and set himself down to a spell of real hard work. He went on without a pause till about eleven o'clock, when he knocked off for a bit to fix his fire and lamp and to make himself a cup of tea. He had always been a tea-drinker, and during his college life had sat late at work and had taken tea late. The rest was a great luxury to him, and he enjoyed it with a sense of delicious, voluptuous ease. The renewed fire leaped and sparkled, and threw quaint shadows through the great old room; and as he sipped his hot tea he revelled in the sense of isolation from his kind. Then it was that he began to notice for the first time what a noise the rats were making.

'Surely,' he thought, 'they cannot have been at it all the time I was reading. Had they been, I must have noticed it!' Presently, when the noise increased, he satisfied himself that it was really new. It was evident that at first the rats had been frightened at the presence of a stranger, and the light of fire and lamp, but that as the time went on they had grown bolder and were now disporting themselves as was their wont.

How busy they were! And hark to the strange noises! Up and down behind the old wainscot, over the ceiling and under the floor they raced, and gnawed, and scratched! Malcolmson smiled to himself as he recalled to mind the saying of Mrs Dempster, 'Bogies is rats, and rats is bogies!' The tea began to have its effect of intellectual and nervous stimulus, he saw with joy another long spell of work to be done before the night was past, and in the sense of security which it gave him, he allowed himself the luxury of a good look round the room. He took his lamp in one hand, and went all round, wondering that so quaint and beautiful an old house had been so long neglected. The carving of the oak on the panels of the wainscot was fine, and on and round the doors and windows it was beautiful and of rare merit. There were some old pictures on the walls, but they were coated so thick with dust and dirt that he could not distinguish any detail of them, though he held his lamp as high as he could over his head. Here and there as he went round he saw some crack or hole blocked for a moment by the face of a rat with its bright eyes glittering in the light, but in an instant it was gone, and a squeak and a scamper followed. The thing that most struck him, however, was the rope of the great alarm bell on the roof, which hung down in a corner of the room on the right-hand side of the fireplace. He pulled up close to the hearth a great high-backed carved oak chair, and sat down to his last cup of tea. When this was done he made up the fire, and went back to his work, sitting at the corner of the table, having the fire to his left. For a little while the rats disturbed him somewhat with their perpetual scampering, but he got accustomed to the noise as one does to the ticking of the clock or to the roar of moving water; and he became so immersed in his work that everything in the world, except the problem which he was trying to solve, passed away from him.

He suddenly looked up, his problem was still unsolved, and there was in the air that sense of the hour before the dawn, which is so dread to doubtful life. The noise of the rats had ceased. Indeed it seemed to him that it must have ceased but lately and that it was the sudden cessation which had disturbed him. The fire had fallen low, but still it threw out a deep red glow. As he looked he started in spite of his *sang froid*.

There on the great high-backed carved oak chair by the right side of the fireplace sat an enormous rat, steadily glaring at him with baleful eyes. He made a motion to it as though to hunt it away, but it did not stir. Then he made the motion of throwing something. Still it did not stir, but showed its great white teeth angrily, and its cruel eyes shone in the lamplight with an added vindictiveness.

Malcolmson felt amazed, and seizing the poker from the hearth ran at it to kill it. Before, however, he could strike it, the rat, with a squeak that sounded like the concentration of hate, jumped upon the floor, and, running up the rope of the alarm bell, disappeared in the darkness beyond the range of the green-shaded lamp. Instantly, strange to say, the noisy scampering of the rats in the wainscot began again.

By this time Malcolmson's mind was quite off the problem; and as a shrill cockcrow outside told him of the approach of morning, he went to bed and to sleep.

He slept so sound that he was not even waked by Mrs Dempster coming in to make up his room. It was only when she had tidied up the place and got his breakfast ready and tapped on the screen which closed in his bed that he woke. He was a little tired still after his night's hard work, but a strong cup of tea soon freshened him up and, taking his book, he went out for his morning walk, bringing with him a few sandwiches lest he should not care to return till dinner time. He found a quiet walk between high elms some way outside the town, and here he spent the greater part of the day studying his Laplace. On his return he looked in to see Mrs Witham and to thank her for her kindness. When she saw him coming through the diamond-paned bay window of her sanctum, she came out to meet him and asked him in. She looked at him searchingly and shook her head as she said: 'You must not overdo it, sir. You are paler this morning than you should be. Too late hours and too hard work on the brain isn't good for any man! But tell me, sir, how did you pass the night? Well, I hope? But, my heart! Sir, I was glad when Mrs Dempster told me this morning that you were all right and sleeping sound when she went in.'

'Oh, I was all right,' he answered smiling. 'The "somethings" didn't worry me, as yet. Only the rats; and they had a circus, I tell you, all over the place. There was one wicked looking old devil that sat up on my own chair by the fire and wouldn't go till I took the poker to him, and then he ran up the rope of the alarm bell and got to somewhere up the wall or the ceiling – I couldn't see where, it was so dark.'

'Mercy on us,' said Mrs Witham, 'an old devil, and sitting on a chair by the fireside! Take care, sir! Take care! There's many a true word spoken in jest.'

'How do you mean? 'Pon my word I don't understand.'

'An old devil! The old devil, perhaps. There! Sir, you needn't laugh,' for Malcolmson had broken into a hearty peal. 'You young folks think it easy to laugh at things that makes older ones shudder.

Never mind, sir! Never mind. Please God, you'll laugh all the time. It's what I wish you myself!' and the good lady beamed all over in sympathy with his enjoyment, her fears gone for a moment.

'Oh, forgive me!' said Malcolmson presently. 'Don't think me rude, but the idea was too much for me – that the old devil himself was on the chair last night!' And at the thought he laughed again. Then he went home to dinner.

This evening the scampering of the rats began earlier; indeed it had been going on before his arrival, and only ceased whilst his presence by its freshness disturbed them. After dinner he sat by the fire for a while and had a smoke; and then, having cleared his table, began to work as before. Tonight the rats disturbed him more than they had done on the previous night. How they scampered up and down and under and over! How they squeaked, and scratched, and gnawed! How they, getting bolder by degrees, came to the mouths of their holes and to the chinks and cracks and crannies in the wainscoting till their eyes shone like tiny lamps as the firelight rose and fell. But to him, now doubtless accustomed to them, their eyes were not wicked; only their playfulness touched him. Sometimes the boldest of them made sallies out on the floor or along the mouldings of the wainscot. Now and again as they disturbed him Malcolmson made a sound to frighten them, smiting the table with his hand or giving a fierce 'Hsh, hsh,' so that they fled straightway to their holes.

And so the early part of the night wore on; and despite the noise Malcolmson got more and more immersed in his work.

All at once he stopped, as on the previous night, being overcome by a sudden sense of silence. There was not the faintest sound of gnaw, or scratch, or squeak. The silence was as of the grave. He remembered the odd occurrence of the previous night, and instinctively he looked at the chair standing close by the fireside. And then a very odd sensation thrilled through him.

There, on the great old high-backed carved oak chair beside the fireplace sat the same enormous rat, steadily glaring at him with baleful eyes.

Instinctively he took the nearest thing to his hand, a book of logarithms, and flung it at it. The book was badly aimed and the rat did not stir, so again the poker performance of the previous night was repeated; and again the rat, being closely pursued, fled up the rope of the alarm bell. Strangely, too, the departure of this rat was instantly followed by the renewal of the noise made by the general rat community. On this occasion, as on the previous one, Malcolmson could not see at what part of the room the rat disappeared, for the green shade of his lamp left the upper part of the room in darkness, and the fire had burned low.

On looking at his watch he found it was close on midnight and, not sorry for the *divertissement*, he made up his fire and made himself his nightly pot of tea. He had got through a good spell of work, and thought himself entitled to a cigarette; and so he sat on the great carved oak chair before the fire and enjoyed it. Whilst smoking he began to think that he would like to know where the rat disappeared to, for he had certain ideas for the morrow not entirely disconnected with a rat trap. Accordingly he lit another lamp and placed it so that it would shine well into the right-hand corner of the wall by the fireplace. Then he got all the books he had with him, and placed them handy to throw at the vermin. Finally he lifted the rope of the alarm bell and placed the end of it on the table, fixing the extreme end under the lamp. As he handled it he could not help noticing how pliable it was, especially for so strong a rope, and one not in use. 'You could hang a man with it,' he thought to himself. When his preparations were made he looked around, and said complacently: 'There now, my friend, I think we shall learn something of you this time!' He began his work again, and though as before somewhat disturbed at first by the noise of the rats, soon lost himself in his proposition and problems.

Again he was called to his immediate surroundings suddenly. This time it might not have been the sudden silence only which took his attention; there was a slight movement of the rope, and the lamp moved. Without stirring, he looked to see if his pile of books was within range, and then cast his eye along the rope. As he looked he saw the great rat drop from the rope on the oak armchair and sit there glaring at him. He raised a book in his right hand, and taking careful aim, flung it at the rat. The latter, with a quick movement, sprang aside and dodged the missile. He then took another book, and a third, and flung them one after another at the rat, but each time unsuccessfully. At last, as he stood with a book poised in his hand to throw, the rat squeaked and seemed afraid. This made Malcolmson more than ever eager to strike, and the book flew and struck the rat a resounding blow. It gave a terrified squeak, and turning on his pursuer a look of terrible malevolence, ran up the chair-back and made a great jump to the rope of the alarm bell and ran up it like lightning. The lamp rocked under the sudden strain, but it was a heavy one and did not topple over. Malcolmson kept his eyes on the rat, and saw it by the light of the second lamp leap to a moulding of the wainscot and disappear through a hole in one of the great pictures which hung on the wall, obscured and invisible through its coating of dirt and dust.

'I shall look up my friend's habitation in the morning,' said the student, as he went over to collect his books. 'The third picture from the fireplace; I shall not forget.' He picked up the books one by one, commenting on them as he lifted them. '*Conic Sections* he does not mind, nor *Cycloidal Oscillations*, nor the *Principia*, nor *Quaternions*, nor *Thermodynamics*. Now for a book that fetched him!' Malcolmson took it up and looked at it. As he did so he started, and a sudden pallor overspread his face. He looked round uneasily and shivered slightly, as he murmured to himself: 'The Bible my mother gave me! What an odd coincidence.' He sat down to work again, and the rats in the wainscot renewed their gambols. They did not disturb him, however; somehow their presence gave him a sense of companionship. But he could not attend to his work, and after striving to master the subject on which he was engaged, gave it up in despair, and went to bed as the first streak of dawn stole in through the eastern window.

He slept heavily but uneasily, and dreamed much; and when Mrs Dempster woke him late in the morning he seemed ill at ease, and for a few minutes did not seem to realise exactly where he was. His first request rather surprised the servant.

'Mrs Dempster, when I am out today I wish you would get the steps and dust or wash those pictures – specially that one the third from the fireplace – I want to see what they are.'

Late in the afternoon Malcolmson worked at his books in the shaded walk, and the cheerfulness of the previous day came back to him as the day wore on, and he found that his reading was progressing well. He had worked out to a satisfactory conclusion all the problems which had as yet baffled him, and it was in a state of jubilation that he paid a visit to Mrs Witham at the Good Traveller. He found a stranger in the cozy sitting room with the landlady, who was introduced to him as Dr Thornhill. She was not quite at ease, and this, combined with the doctor's plunging at once into a series of questions, made Malcolmson come to the conclusion that his presence was not an accident, so without preliminary he said: 'Dr Thornhill, I shall with pleasure answer you any question you may choose to ask me if you will answer me one question first.'

The doctor seemed surprised, but he smiled and answered at once, 'Done! What is it?'

'Did Mrs Witham ask you to come here and see me and advise me?'

Dr Thornhill for a moment was taken aback, and Mrs Witham got fiery red and turned away; but the doctor was a frank and ready man, and he answered at once and openly: 'She did, but she didn't intend you to know it. I suppose it was my clumsy haste that made you suspect. She told me that she did not like the idea of your being in that house all by yourself, and that she thought you took too much strong tea. In fact, she wants me to advise you if possible to give up the tea and the very late hours. I was a keen student in my time, so I suppose I may take the liberty of a college man, and without offence, advise you not quite as a stranger.'

Malcolmson with a bright smile held out his hand. 'Shake! as they say in America,' he said. 'I must thank you for your kindness and Mrs Witham too, and your kindness deserves a return on my part. I promise to take no more strong tea – no tea at all till you let me – and I shall go to bed tonight at one o'clock at latest. Will that do?'

'Capital,' said the doctor. 'Now tell us all that you noticed in the old house,' and so Malcolmson then and there told in minute detail all that had happened in the last two nights. He was inter-rupted every now and then by some exclamation from Mrs Witham, till finally when he told of the episode of the Bible the landlady's pent-up emotions found vent in a shriek; and it was not till a stiff glass of brandy and water had been administered that she grew composed again. Dr Thornhill listened with a face of growing grav-ity, and when the narrative was complete and Mrs Witham had been restored, he asked: 'The rat always went up the rope of the alarm bell?'

'I suppose you know,' said the doctor after a pause, 'what the rope is?'

'It is,' said the doctor slowly, 'the very rope which the hangman used for all the victims of the judge's judicial rancour!' Here he was interrupted by another scream from Mrs Witham, and steps had to be taken for her recovery. Malcolmson having looked at his watch, and found that it was close to his dinner hour, had gone home before her complete recovery.

When Mrs Witham was herself again she almost assailed the doctor with angry questions as to what he meant by putting such horrible ideas into the poor young man's mind. 'He has quite enough there already to upset him,' she added. Dr Thornhill replied: 'My dear madam, I had a distinct purpose in it! I wanted to draw his attention to the bell rope, and to fix it there. It may be that he is in a highly overwrought state, and has been studying too much, although I am bound to say that he seems as sound and healthy a young man, mentally and bodily, as ever I saw – but then the rats – and that suggestion of the devil.' The doctor shook his head and went on. 'I would have offered to go and stay the first night with him but that I felt sure it would have been a cause of offence. He may get in the night some strange fright or hallucination and if he does I want him to pull that rope. All alone as he is, it will give us warning, and we may reach him in time to be of service. I shall be sitting up pretty late tonight and shall keep my ears open. Do not be alarmed if Benchurch gets a surprise before morning.'

'Oh, doctor, what do you mean? What do you mean?'

'I mean this; that possibly – nay, more probably – we shall hear the great alarm bell from the Judge's House tonight,' and the doctor made about as effective an exit as could be thought of.

When Malcolmson arrived home he found that it was a little after his usual time, and Mrs Dempster had gone away – the rules of Greenhow's Charity were not to be neglected. He was glad to see that the place was bright and tidy with a cheerful fire and a well-trimmed lamp. The evening was colder than might have been expected in April, and a heavy wind was blowing with such rapidly-increasing strength that there was every promise of a storm during the night. For a few minutes after his entrance the noise of the rats ceased; but so soon as they became accustomed to his presence they began again. He was glad to hear them, for he felt once more the feeling of companionship in their noise, and his mind ran back to the strange fact that they only ceased to manifest themselves when that other – the great rat with the baleful eyes – came upon the scene. The reading lamp only was lit and its green shade kept the ceiling and the upper part of the room in darkness, so that the cheerful light from the hearth spreading over the floor and shining on the white cloth laid over the end of the table was warm and cheery. Malcolmson sat down to his dinner with a good appetite and a buoyant spirit. After his dinner and a cigarette he sat steadily down to work, determined not to let anything disturb him, for he remembered his promise to the doctor, and made up his mind to make the best of the time at his disposal.

For an hour or so he worked all right, and then his thoughts began to wander from his books. The actual circumstances around him, the calls on his physical attention, and his nervous suscepti-bility were not to be denied. By this time the wind had become a gale, and the gale a storm. The old house, solid though it was, seemed to shake to its foundations, and the storm roared and raged through its many chimneys and its queer old gables, producing strange, unearthly sounds in the empty rooms and corridors. Even the great alarm bell on the roof must have felt the force of the wind, for the rope rose and fell slightly, as though the bell were moved a little from time to time, and the limber rope fell on the oak floor with a hard and hollow sound.

As Malcolmson listened to it he bethought himself of the doctor's words, 'It is the rope which the hangman used for the victims of the judge's judicial rancour,' and he went over to the corner of the fireplace and took it in his hand to look at it. There seemed a sort of deadly interest in it, and as he stood there he lost himself for a moment in speculation as to who these victims were, and the grim wish of the judge to have such a ghastly relic ever under his eyes. As he stood there the swaying of the bell on the roof still lifted the rope now and again; but presently there came a new sensation – a sort of tremor in the rope, as though something was moving along it.

Looking up instinctively Malcolmson saw the great rat coming slowly down towards him, glaring at him steadily. He dropped the rope and started back with a muttered curse, and the rat turning ran up the rope again and disappeared, and at the same instant Malcolmson became conscious that the noise of the other rats, which had ceased for a while, began again.

All this set him thinking, and it occurred to him that he had not investigated the lair of the rat or looked at the pictures, as he had intended. He lit the other lamp without the shade, and, holding it up, went and stood opposite the third picture from the fireplace on the right-hand side where he had seen the rat disappear on the previous night.

At the first glance he started back so suddenly that he almost dropped the lamp, and a deadly pallor overspread his face. His knees shook, and heavy drops of sweat came on his forehead, and he trembled like an aspen. But he was young and plucky, and pulled himself together, and after the pause of a few seconds stepped forward again, raised the lamp, and examined the picture which had been dusted and washed, and now stood out clearly.

It was of a judge dressed in his robes of scarlet and ermine. His face was strong and merciless, evil, crafty, and vindictive, with a sensual mouth, hooked nose of ruddy colour, and shaped like the beak of a bird of prey. The rest of the face was of a cadaverous colour. The eyes were of peculiar brilliance and with a terribly malignant expression. As he looked at them Malcolmson grew cold, for he saw there the very counterpart of the eyes of the great rat. The lamp almost fell from his hand, he saw the rat with its baleful eyes peering out through the hole in the corner of the picture, and noted the sudden cessation of the noise of the other rats. However, he pulled himself together, and went on with his examination of the picture.

The judge was seated in a great high-backed carved oak chair, on the right-hand side of a great stone fireplace where, in the corner, a rope hung down from the ceiling, its end lying coiled on the floor. With a feeling of something like horror, Malcolmson recognised the scene of the room as it stood, and gazed around him in an awestruck manner as though he expected to find some strange presence behind him. Then he looked over to the corner of the fireplace – and with a loud cry he let the lamp fall from his hand.

There, in the judge's armchair, with the rope hanging behind, sat the rat with the judge's baleful eyes, now intensified and with a fiendish leer. Save for the howling of the storm without there was silence.

The fallen lamp recalled Malcolmson to himself. Fortunately it was of metal, and so the oil was not spilt. However, the practical need of attending to it settled at once his nervous apprehensions. When he had turned it out, he wiped his brow and thought for a moment.

'This will not do,' he said to himself. 'If I go on like this I shall become a crazy fool. This must stop! I promised the doctor I would not take tea. Faith, he was pretty right! My nerves must have been getting into a queer state. Funny I did not notice it. I never felt better in my life. However, it is all right now, and I shall not be such a fool again.'

Then he mixed himself a good stiff glass of brandy and water and resolutely sat down to his work.

It was nearly an hour later when he looked up from his book, disturbed by the sudden stillness. Without, the wind howled and roared louder than ever, and the rain drove in sheets against the windows, beating like hail on the glass; but within there was no sound whatever save the echo of the wind as it roared in the great chimney, and now and then a hiss as a few raindrops found their way down the chimney in a lull of the storm. The fire had fallen low and had ceased to flame, though it threw out a red glow. Malcolmson listened attentively, and presently heard a thin, squeaking noise, very faint. It came from the corner of the room where the rope hung down, and he thought it was the creaking of the rope on the floor as the swaying of the bell raised and lowered it. Looking up, however, he saw in the dim light the great rat clinging to the rope and gnawing it. The rope was already nearly gnawed through – he could see the lighter colour where the strands were laid bare. As he looked the job was completed, and the severed end of the rope fell clattering on the oaken floor, whilst for an instant the great rat remained like a knob or tassel at the end of the rope, which now began to sway to and fro. Malcolmson felt for a moment another pang of terror as he thought that now the possibility of calling the outer world to his assistance was cut off, but an intense anger took its place, and seizing the book he was reading he hurled it at the rat. The blow was well aimed, but before the missile could reach him the rat dropped off and struck the floor with a soft thud. Malcolmson instantly rushed over towards him, but it darted away and disappeared in the darkness of the shadows of the room. Malcolmson felt that his work was over for the night, and determined then and there to vary the monotony of the proceedings by a hunt for the rat, and took off the green shade of the lamp so as to insure a wider spreading light. As he did so the gloom of the upper part of the room was relieved, and in the new flood of light, great by comparison with the previous darkness, the pictures on the wall stood out boldly. From where he stood, Malcolmson saw right opposite to him the third picture on the wall from the right of the fireplace. He rubbed his eyes in surprise, and then a great fear began to come upon him.

In the centre of the picture was a great irregular patch of brown canvas, as fresh as when it was stretched on the frame. The background was as before, with chair and chimney-corner and rope, but the figure of the judge had disappeared.

Malcolmson, almost in a chill of horror, turned slowly round, and then he began to shake and tremble like a man in a palsy. His strength seemed to have left him, and he was incapable of action or movement, hardly even of thought. He could only see and hear.

There, on the great high-backed carved oak chair sat the judge in his robes of scarlet and ermine, with his baleful eyes glaring vindictively, and a smile of triumph on the resolute, cruel mouth, as he lifted with his hands a *black cap*. Malcolmson felt as if the blood was running from his heart, as one does in moments of prolonged suspense. There was a ringing in his ears. Without, he could hear the roar and howl of the tempest, and through it, swept on the storm, came the striking of midnight by the great chimes in the market-place. He stood for a space of time that seemed to him endless still as a statue, and with wide-open, horror-struck eyes, breathless. As the clock struck, so the smile of triumph on the judge's face inten-sified, and at the last stroke of midnight he placed the black cap on his head.

Slowly and deliberately the judge rose from his chair and picked up the piece of the rope of the alarm bell which lay on the floor, drew it through his hands as if he enjoyed its touch, and then delib-erately began to knot one end of it, fashioning it into a noose. This he tightened and tested with his foot, pulling hard at it till he was satisfied and then making a running noose of it, which he held in his hand. Then he began to move along the table on the opposite side to Malcolmson keeping his eyes on him until he had passed him, when with a quick movement he stood in front of the door. Malcolmson then began to feel that he was trapped, and tried to think of what he should do. There was some fascination in the judge's eyes, which he never took off him, and he had, perforce, to look. He saw the judge approach – still keeping between him and the door – and raise the noose and throw it towards him as if to entangle him. With a great effort he made a quick movement to one side, and saw the rope fall beside him, and heard it strike the oaken floor. Again the judge raised the noose and tried to ensnare him, ever keeping his baleful eyes fixed on him, and each time by a mighty effort the student just managed to evade it. So this went on for many times, the judge seeming never discouraged nor discomposed at failure, but playing as a cat does with a mouse. At last in despair, which had reached its climax, Malcolmson cast a quick glance round him. The lamp seemed to have blazed up, and there was a fairly good light in the room. At the many rat-holes and in the chinks and crannies of the wainscot he saw the rats' eyes; and this aspect, that was purely physical, gave him a gleam of comfort. He looked round and saw that the rope of the great alarm bell was laden with rats. Every inch of it was covered with them, and more and more were pouring through the small circular hole in the ceiling whence it emerged, so that with their weight the bell was beginning to sway.

Hark! It had swayed till the clapper had touched the bell. The sound was but a tiny one, but the bell was only beginning to sway, and it would increase.

At the sound the judge, who had been keeping his eyes fixed on Malcolmson, looked up, and a scowl of diabolical anger overspread his face. His eyes fairly glowed like hot coals, and he stamped his foot with a sound that seemed to make the house shake. A dreadful peal of thunder broke overhead as he raised the rope again, whilst the rats kept running up and down the rope as though working against time. This time, instead of throwing it, he drew close to his victim, and held open the noose as he approached. As he came closer there seemed something paralysing in his very presence, and Malcolmson stood rigid as a corpse. He felt the judge's icy fingers touch his throat as he adjusted the rope. The noose tightened – tightened. Then the judge, taking the rigid form of the student in his arms, carried him over and placed him standing in the oak chair, and stepping up beside him, put his hand up and caught the end of the swaying rope of the alarm bell. As he raised his hand the rats fled squeaking, and disappeared through the hole in the ceiling. Taking the end of the noose which was round Malcolmson's neck he tied it to the hanging bell-rope, and then descending pulled away the chair.

When the alarm bell of the Judge's House began to sound, a crowd soon assembled. Lights and torches of various kinds appeared, and soon a silent crowd was hurrying to the spot. They knocked loudly at the door, but there was no reply. Then they burst in the door, and poured into the great dining room, the doctor at the head.

There at the end of the rope of the great alarm bell hung the body of the student, and on the face of the judge in the picture was a malignant smile.

THE OPEN WINDOW

SAKI

(1914)

Ghostly endeavours can be fun. Certainly, if introduced by a self-possessed fifteen-year-old who might as well be ninety. And, at her mercy, a self-obsessed middle-aged man who has arrived with his nerves and his letters of introduction. Once Vera has established the visitor knows nothing of her aunt, out steps her inner minx — a gleeful ghost of human design. An oral narrative wonderfully becomes a ghost story, giving us a laugh-out-loud scare. Oh, how I want to be Vera!

Y AUNT WILL BE down presently, Mr Nuttel,' said a very self-possessed young lady of fifteen. 'In the meantime you must try and put up with me.'

Framton Nuttel endeavoured to say the correct something which should duly flatter the niece of the moment without unduly discounting the aunt that was to come. Privately he doubted more than ever whether these formal visits on a succession of total strangers would do much towards helping the nerve cure which he was supposed to be undergoing.

'I know how it will be,' his sister had said when he was preparing to migrate to this rural retreat. 'You will bury yourself down there and not speak to a living soul, and your nerves will be worse than ever from moping. I shall just give you letters of introduction to all the people I know there. Some of them, as far as I can remember, were quite nice.'

Framton wondered whether Mrs Sappleton, the lady to whom he was presenting one of the letters of introduction, came into the nice division.

'Do you know many of the people round here?' asked the niece, when she judged that they had had sufficient silent communion.

'Hardly a soul,' said Framton. 'My sister was staying here, at the rectory, you know, some four years ago, and she gave me letters of introduction to some of the people here.'

He made the last statement in a tone of distinct regret.

'Then you know practically nothing about my aunt?' pursued the self-possessed young lady.

'Only her name and address,' admitted the caller. He was wondering whether Mrs Sappleton was in the married or widowed state. An undefinable something about the room seemed to suggest masculine habitation.

'Her great tragedy happened just three years ago,' said the child. 'That would be since your sister's time.'

'Her tragedy?' asked Framton; somehow in this restful country spot tragedies seemed out of place.

'You may wonder why we keep that window wide open on an October afternoon,' said the niece, indicating a large French window that opened on to a lawn.

'It is quite warm for the time of the year,' said Framton, 'but has that window got anything to do with the tragedy?'

'Out through that window, three years ago to a day, her husband and her two young brothers went off for their day's shooting. They never came back. In crossing the moor to their favourite snipe-shooting ground they were all three engulfed in a treacherous piece of bog. It had been that dreadful wet summer, you know, and places that were safe in other years gave way suddenly without warning. Their bodies were never recovered. That was the dreadful part of it.' Here the child's voice lost its self-possessed note and became falteringly human. 'Poor aunt always thinks that they will come back some day, they and the little brown spaniel that was lost with them, and walk in at that window just as they used to do. That is why the window is kept open every evening till it is quite dusk. Poor dear aunt, she has often told me how they went out, her husband with his white waterproof coat over his arm, and Ronnie, her youngest brother, singing 'Bertie, why do you bound?' as he always did to tease her, because she said it got on her nerves. Do you know, sometimes on still, quiet evenings like this, I almost get a creepy feeling that they will all walk in through that window – '

She broke off with a little shudder. It was a relief to Framton when the aunt bustled into the room with a whirl of apologies for being late in making her appearance.

'I hope Vera has been amusing you?' she said.

'She has been very interesting,' said Framton.

'I hope you don't mind the open window,' said Mrs Sappleton briskly. 'My husband and brothers will be home directly from shooting, and they always come in this way. They've been out for snipe in the marshes today, so they'll make a fine mess over my poor carpets. So like you menfolk, isn't it?'

She rattled on cheerfully about the shooting and the scarcity of birds, and the prospects for duck in the winter. To Framton it was all purely horrible. He made a desperate but only partially successful effort to turn the talk on to a less ghastly topic; he was conscious that his hostess was giving him only a fragment of her attention, and her eyes were constantly straying past him to the open window and the lawn beyond. It was certainly an unfortunate coincidence that he should have paid his visit on this tragic anniversary.

'The doctors agree in ordering me complete rest, an absence of mental excitement, and avoidance of anything in the nature of violent physical exercise,' announced Framton, who laboured under the tolerably widespread delusion that total strangers and chance acquaintances are hungry for the least detail of one's ailments and infirmities, their cause and cure. 'On the matter of diet they are not so much in agreement,' he continued.

'No?' said Mrs Sappleton, in a voice which only replaced a yawn at the last moment. Then she suddenly brightened into alert attention – but not to what Framton was saying.

'Here they are at last!' she cried. 'Just in time for tea, and don't they look as if they were muddy up to the eyes!'

Framton shivered slightly and turned towards the niece with a look intended to convey sympathetic comprehension. The child was staring out through the open window with dazed horror in her eyes. In a chill shock of nameless fear Framton swung round in his seat and looked in the same direction.

In the deepening twilight three figures were walking across the lawn towards the window; they all carried guns under their arms, and one of them was additionally burdened with a white coat hung over his shoulders. A tired brown spaniel kept close at their heels. Noiselessly they neared the house, and then a hoarse young voice chanted out of the dusk: 'I said, Bertie, why do you bound?'

Framton grabbed wildly at his stick and hat; the hall door, the gravel drive, and the front gate were dimly-noted stages in his headlong retreat. A cyclist coming along the road had to run into the hedge to avoid an imminent collision.

'Here we are, my dear;' said the bearer of the white mackintosh, coming in through the window, 'fairly muddy, but most of it's dry. Who was that who bolted out as we came up?'

'A most extraordinary man, a Mr Nuttel,' said Mrs Sappleton. 'Could only talk about his illnesses, and dashed off without a word

civica

Issued

Branch: South Dublin Lucan
Date: 27/02/2024 Time: 10:17 AI
Name: Cahill, Brendan
ID: D4000000573210

ITEM(S) DUE DATI

Tales of the otherworld :_ 08 Mar 202·
SD200000056841
Item Value: €24.99

Total value of item(s): €24.99
Your current loan(s): 1
Your current reservation(s): 0
Your current active request(s): 0

To renew your items please log onto My
Account on the OPAC at
https://southdublin.spydus.ie

Thank you for using your local library

of goodbye or apology when you arrived. One would think he had seen a ghost.'

'I expect it was the spaniel,' said the niece calmly. 'He told me he had a horror of dogs. He was once hunted into a cemetery some-where on the banks of the Ganges by a pack of pariah dogs, and had to spend the night in a newly dug grave with the creatures snarling and grinning and foaming just above him. Enough to make anyone lose their nerve.'

Romance at short notice was her speciality.

THE PORTRAIT OF ROISIN DHU

DOROTHY MACARDLE

(1924)

As a student, I often stopped at the bust of James Clarence Mangan in Saint Stephen's Green. It was a time for the romantic dreams of youth, and the description of this story's paintings are redolent of another time. This strange and haunting story has a vampiric feel; the artist genius has no further interest in beauty once he has captured it. Or so it seems.

IT WAS A YEAR after the artist was drowned that the loan exhibition of Hugo Blake's paintings was opened in Philadelphia by Maeve. 'Whom the gods love die young,' people said.

To remember those paintings is like remembering a dream-life spent with the Ever-living in an Ireland untrodden by men.

Except once he never painted a human face or any form of life, human or fairy, yet the very light and air of them thrilled with life – it was as though he had painted life itself. There was the great 'Sliav Gullion' – stony, austere – the naked mountain against the northern sky, and to look at it was to be filled with a young, fierce hunger for heroic deeds, with the might of Cuchulain and Fionn. There was 'Loch Corrib' like a mirage from the first day of Creation – there was Una's 'Dawn' …

The critics, inarticulate with wonder, made meaningless phrases: 'Blake paints as a seer,' 'He paints on the astral plane.'

At the end of the room, alone on a grey wall, hung the 'Portrait of Roisin Dhu'. Before her, Irish men and women stood worshipping, the old with tears, the young with fire in their eyes. There were men whom it sent home.

Had Blake seen, anywhere on earth, others were asking, that heartbreaking, entrancing face? Knowledge of the secrets of God was in the eyes; on the lips was the memory, the endurance and the foreknowledge of endless pain; yet from the luminous, serene face shone out a beauty that made one crave for the spaces beyond death.

No woman in the world, we said, had been Hugo's Roisin Dhu; no mortal face had troubled him when he painted that immortal dream – that ecstasy beyond fear, that splendour beyond anguish – that wild, sweet holiness of Ireland for which men die.

Maeve, as we knew, had been his old friend. When strangers clamoured, 'Was there a woman?' she would not tell. But one evening when we were five only around Una's fire she told us the strange, incredible tale.

'I will not tell everyone for a while,' she said, 'because so few would understand, and Hugo, unless one understood to the heights and depths, might seem to have been ... unkind. But I will tell you: there was a girl.'

'It is almost impossible to believe,' Liam said. 'It is not a human body he has painted; nor even a human soul!'

'That is true in a way,' Maeve answered, hesitating. 'I will try to make you understand.

'He was the loneliest being I have ever known. He was a little atom of misery and rebellion when my godmother rescued him in France. She bought the child from a drunkard who was starving him almost to death. His mother, you know, was Nora Raftery, the actress; she ran away from her husband with François Raoul, taking the child, and died. Poor Blake rode over a precipice while hunting – mad with grief, and the boy was left without a friend in the world. It was I who taught him to read and write: already he could draw.

To the end he was the same passionate, lonely child. The anguish of pity and love he had had for his mother he gave to her country when he came home: he suffered unbearable 'heim-weh' all the years he was studying abroad. The 'Dark Tower' as we called it, of our godmother's house on Loch Corrib was the place he loved best.

I have known no one who lived in such extremes, always, of misery or of joy. In any medium but paint he was helpless – chaotic or dumb, yet I think that his pictures came to him first not visually at all, but as intense perceptions of a *mood*. And between that moment of perception and the moment when it took form and colour in his mind he used to be like a wild creature in pain. He would prowl day and night around the region he meant to paint, waiting in a rage of impatience for the right moment of light and shadow to come, the incarnation of the soul … Then, when he had found it, the blessed mood of contentment would come and he would paint, day after day, until it was done. At those times, in the evenings, he would be exhausted and friendly and grateful like a child.

For all the vehemence that you feel in his work he painted very slowly, with intense, exquisite care, like a man in love. That is indeed what he was – in love, obliviously, with whatever spirit had enthralled his imagination at the time. And when the picture was finished and the vision gone he fell into a mood of desolation in which he wanted to die. He was very young.

I tried to scold Hugo out of those moods. I was with him in April just after he had finished his 'Loch Corrib' – you know the innocence, the angelic tranquillity in it, like the soul of a child.

He would not go near the lake: 'It is nothing to me now,' he said sombrely, 'I have done with it.'

'Hugo!' I said, laughing, 'you are a vampire! The loch has given you its soul.' He answered, 'Yes: that is true; corpses are ugly things.'

For a month that empty, dead mood lasted and Hugo hated all the world. I took him to London to give him something to hate. After two days he fled back to his tower and breathed the smell of the peat and sea wind, and the sweet, home-welcome of burning turf, and looked out on Ireland with eyes of love. The next morning he came in from a bathe in the loch with the awakened, wondering look I had longed to see and said, 'I am going to paint Roisin Dhu.' Then he went off to walk the west of Ireland seeking a woman for his need.

I was astonished and excited beyond words; he had been so contemptuous of human subjects, although I remembered, in his student days, studies for heads and hands that had made one artist whisper, 'Leonardo!' under his breath.

I wondered what woman he would bring home.

They came about two weeks later, after dark, rowing over the loch, Hugo and the girl alone.

After supper, sitting over the turf fire in the round hall of the tower, Hugo told me that she was the daughter of a king.

She smiled at him, knowing that he spoke of her although she had no English at all, and I told her in Irish what he had said. She answered gravely, 'It is true.'

I looked at her then as she moved from the window to her chair, and I felt almost afraid – her beauty was so delicate and so remote …

'Those red lips with all their mournful pride' … Poems of Yeats were haunting me while I looked at her. But it was the beauty of one asleep, unaware of life or of sorrow or love … the face of a woman whose light is hidden …

She sat in the shadowed corner, brooding, while Hugo talked. He was at his happiest, overflowing with childish delight in his achievement and with eagerness for tomorrow's sun.

Nuala was her name. The King of the Blasket Isles was her father – a superstitious, tyrannical old man. Hugo had been able to make no way with him or his sons.

'I invited one of them to come too, and take care of her,' he said, 'but they would not hear of it at all.

'The old man was as dignified as a Spanish Grandee.

'"It is not that I would be misdoubting you, honest man," says he, "but my daughter is my daughter and there is no call for her to be going abroad to the world."

'And her brothers was as obstinate:

'"'Tis not good to be put in a picture: it takes from you," they said.'

'They got me into a boat by a ruse, rowed me "back to Ireland", and when they had landed me pulled off.

'"The blessing of God on your far travelling!" they called to me gravely: a hint that I would not be welcome to the island again.

'You can imagine the frenzy I was in!' he said. And I could, well. He had walked night after night on the rocks of the mainland planning some desperate thing, but one night Nuala came to him, rowed out through the darkness by some boys who braved the vengeance of the old king for her sake. He rewarded them extravagantly and brought Nuala home.

He told it all triumphantly, and Nuala looked up at him from time to time with a gentle gaze full of content and rest. But my heart sank: there was only one possible end to this; Hugo, at his best, was loving and kind and selfless – all might be well – but I knew my Hugo after work.

She slept in my room and talked to me, softly, in the dark, asking me questions about Hugo's work. 'He told me you were his sister-friend,' she said.

I told her about his childhood, his suffering and his genius: she listened and sighed.

'It is a pity of him to be so long lonely,' she said, 'but he will not be lonely any more.'

'Why, Nuala?' I asked, my heart heavy with dread for her. Her answer left me silent.

'I myself will be giving him love.'

Hugo had found a being as lost to the world as himself. How would it end for her, I wondered. She slept peacefully, but I lay long awake.

The next morning work began in the studio at the top of the tower. I gave up all thought of going home. Nuala would need me.

Hugo was working faster than usual it seemed, beginning as soon as the light was clear and never pausing until it failed. I marvelled at Nuala's endurance, but I dared not plead for her. I had wrecked a picture of Hugo's once by going into his studio while he painted: his vision fled from him at the least intrusion and I had learned to keep aloof.

Day after day, when they came down at last to rest and eat, I could measure his progress by the sombre glow of power in his eyes. I could imagine some young druid when his spells proved potent, looking like that.

But the change that came over Nuala frightened me; he was wearing her away: her face had a clear, luminous look, her eyes were large and dark; I saw an expression in them sometimes as of one gazing into an abyss of pain. The change that might come to a lovely woman in years, seemed to come to her in days: the beauty of her, as she sat in the candlelight, gazing at her own thoughts in the shadows, would still your breathing. It grew more wonderful, more tragic, from day to day.

One night after she had stolen away to bed, exhausted, while Hugo sat by the fire in a kind of trance, I forced myself to question him.

'Hugo,' I said, as lightly as I could, with my heart throbbing: 'Is it that you are in love with your Roisin Dhu?'

He looked up suddenly, with a dark fire in his eyes. 'Love,' he whispered in a voice aching with passion. He rose and threw back his head and cried out in tones like deep music –

'I could plough the blue air!
I could climb the high hills!
O, I could kneel all night in prayer
To heal your many ills!'

Then he sighed and went away.

Nuala's look was becoming, day by day, a look of endurance and resignation that I could not bear, as of one despairing of all human happiness yet serene.

At last I questioned him again:

'Will you be marrying your Roisin Dhu?'

He turned on me startled, with a laugh, both angry and amazed.

'What a question! What an outrageous question, Maeve!'

I was unanswered still.

When seven weeks had gone I grew gravely anxious. I feared that Nuala would die: she had the beauty you could imagine in a spirit new-awakened from death, a look of anguish and ecstasy in one … She was frail and spent; she scarcely spoke to me or seemed to know me; she slept always in the garden alone.

It was towards the end of June that I said to Hugo, 'You are wearing your model out.'

'I am painting her better than God created her,' he answered. Then he said, contentedly, 'I shall have done with her very soon.'

I cannot express the dread that fell on me then; I was torn with irresolution. To interfere with Hugo – to break the spell of his vision, would not only sacrifice the picture, it might destroy him. I thought his reason would not survive the laceration, the passion that would follow the shattering of that dream.

That night I found Nuala utterly changed. She came down from the studio dull-eyed and ugly and went straight to bed in my room.

Hugo told me he did not want her any more.

I rowed her out next morning across the loch: it was one of those grey, misty days when it is loveliest; the Twelve Bens in the distance looked like mountains of Hy Breasail, the weeds and sedges glimmering silvery-gold ... but she had no eyes for its beauty, no beauty of her own, no light ... she lay drowsy and unresponsive on her cushions; her hands and face were like wax.

I would have rebelled that night, taken any risk, to make Hugo undo what he had done. She lay down to sleep under a willow by the water's edge and I went to him in the hall. He was standing by the fire and turned to me as I came in; there was a look of wondering humility in his face, as if his own achievement were a thing to worship – a thing he could not understand.

'Tomorrow!' he said. 'It will be finished in an hour: you shall see it.'

Then he came and took my hands in his old, affectionate way and said:

'You have been such a good sister-friend!'

One hour more! She must endure it: I would not sacrifice him for that. But I lay awake all night oppressed with a sense of fear and cruelty and guilt.

At breakfast time there was no Hugo: he had eaten and started work. Old Kate rang the bell in the garden but Nuala did not come. My fears had vanished with the sweet air and sunshine of the early morning: larks were singing; it was mid-June: the joy of Hugo's triumph was my own joy. I went down to the willow where I had left Nuala asleep. She was lying there still; she never stirred when I touched her. She was cold.

I called no one, I ran madly up the spiral stair to Hugo's studio in the tower. Outside his door I paused: the memory of the last time I had broken in and the devastating consequences arrested me even then. I pushed the door open without a sound and stood inside, transfixed.

I looked for a moment and grew dizzy, so amazing was the thing I saw. Hugo stood by his easel: before him on the dais, glimmering in the misty silver light, stood Nuala, gazing at him, all a radiance of consummated sacrifice and sweet, unconquerable love – Nuala, as you have seen her in the portrait of Roisin Dhu.

Hugo stumbled, laid down his brush, drew his hand over his eyes, then turned and, seeing me, said, 'It is done.'

When I looked again at the dais she was gone.

I was shaken to the heart with fear. I cried out, 'Come to her! She is dead.'

He ran with me down to the water's edge.

I believe I had hoped that he would be able to waken her, but she was cold and dead, lying with wide-open eyes.

Hugo knelt down and touched her, then rose quickly and turned away: 'How unbeautiful!' he said.

I called out to him sternly, angrily, and he looked down at her again, then stooped and lifted her in his arms.

'Maeve, Maeve!' he cried then, piteously. 'Have I done this?'

He brought her home with state to the Island, told them she had been his bride and gave her such a burial as the old King's heart approved. Then he came home again to his lonely house. I left it before he came; he had told me he wanted to be alone.

I heard nothing of him then for a long time and felt uneasy and afraid. After I had written many anxious letters a strange, disjointed answer came.

'She has never left me,' he wrote. 'She is waiting, near, quite near. But what can I do? This imprisoning body – this suffocating life – this burdenous mortality – this dead world.

'The picture is for you, Sister-friend, and for Ireland when you die.'

Before I could go to him the picture came and with it the news that he was drowned.

They found the boat far out on the loch.'

Maeve's face was pale when she ended: she covered her eyes for a moment with her hand.

'He had seen the hidden vision …' one of us said.

Nesta was looking into the fire, her dark eyes wide with foreboding.

'It is written in Destiny,' she said, 'the lovers of Roisin Dhu must die.'

ENCOUNTER AT NIGHT

MARY FRANCES MCHUGH

(1935)

Ghostly graveyards and haunted castles may make us shiver, but cities are ghostly places too. As life drifts away from the busy streets, ghosts linger in the heads of the few living who remain. How strange that the loneliness haunting our narrator never recognised the same spectre in the friend he regarded as jolly little Terry Shaughnessy, a safe harbour of good cheer. How little we know of each other's ghosts.

UBLIN WAS GROWING DESERTED; only an odd car slid by in the dark, rainy night, for the second of its passing throwing a dazzle on the shiny pavements and lighting up the shuttered shops. Figures would pass, hurrying by with hunched shoulders – but less and less frequently.

Tom Donovan and his three friends scarcely felt the rain. They were hot and happy and bemused. All that each of them wanted was somehow to continue talking and drinking and smoking in genial company ... But Jim, the red-haired barman at Flynn's, had gradually edged them out into the night, and bolted the doors against them. There was nothing for it but to go home.

'Take care of yourself, Joe!'

'Well, goodnight, boys!'

'Take care – see you tomorrow.'

The milk of human kindness flowed in them, and they patted one another's backs affectionately again and again before each went his separate way. Donovan, the shiftless poet, was left standing on the pavement, last and lonely. Slowly there faded from his face its smile of convivial bliss, and into his sobering mind crept back those thoughts which now, with the fleeting years, possessed him more and more in his solitary moments.

Wretched, killing thoughts. No, not thoughts – not thoughts, but feelings – or one feeling only, corroding unhappiness. A sense that life was vain and empty, with comfort nowhere – not even in drinking, in friendship, or in love. If even he knew friendship or love! A certainty that never, during all his existence, even when he had been young and gay and roistering, had he known ease; always a shadow had been lurking at his elbow. And it whispered to him that he was a fool to go on with the sham from day to day, that there was only one solution to everything: a knife or a rope for his throat.

Cruel memories came thronging. He saw a miserable, beaten peasant child: himself. All that child had really known was suffering, though the man had made sweet lilting songs of a boy, barefooted, in the West, birds'-nesting or tickling for trout in a mountain stream. The boy had been there, the sun, the stream, the idyllic sky, the irrational light-heartedness of childhood. These were the stuff of his verse – but not the harsh home, the pain and puzzled grief, the cold and hunger which had been more true and near. These things had made him! They were with him even now.

Later, there was the man. A poet he was now, praised and wondered at for the clear innocency of his songs, toys fashioned for the cultured mind by a queer bohemian fellow. That he was so different from his poetry merely gave it zest. He knew this, and cultivated his oddity; and it was partly to curry favour with his admirers that he drank and sang his way through Europe without a word of any language but his own. Here, standing on a Dublin pavement in the night, he recalled the troubadour adventure and shivered – not because the steely rain was stinging his face and sending cold arrows through his clothing. No; but because from those wanderings from which he had so triumphantly returned he could now remember only a haunting horror. He evoked without willing it a night in Russia, when he lay in a country tavern with his familiar spirit beside him. There, in a big common room, several poor travellers slept about the stove. The air was humid with their breath and the odorous damp of their clothing, and the windows were sealed to blindness by the snow outside. In the yard there suddenly arose the commotion of a sledge being unharnessed; a bulky figure stepped into the room and looked stealthily around at the sleepers and fixedly at him, Donovan, before flinging itself likewise down in a corner. Donovan through half-closed eyes saw the stranger's Mongolian face, and as though he were a child it smote him with its mystery of a locked mind, of a race other than and alien to his own. There was no reason for his sudden panic of fear, or for the anguish of loneliness which overcame him then. It was simply part of the encompassing oppression of the world to his soul, driving him whither he knew not.

He tossed his head, heedless of the rain, appealing to the sky above him to protect and save. There must be rest somewhere, a cooling of this fever: why should he, more than other men, be so tormented? Why could he not be like little Terry Shaughnessy, caring nothing for anyone, whether drunk or sober, in funds or out of them? Now, there was an idea! Why go back, in this mood and in this weather, to his cold room and unwelcoming bed, when Terry would be glad enough for him to drop in for a smoke and a talk? He'd be there, sure enough, in his attic in Eustace Street. He wouldn't be in bed. Who ever heard of little Terry being in bed?

He'd have a warm fire, and maybe a taste of something – 'one for the worms,' as he called it … Donovan turned towards Eustace Street.

He trotted along mechanically, now thinking cheerfully of himself and Terry. They were the only bachelors among the boys – and taking it all in all, he'd swear they were as well off like that. He thought of Ned Buckley's wife, and grinned to himself. A nice exhibition she made of the poor man, running to his newspaper office or writing to the editor when she wanted money. Ned was a good sort – but what kind of man was he to put up with that? Now, if any woman tried to manage *him* – ! Or Terry: he'd swear Terry would know how to deal with her, too. Keep a firm hand. That was it.

Yet, maybe – Terry as well as himself – in their hearts they'd like to have a home, and a woman waiting for them, and children. Maybe they'd die in the workhouse, no one caring enough for them to follow them to the grave … At these sad thoughts Donovan's mouth turned down again behind his coat collar, and he felt nearly dismal enough to cry. But resolutely he clung to the advantages of his state. He was his own master, anyway. He could drop in on Terry like this, tonight, and Terry be welcome to drop in on him, any hour he liked.

The rain beat on his face, stood in tears on his eyelashes till the street lamps carried a halo, each of them. Then he blinked and shook his head, and the long, deserted street shone straight before him again. A clock struck twelve. Ah, here was Terry's door. God, it was good to get in out of the rain!

The door stood ajar. That saved ringing the bell. Probably someone had left it like that on purpose – goodness knew how many lived in the old rookery. Not a glimmer of light. But Donovan felt his way to the banisters, gripped them, and mounted, cautiously counting the stairs.

Terry's door was opposite the fourth turn. Two … three … The next one … *Mother of God, what was that?*

Someone, coming out of the darkness, had struck him softly. A blow of a doubled-up fist in the face. Like a joke, by the Lord! But where had the fellow got to?

'Who's that?' called out Donovan, his voice a little startled in the night. 'Who's there? What the blazes are you doing?'

There was no answer. Donovan crouched a moment in the darkness, very still, then changed his walking stick to the other hand. But he must have been flustered, for his fingers didn't catch on it, and down it went clattering against the uncarpeted stairs, stopping once, clattering again, staying finally where it was. He stopped and groped, but thought better of going back for it. He stared about him and in the blackness thought he saw a solider patch, a man facing him a couple of steps up. That was the man who had struck him. But why on earth didn't he say something?

'Who's there?' he shouted again. 'Speak up, whoever you are!'

There was no answer, so he stepped forward boldly. But again someone pushed him – pushed him so plainly, as though with a playful gentleness, that he could feel the woollen jacket of the shoulder thrust against him. As in indignant alarm he tried to grasp it, it silently eluded him, moving soundlessly, eerily, out of reach.

Donovan's blood crept in his veins, and his heart seemed to lunge downwards in his body. Suddenly he wished he felt steadier, that he hadn't had so many drinks. Then he thought instinctively how another good stiff whisky would hearten him – yes, give him fire to tell this sly fellow, whoever the hell he was, what he thought of him.

He paused and gasped, listening with all his ears. Not a sound could he catch; and swiftly changing mood, convinced that it was only some silly trick being played on him, he became wildly angry.

'Come on!' he shouted, his excited voice falling back to the cadence of his native West. 'Come on, you puppy! Come on, you coward you, if you're a man at all, and I'll wrastle you in the Connemara fashion!'

He bent down over his right knee in an attitude of defence. 'I'll fight you! I'll wrastle you!' he repeated belligerently.

For a few seconds he held up his fists, awaiting his assailant. But the latter did not move. Then, like a bull, Donovan made to rush up the stairs. *Ah*! – With a soft thud he struck his head into the stomach of the lurking enemy. The invisible man, silent and unshocked, moved stealthily away.

But Donovan followed him, and as he did so was surprised to find the other coming towards him. He flung away caution and grasped his man about the body. Something rigid but yielding, human yet cold, lay unprotestingly within his arms. He released it and stepped back, weak and shuddering.

It swung – it hung … Ah, God!

Donovan recoiled, as sober as at morning. For a full minute he waited where he stood, overwhelmed with a nameless dread. Then he struck a match and, peering up, saw above him the blackened face of little Terry Shaughnessy, hanging from his attic banisters …

THE DEMON LOVER

ELIZABETH BOWEN

(1941)

I love the prosaic visit to a family home to collect a few personal belongings. This story takes place on a hot, steamy August day, but then ghosts don't always go bump in the night. Enter the uneasy feeling of time out of time, the hint that what should be normal is not. I am reminded of chancing on a rather nice flat in a leafy Dublin suburb at an unusually reasonable rent. The Promised Land! But there was an uneasy feel to it – inexplicable noises on the stairs, and a sense, sometimes, of something rushing by. I lasted a month but left safely, unlike someone who is pursued by a love that reaches from the grave.

OWARDS THE END OF her day in London Mrs Drover went round to her shut-up house to look for several things she wanted to take away. Some belonged to herself, some to her family, who were by now used to their country life. It was late August; it had been a steamy, showery day: at the moment the trees down the pavement glittered in an escape of humid yellow afternoon sun. Against the next batch of clouds, already piling up ink-dark, broken chimneys and parapets stood out. In her once familiar street, as in any unused channel, an unfamiliar queerness had silted up; a cat wove itself in and out of railings, but no human eye watched Mrs Drover's return. Shifting some parcels under her arm, she slowly forced round her latchkey in an unwilling lock, then gave the door, which had warped, a push with her knee. Dead air came out to meet her as she went in.

The staircase window having been boarded up, no light came down into the hall. But one door, she could just see, stood ajar, so she went quickly through into the room and unshuttered the big window in there. Now the prosaic woman, looking about her, was more perplexed than she knew by everything that she saw, by traces of her long former habit of life – the yellow smoke stain up the white marble mantelpiece, the ring left by a vase on the top of the escritoire; the bruise in the wallpaper where, on the door being thrown open widely, the china handle had always hit the wall. The piano, having gone away to be stored, had left what looked like claw marks on its part of the parquet. Though not much dust had seeped in, each object wore a film of another kind; and, the only ventilation being the chimney, the whole drawing-room smelled of the cold hearth. Mrs Drover put down her parcels on the escritoire and left the room to proceed upstairs; the things she wanted were in a bedroom chest.

She had been anxious to see how the house was – the part-time caretaker she shared with some neighbours was away this week on his holiday, known to be not yet back. At the best of times he did not look in often, and she was never sure that she trusted him. There were some cracks in the structure, left by the last bombing, on which she was anxious to keep an eye. Not that one could do anything –

A shaft of refracted daylight now lay across the hall. She stopped dead and stared at the hall table – on this lay a letter addressed to her.

She thought first – then the caretaker *must* be back. All the same, who, seeing the house shuttered, would have dropped a letter in at the box? It was not a circular, it was not a bill. And the post office redirected, to the address in the country, everything for her that came through the post. The caretaker (even if he *were* back) did not know she was due in London today – her call here had been planned to be a surprise – so his negligence in the manner of this letter, leaving it to wait in the dusk and the dust, annoyed her.

Annoyed, she picked up the letter, which bore no stamp. But it cannot be important, or they would know ... She took the letter rapidly upstairs with her, without a stop to look at the writing till she reached what had been her bedroom, where she let in light. The room looked over the garden and other gardens: the sun had gone in; as the clouds sharpened and lowered, the trees and rank lawns seemed already to smoke with dark. Her reluctance to look again at the letter came from the fact that she felt intruded upon – and by someone contemptuous of her ways. However, in the tenseness preceding the fall of rain she read it: it was a few lines.

Dear Kathleen: You will not have forgotten that today is our anniversary, and the day we said. The years have gone by at once slowly and fast. In view of the fact that nothing has changed, I shall rely upon you to keep your promise. I was sorry to see you leave London, but was satisfied that you would be back in time. You may expect me, therefore, at the hour arranged. Until then ...

K.

Mrs Drover looked for the date: it was today's. She dropped the letter on to the bed-springs, then picked it up to see the writing again – her lips, beneath the remains of lipstick, beginning to go white. She felt so much the change in her own face that she went to the mirror, polished a clear patch in it and looked at once urgently and stealthily in. She was confronted by a woman of forty-four, with eyes starting out under a hat-brim that had been rather carelessly pulled down. She had not put on any more powder since she left the shop where she ate her solitary tea. The pearls her husband had given her on their marriage hung loose round her now rather thinner throat, slipping in the V of the pink wool jumper her sister knitted last autumn as they sat round the fire. Mrs Drover's most normal expression was one of controlled worry, but of assent. Since the birth of the third of her little boys, attended by a quite serious illness, she had had an intermittent muscular flicker to the left of her mouth, but in spite of this she could always sustain a manner that was at once energetic and calm.

Turning from her own face as precipitately as she had gone to meet it, she went to the chest where the things were, unlocked it, threw up the lid and knelt to search. But as rain began to come crashing down she could not keep from looking over her shoulder at the stripped bed on which the letter lay. Behind the blanket of rain the clock of the church that still stood struck six – with rapidly heightening apprehension she counted each of the slow strokes. 'The hour arranged … My God,' she said, '*what* hour? How should I …? After twenty-five years …'

The young girl talking to the soldier in the garden had not ever completely seen his face. It was dark; they were saying goodbye under a tree. Now and then – for it felt, from not seeing him at this intense moment, as though she had never seen him at all – she verified his presence for these few moments longer by putting out a hand, which he each time pressed, without very much kindness, and painfully, on to one of the breast buttons of his uniform. That cut of the button on the palm of her hand was principally what she was to carry away. This was so near the end of a leave from France that she could only wish him already gone. It was August 1916. Being not kissed, being drawn away from and looked at intimidated Kathleen till she imagined spectral glitters in the place of his eyes. Turning away and looking back up the lawn she saw, through branches of trees, the drawing-room window alight: she caught a breath for the moment when she could go running back there into the safe arms of her mother and sister, and cry: 'What shall I do, what shall I do? He has gone.'

Hearing her catch her breath, her fiancé said, without feeling: 'Cold?'

'You're going away such a long way.'

'Not so far as you think.'

'I don't understand?'

'You don't have to,' he said. 'You will. You know what we said.'

'But that was – suppose you – I mean, suppose.'

'I shall be with you,' he said, 'sooner or later. You won't forget that. You need do nothing but wait.'

Only a little more than a minute later she was free to run up the silent lawn. Looking in through the window at her mother and sister, who did not for the moment perceive her, she already felt that unnatural promise drive down between her and the rest of all human kind. No other way of having given herself could have made her feel so apart, lost and foresworn. She could not have plighted a more sinister troth.

Kathleen behaved well when, some months later, her fiancé was reported missing, presumed killed. Her family not only supported her but were able to praise her courage without stint because they could not regret, as a husband for her, the man they knew almost nothing about. They hoped she would, in a year or two, console herself – and had it been only a question of consolation things might have gone much straighter ahead. But her trouble, behind just a little grief, was a complete dislocation from everything. She did not reject other lovers, for these failed to appear: for years she failed to attract men – and with the approach of her thirties she became natural enough to share her family's anxiousness on this score. She began to put herself out, to wonder; and at thirty-two she was very greatly relieved to find herself being courted by William Drover. She married him, and the two of them settled down in this quiet, arboreal part of Kensington: in this house the years piled up, her children were born and they all lived till they were driven out by the bombs of the next war. Her movements as Mrs Drover were circumscribed, and she dismissed any idea that they were still watched.

As things were – dead or living the letter-writer sent her only a threat. Unable, for some minutes, to go on kneeling with her back exposed to the empty room, Mrs Drover rose from the chest to sit on an upright chair whose back was firmly against the wall. The desuetude of her former bedroom, her married London home's whole air of being a cracked cup from which memory, with its reassuring power, had either evaporated or leaked away, made a crisis – and at just this crisis the letter-writer had, knowledgeably, struck. The hollowness of the house this evening cancelled years on years of voices, habits and steps. Through the shut windows she only heard rain fall on the roofs around. To rally herself, she said she was in a mood – and for two or three seconds shutting her eyes, told herself that she had imagined the letter. But she opened them – there it lay on the bed.

On the supernatural side of the letter's entrance she was not permitting her mind to dwell. Who, in London, knew she meant to call at the house today? Evidently, however, this had been known. The caretaker, *had* he come back, had had no cause to expect her: he would have taken the letter in his pocket, to forward it, at his own time, through the post. There was no other sign that the caretaker had been in – but, if not? Letters dropped in at doors of deserted houses do not fly or walk to tables in halls. They do not sit on the dust of empty tables with the air of certainty that they will be found. There is needed some human hand – but nobody but the caretaker had a key. Under circumstances she did not care to consider, a house can be entered without a key. It was possible that she was not alone now. She might be being waited for, downstairs. Waited for – until when? Until 'the hour arranged'. At least that was not six o'clock: six has struck.

She rose from the chair and went over and locked the door.

The thing was, to get out. To fly? No, not that: she had to catch her train. As a woman whose utter dependability was the keystone of her family life she was not willing to return to the country, to her husband, her little boys and her sister, without the objects she had come up to fetch. Resuming work at the chest she set about making up a number of parcels in a rapid, fumbling-decisive way. These, with her shopping parcels, would be too much to carry; these meant a taxi – at the thought of the taxi her heart went up and her normal breathing resumed. I will ring up the taxi now; the taxi cannot come too soon: I shall hear the taxi out there running its engine, till I walk calmly down to it through the hall. I'll ring up – But no: the telephone is cut off ... She tugged at a knot she had tied wrong.

The idea of flight ... He was never kind to me, not really. I don't remember him kind at all. Mother said he never considered me. He was set on me, that was what it was – not love. Not love, not meaning a person well. What did he do, to make me promise like that? I can't remember – But she found that she could.

She remembered with such dreadful acuteness that the twenty-five years since then dissolved like smoke and she instinctively looked for the weal left by the button on the palm of her hand. She remembered not only all that he said and did but the complete suspension of *her* existence during that August week. I was not myself –

215

they all told me so at the time. She remembered – but with one white burning blank as where acid has dropped on a photograph: *under no conditions* could she remember his face.

So, wherever he may be waiting, I shall not know him. You have no time to run from a face you do not expect.

The thing was to get to the taxi before any clock struck what could be the hour. She would slip down the street and round the side of the square to where the square gave on the main road. She would return in the taxi, safe, to her own door, and bring the solid driver into the house with her to pick up the parcels from room to room. The idea of the taxi driver made her decisive, bold: she unlocked her door, went to the top of the staircase and listened down.

She heard nothing – but while she was hearing nothing the *passé* air of the staircase was disturbed by a draught that travelled up to her face. It emanated from the basement: down there a door or window was being opened by someone who chose this moment to leave the house.

The rain had stopped; the pavements steamily shone as Mrs Drover let herself out by inches from her own front door into the empty street. The unoccupied houses opposite continued to meet her look with their damaged stare. Making towards the thoroughfare and the taxi, she tried not to keep looking behind. Indeed, the silence was so intense – one of those creeks of London silence exaggerated this summer by the damage of war – that no tread could have gained on hers unheard. Where her street debouched on the square where people went on living, she grew conscious of, and checked, her unnatural pace. Across the open end of the square two buses impassively passed each other: women, a perambulator, cyclists, a man wheeling a barrow signalised, once again, the ordinary flow of life. At the square's most populous corner should be – and was – the short taxi rank. This evening, only one taxi – but this, although it presented its blank rump, appeared already to be alertly waiting for her. Indeed, without looking round the driver started his engine as she panted up from behind and put her hand on the door. As she did so, the clock struck seven. The taxi faced the main road: to make the trip back to her house it would have to turn – she had settled back on the seat and the taxi *had* turned before she, surprised by its knowing movement, recollected that she had not 'said where'. She leaned forward to scratch at the glass panel that divided the driver's head from her own.

The driver braked to what was almost a stop, turned round and slid the glass panel back: the jolt of this flung Mrs Drover forward till her face was almost into the glass. Through the aperture driver and passenger, not six inches between them, remained for an eternity eye to eye. Mrs Drover's mouth hung open for some seconds before she could issue her first scream. After that she continued to scream freely and to beat with her gloved hands on the glass all round as the taxi, accelerating without mercy, made off with her into the hinterland of deserted streets.

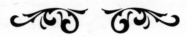

TWO IN ONE

FLANN O'BRIEN

(1954)

Flann O'Brien is one of my favourite writers, and I credit rereading The Third Policeman *with being my saviour during the interminable lockdowns of the pandemic. When the world shifted in such a frightening way, who better to turn to? For some years, there was a wonderful shop near to where I live called The Third Policeman. I had the joy of one day hearing a fellow customer remark that the shop was named after her brother-in-law's book. And serendipity didn't end there that day – I also found a pair of bicycle clips. You'll find a pair in this story, too. Along with interesting questions about the danger of becoming someone else – intentionally or not – with or without murder!*

HE STORY I HAVE to tell is a strange one, perhaps unbelievable. I will try to set it down as simply as I can. I do not expect to be disturbed in my literary labours, for I am writing this in the condemned cell.

Let us say my name is Murphy. The unusual occurrence which led me here concerns my relations with another man whom we shall call Kelly. Both of us were taxidermists.

I will not attempt a treatise on what a taxidermist is. The word is ugly and inadequate. Certainly it does not convey to the layman that such an operator must combine the qualities of zoologist, naturalist, chemist, sculptor, artist, and carpenter. Who would blame such a person for showing some temperament now and again, as I did?

It is necessary, however, to say a brief word about this science. First, there is no such thing in modern practice as 'stuffing' an animal. There is a record of stuffed gorillas having been in Carthage in the 5th century, and it is a fact that an Austrian prince, Siegmund

Herberstein, had stuffed bison in the great hall of his castle in the 16th century – it was then the practice to draw the entrails of animals and to substitute spices and various preservative substances. There is a variety of methods in use today but, except in particular cases – snakes, for example, where preserving the translucency of the skin is a problem calling for special measures – the basis of all modern methods is simply this: you skin the animal very carefully according to a certain pattern, and you encase the skinless body in plaster of Paris. You bisect the plaster when cast providing yourself with two complementary moulds from which you can make a casting of the animal's body – there are several substances, all very light, from which such castings can be made. The next step, calling for infinite skill and patience, is to mount the skin on the casting of the body. That is all I need explain here, I think.

Kelly carried on a taxidermy business and I was his assistant. He was the boss – a swinish, overbearing mean boss, a bully, a sadist. He hated me, but enjoyed his hatred too much to sack me. He knew I had a real interest in the work, and a desire to broaden my experience. For that reason, he threw me all the commonplace jobs that came in. If some old lady sent her favourite terrier to be done, that was me; foxes and cats and Shetland ponies and white rabbits – they were all strictly *my* department. I could do a perfect job on such animals in my sleep, and got to hate them. But if a crocodile came in, or a Great Borneo spider, or (as once happened) a giraffe – Kelly kept them all for himself. In the meantime he would treat my own painstaking work with sourness and sneers and complaints.

One day the atmosphere in the workshop had been even fouler than usual, with Kelly in a filthier temper than usual. I had spent the forenoon finishing a cat, and at about lunchtime put it on the shelf where he left completed orders.

I could nearly *hear* him glaring at it. Where was the tail? I told him there was no tail, that it was a Manx cat. How did I know it was a Manx cat, how did I know it was not an ordinary cat which had lost its tail in a motor accident or something? I got so mad that I permitted myself a disquisition on cats in general, mentioning the distinctions as between *Felis manul*, *Felis silvestris*, and *Felis lybica*, and on the unique structure of the Manx cat. His reply to that? He called me a slob. That was the sort of life *I* was having.

On this occasion something within me snapped. I was sure I could hear the snap. I had moved up to where he was to answer his last insult. The loathsome creature had his back to me, bending down to put on his bicycle clips. Just to my hand on the bench was one of the long, flat, steel instruments we use for certain operations with plaster. I picked it up and hit him a blow with it on the back of the head. He gave a cry and slumped forward. I hit him again. I rained blow after blow on him. Then I threw the tool away. I was upset. I went out into the yard and looked around. I remembered he had a weak heart. Was he dead? I remember adjusting the position of a barrel we had in the yard to catch rainwater, the only sort of water suitable for some of the mixtures we used. I found I was in a cold sweat but strangely calm. I went back into the workshop.

Kelly was just as I had left him. I could find no pulse. I rolled him over on his back and examined his eyes, for I have seen more lifeless eyes in my day than most people. Yes, there was no doubt: Kelly was dead. I had killed him. I was a murderer. I put on my coat and hat and left the place. I walked the streets for a while, trying to avoid panic, trying to think rationally. Inevitably, I was soon in a public house. I drank a lot of whiskey and finally went home to my digs. The next morning I was very sick indeed from this terrible mixture of drink and worry. Was the Kelly affair merely a fancy, a drunken fancy? No, there was no consolation in that sort of hope. He was dead all right.

It was as I lay in bed there, shaking, thinking, and smoking, that the mad idea came into my head. No doubt this sounds incredible, grotesque, even disgusting, but I decided I would treat Kelly the same as any other dead creature that found its way to the workshop.

Once one enters a climate of horror, distinction of degree as between one infamy and another seems slight, sometimes undetectable. That evening I went to the workshop and made my preparations. I worked steadily all next day. I will not appall the reader with gruesome detail. I need only say that I applied the general technique and flaying pattern appropriate to apes. The job took me four days at the end of which I had a perfect skin, face and all. I made the usual castings before committing the remains of, so to speak, the remains, to the furnace. My plan was to have Kelly on view asleep on a chair, for the benefit of anybody who might call. Reflection convinced me that this would be far too dangerous. I had to think again.

A further idea began to form. It was so macabre that it shocked even myself. For days I had been treating the inside of the skin with the usual preservatives – cellulose acetate and the like – thinking all the time. The new illumination came upon me like a thunderbolt. *I would don his skin and, when the need arose, BECOME Kelly!* His clothes fitted me. So would his skin. Why not?

Another day's agonised work went on various alterations and adjustments but that night I was able to look into a glass and see Kelly looking back at me, perfect in every detail except for the teeth and eyes, which had to be my own but which I knew other people would never notice.

Naturally I wore Kelly's clothes, and had no trouble in imitating his unpleasant voice and mannerisms. On the second day, having 'dressed,' so to speak, I went for a walk, receiving salutes from newsboys and other people who had known Kelly. And on the day after, I was foolhardy enough to visit Kelly's lodgings. Where on earth had I been, his landlady wanted to know. (She had noticed nothing.) What, I asked – had that fool Murphy not told her that I had to go to the country for a few days? No? I had told the good-for-nothing to convey the message.

I slept that night in Kelly's bed. I was a little worried about what the other landlady would think of my own absence. I decided not to remove Kelly's skin the first night I spent in his bed but to try to get the rest of my plan of campaign perfected and into sharper focus. I eventually decided that Kelly should announce to various people that he was going to a very good job in Canada, and that he had sold his business to his assistant Murphy. I would then burn the skin, I would own a business and – what is more stupid than vanity! – I could secretly flatter myself that I had committed the perfect crime.

Need I say that I had overlooked something?

The mummifying preparation with which I had dressed the inside of the skin was, of course, quite stable for the ordinary purposes of taxidermy. It had not occurred to me that a night in a warm bed would make it behave differently. The horrible truth dawned on me the next day when I reached the workshop and tried to take the skin off. *It wouldn't come off!* It had literally fused with my own! And in the days that followed, this process kept rapidly advancing. Kelly's skin got to live again, to breathe, to perspire.

Then followed more days of terrible tension. My own landlady called one day, inquiring about me of 'Kelly.' I told her I had been on the point of calling on *her* to find out where I was. She was disturbed about my disappearance – it was so unlike me – and said she thought she should inform the police. I thought it wise not to try to dissuade her. My disappearance would eventually come to be accepted, I thought. My Kelliness, so to speak, was permanent. It was horrible, but it was a choice of that or the scaffold.

I kept drinking a lot. One night, after many drinks, I went to the club for a game of snooker. This club was in fact one of the causes of Kelly's bitterness towards me. I had joined it without having been aware that Kelly was a member. His resentment was boundless. He thought I was watching him, and taking note of the attentions he paid the lady members.

On this occasion I nearly made a catastrophic mistake. It is a simple fact that I am a very good snooker player, easily the best in that club. As I was standing watching another game in progress awaiting my turn for the table, *I suddenly realised that Kelly did not play snooker at all!* For some moments, a cold sweat stood out on Kelly's brow at the narrowness of this escape. I went to the bar. There, a garrulous lady (who thinks her unsolicited conversation is a fair exchange for a drink) began talking to me. She remarked the long absence of my nice Mr Murphy. She said he was missed a lot in the snooker room. I was hot and embarrassed and soon went home. To Kelly's place, of course.

Not embarrassment, but a real sense of danger, was to be my next portion in this adventure. One afternoon, two very casual strangers strolled into the workshop, saying they would like a little chat with me. Cigarettes were produced. Yes indeed, they were plain-clothes men making a few routine inquiries. This man Murphy had been reported missing by several people. Any idea where he was? None at all. When had I last seen him? Did he seem upset or disturbed? No, but he was an impetuous type. I had recently reprimanded him for bad work. On similar other occasions he had threatened to leave and seek work in England. Had I been away for a few days myself?

Yes, down in Cork for a few days. On business. Yes … yes … some people thinking of starting a natural museum down there, technical school people – that sort of thing.

The casual manner of these men worried me, but I was sure they did not suspect the truth and that they were genuinely interested in tracing Murphy. Still, I knew I was in danger, without knowing the exact nature of the threat I had to counter. Whiskey cheered me somewhat.

Then it happened. The two detectives came back accompanied by two other men in uniform. They showed me a search warrant. It was purely a formality; it had to be done in the case of all missing persons. They had already searched Murphy's digs and had found nothing of interest. They were very sorry for upsetting the place during my working hours.

A few days later the casual gentlemen called and put me under arrest for the wilful murder of Murphy, of myself. They proved the charge in due course with all sorts of painfully amassed evidence, including the remains of human bones in the furnace. I was sentenced to be hanged. Even if I could now prove that Murphy still lived by shedding the accursed skin, what help would that be? Where, they would ask, is Kelly?

This is my strange and tragic story. And I end it with the thought that if Kelly and I must each be either murderer or murdered, it is perhaps better to accept my present fate as philosophically as I can and be cherished in the public mind as the victim of this murderous monster, Kelly. He *was* a murderer, anyway.

ARACHNOPHOBIA

CATHERINE BROPHY

(1995)

For heaven's sake, don't read this story if you're afraid of spiders! And be very careful if you are loved by someone who wants to own you. But the counselling sessions are wonderfully entertaining, and the end is startling stuff. I never pay much attention to spiders apart from keeping an eye out for the False Widow. This story will make you keep an eye out for a lot more hidden terrors!

RACHNOPHOBIA: AN INORDINATE FEAR ... yes that was true, an inordinate fear ... she couldn't bring herself to think the rest. Dr Bishop was right, that's what she had, arachnophobia. It was a proper disease, the doctor said so, written up in the big serious books on his shelves. He'd even taken one down to show her. She wasn't depressed or mad or anything, she was arachnophobic and he said he could cure it. The relief ... A bus came into view and she put out her hand. It squealed to a halt and she handed the correct change to the driver.

'No drugs,' he'd said, 'there's no need for that, we'll use operant conditioning. It will take time of course ...'

She smiled out of the window at the sliding-away shop fronts. No drugs! She definitely wasn't mad. Isn't that the first thing they do when you're mad, drugs, injections, strong-arm nurses ... she shivered and remembered, no drugs, we can cure you. 'I suffer from arachnophobia,' she told herself over and over.

She hadn't told him about her brother … couldn't. The sudden jerk on the back of her collar, the threats, the choking in her throat … and it didn't matter what she did, he would still drop them down her neck, the … the things, the awful … She wanted to scream and scream and scream and tear her clothes but she couldn't on the bus, they'd take her away, they'd think her mad. She felt physically ill, her skin began to crawl … they were down her back, all black and hairy, her stomach heaved and she rushed off the bus four stops too soon.

She clung to a railing holding her breath, torn, buffeted by her crawling spine, heaving stomach and the little voice that shrieked 'Get a grip, they'll think you're mad, they'll think you're mad.'

'Breathe,' the doctor'd said, 'breathe, Ann, breathe. The brain needs oxygen and the muscles, it helps you to take control.'

She gulped in air but it wasn't till she grasped her thumbs, the right one in her left hand, the left one in her right, and repeated 'Mama's here, Mama's here' twenty-three times that she could find the strength to move.

She walked quickly and when she reached the corner of her road she ran. Running was difficult with her bag squashed under her arm and her elbows tight to her sides, but she couldn't let her thumbs go or the creepy-crawling would start again. It was hard to get the key out and twice she dropped it before she got the door open and could dash up the stairs and tear off her clothes.

Wash, she had to wash but they'd be in there. Waiting in the black plugholes. Her brother, Brian, said that was nonsense, they didn't live in plugholes, they fell from the ceiling, but she found that hard to believe. She had seen the black legs waving from the dark and the fat black heaving out of the drain …

'Mama's here, Mama's here …' she gasped and gasped and kept losing count and having to start again.

When she was absolutely sure she'd said it twenty-three times she was calm again. She looked round the bathroom warily … nothing, the floor, the ceiling … nothing. She poked a bamboo cane down the plughole … nothing, so she stuck in the plug. She could have a shower now. When she'd dried herself and put on clean clothes, every garment straight from its sealed plastic bag, she felt a whole lot better.

'I'm sure that was the beginning of your trouble,' Dr Bishop said, 'the trauma which initiated your phobia.'

She was glad now she'd told him about Brian.

'But, however interesting the cause,' he continued, 'it's the symptoms that create trouble, the fear, the sense of paralysis, that's what we're dealing with here, we're learning to control them.'

'The worst is in the kitchen.'

'The worst?'

'Yes, there's one always in the kitchen.'

'Ah, there's a spider in the kitchen is there?'

'Yes.'

'Do you think you could describe it?'

She felt the panic rising. She could see it at the table with its knees apart and its surgical stockings. The head resting in the palm, the elbow pushed amongst the dirty delft and crumbs. The table-cloth was skew-ways. She held her breath.

'Breathe, Ann, breathe.'

She held her thumbs tightly.

'Now tell me,' his voice was calm, reassuring, commanding. 'Take your time.'

'Mama's here, Mama's here …' she mouthed twenty-three times, and was safe.

'It's fat and black and hairy,' she said in a little girl voice.

'There now, Ann, that wasn't so bad, was it? Relax now, close your eyes. I think we're doing pretty well, don't you?'

'Yes.'

But she held her thumbs securely.

When she got home it was in the kitchen of course, as usual, so she went up to her room.

'Are you all right, Ann?' it called up the stairs.

'Yes.'

'Your dinner will be ready soon.'

'All right.'

As long as she didn't look directly at it she was all right. It thought that she was shy, introverted, depressed, mad ... that's why it insisted that she see the doctor. Well, she was seeing the doctor and he was helping her. She'd talked about it today, not said ... the ... word but talked about it.

'Sp ... sp ... spider, now, there I've said it,' she gasped and laughed and held her thumbs close to herself.

'Wonderful ... good girl. My, we are making progress! Do you think you could name any types of spiders?'

'The Common House sp ... sp ... spider ... Tarantula ... and the ... the ...' She could see it from the corner of her eye, the white podgy fingers, swollen round the ring, creeping along the kitchen table on its way to the cooker.

'I'll always look after you,' it said, 'you know I always will, as long as these poor legs can carry me.'

It grunted and bent to the oven. Ann gagged and was afraid she might vomit on Dr Bishop's lovely carpet but she couldn't get a tissue from her bag without letting go her thumbs. She swallowed back the bile and repeated to herself, 'Mama's here, Mama's here, oh Mama's here …'

'Just breathe, Ann, breathe … that's very good. Tarantula and … ?'

'… and … and … the … the Black Widow.'

'Good, that's very good. Now relax.'

Black Widow was what her brother called it when it first came to look after them after Mama had gone away forever. She didn't remember much of Mama, she was too young, but she remembered her cheek against a pink flowered apron and Mama rocking her and saying something lovely in her ear. The Widow never wore an apron, she wore black. She opened her eyes quickly.

'The one in the kitchen … the one I told you about before … it's a Black Widow,' she whispered.

The doctor laughed indulgently.

'Well now, Ann, that's a bit unlikely,' he said, 'they couldn't survive here, it's too cold, they only live in hot climates. It's just a common house spider.'

'But it frightens me … I can't get away.'

'Yes, I know it frightens you. Now take a breath, relax, and close your eyes. Imagine that the sun is shining on you, feel the warmth … now imagine that you are going to a safe place, a very safe place, where nothing at all can harm you …'

The sun was shining somewhere outside but she crouched in the dark, hiding, safe, under the stairs. Her brother was beside her, big and strong. It would never catch them there. She could hear the voice call for them out the back.

'She killed her husband,' Brian whispered in her ear.

'No!'

'Oh yes, that's what Black Widows do, they kill their husbands right after mating.'

'No!'

'Then why's she called the Black Widow? She poisoned her husband and sucked his brains through the top of his head.'

'Stop, I don't want to hear.' She tried to cover her ears but Brian grabbed her hands and wouldn't let her.

'And then she sucked out his lungs and heart and liver and all his guts and all the piss and ca-ca through the hole in his head.'

'Stop, please stop.'

'And all the insides of his legs and feet and left him like a burst balloon.'

She was crying now.

'And she'll do the same to you.'

'You too, you too,' she said, trying to hit him.

'Oh no she won't. I'm going away to school and you'll be all alone with her ...'

'Mama's here, Mama's here, oh Mama's here ...'

'Now I want you to imagine,' Dr Bishop's voice interrupted.

Oh yes, imagine, yes, she was safe with her brother under the stairs, the Widow couldn't suck her brains out here.

'Imagine,' the doctor continued, 'that away in the distance there is a spider, a very tiny ...'

The Widow's step came closer, her voice louder, her hand on the door ... she started screaming then.

'Open your eyes,' the doctor commanded. 'Ann! Open your eyes and look at me.'

She looked into his grey-blue eyes, her brother faded and the dark grew light, he had grizzled eyebrows.

'Now look around the room.'

The room was soothing, all plants and big fat books and carpets from Turkey. He was talking to her calm and quiet, she didn't really know what he was saying but his voice was soothing and he kept his distance at the other side of his shiny desk. She liked that. She hated when people touched or came too close. He put on his spectacles and took them off again, pinched his nose, rubbed his eyes and smiled. He must be what, fifty … fifty-five?

'Are we going a bit too fast?' he asked.

'Yes, a bit,' she replied.

As long as he covered the pictures with a piece of paper she was all right. And she could read as long as she didn't have to touch the book.

'Spiders weave complex webs of great delicacy as a safeguard against falling, to catch prey and to nest,' she read in a rush.

'Keep breathing, Ann, keep breathing.'

That was right, that's what the Widow did. She wove her web right there in the kitchen, making savoury casserole and apple pie and listening to the radio.

'Can you read another bit?'

'They do not hunt, they wait. And when an insect flies into the web they do not kill, they scuttle out and paralyse their victims and store them in their larder.'

'You're perfectly safe, Ann, keep breathing.'

She had been the Widow's prey a long time now, since Brian went away to school. The Widow washed and dressed and fed her. She chose her friends and kept her home from school if she thought she had a sniffle. 'She's delicate,' the Widow used to tell people on the phone, 'I have to mind her health.'

In the winter the Widow kept her indoors and when she must go out swaddled her in woolly vests, extra cardigans, mittens, thick tweed coats, knitted hat and scarves.

'Keep your throat covered,' she warned, 'or you'll catch your death of cold.'

And when she finally left school the Widow told her that she had no need to work.

'There's plenty of money, you know, besides, you're delicate, a job would kill you.'

Ann protested but it was no good.

'We can look after one another,' the Widow said. 'I'm not getting any younger.'

The Widow had her caught and wrapped in silk and paralysed she held her breath so long she started to go blue in the face.

'Breathe, Ann, breathe.' Dr Bishop shook her shoulder.

She gulped the air and grasped both thumbs.

'Mama's here, Mama's here,' she told herself. 'Mama's here, Mama's here, Mama's here …'

There, she only had to say it ten times now. She would not stay wrapped and helpless. Dr Bishop was helping her to get out, to make her free. It was working already, his operant conditioning. He had even touched her shoulder and she didn't mind. She went home happy.

'Do you think you're ready?'

'Yes.'

Her stomach churned and she shivered but she did not flinch. She was determined now. Dr Bishop was very kind and she would not let him down. He propped the picture on his desk. She gulped and grasped the arms of the leather chair, pushing into it as though she were trying to fade backwards through the upholstery.

'If it's too close I can move it further back,' he said.

'No, no … it's all right … I'll … I'll just … just breathe.'

She closed her eyes and grasped her thumbs.

'Mama's here, Mama's here …' ten times, and she looked again.

'What kind is it?' she asked faintly.

'Black Widow,' he said, 'they're not nearly as dangerous as people think.'

The body was round and shiny with the red markings and the legs, oh God, the legs, all sticking out like … like the Widow's sticks. The black walking sticks she hobbled down to Mass on. She felt like screaming but grasped her thumbs instead.

'Mama's here, Mama's here …'

'Breathe, Ann, breathe.'

The legs, the hideous legs, like that photograph with the Widow sitting behind her, black arms creeping round her white Communion dress, the surgical stockings … Bile surged into her throat and made her cough and splutter and spit in her tissue.

'Breathe, Ann, breathe.'

The Widow had a photo taken every year in Mr McEvoy's studio and sent a copy to her only sister in England. 'Me and my little darling,' she wrote on the back or, 'Happy Christmas from my little angel and me.'

Ann was angry. I am not her darling, she thought, I'm not her angel, I'm not, I'm not. And she is not my Mama!

'I think she's dangerous,' she said aloud, nodding at the picture.

Dr Bishop chuckled.

'I know you do, but a picture couldn't harm you, now could it?'

'No.'

She did not run upstairs when she returned home. It was the first time she hadn't. Instead she went straight to the living room. There they were! Years of photographs in their silver frames. They covered every surface, the mantelpiece, piano, little tables, whatnot. She gathered them up and sat in the middle of the floor systematically tearing them out of their frames and ripping them in halves, quarters, eighths and sixteenths, every one, every single one and left them scattered on the floor.

'What on earth did you do that for?' the Widow wailed when she found them.

'I'm sorry. I was angry,' Ann said, not looking.

'You're not well, Ann, better lie down, you're not well at all.'

'I'm perfectly all right.' Ann could barely contain her anger.

'Well, we'd better clean up the mess,' the Widow said and hobbled to the bureau, sticks clattering against the furniture. 'Fortunately I have copies.'

Ann ran upstairs and screamed and screamed and screamed into her pillow.

'I think it's time to look now.'

She started breathing quickly. Out of the drawer of his desk he took a matchbox and opened it. She grasped her thumbs.

'Don't worry, it can't escape,' he said and put it on his desk. There was Cling-Film over the inside part of the box where … where … where it was … It grew huge and fat … big round belly, red hourglass marking …

'She'll suck your brains and guts out,' Brian whispered in her ear.

The legs all swollen, surgical stockings …

'You'll kill me,' she screamed at it.

'Ann, Ann, calm yourself. Breathe. Look, I've closed the box.' Dr Bishop put it back in the drawer.

'… kill me, kill me.' She broke down sobbing.

'I'm trying to help you, Ann, that's all. Just breathe, relax …'

'No, no, not you, the, the ...' she pointed to the drawer where the Widow had retreated.

'Ah ... so that's what this is all about. You thought it was a Black Widow! No, no, my dear, it's just an ordinary house spider. They're harmless, you know that. In fact they help mankind by catching flies and insects. House spiders can even become pets. My grandfather had one that came down from the ceiling every time he sat down at his writing desk and kept him company. He became very fond of it. Always said it had a personality of its own ...'

'Oh Mama's here, Mama's here, Mama's here, Mama's here ...' She grasped her thumbs and didn't listen to his talk ... 'Mama's here, yes, Mama's here ...'

Eventually she calmed enough to dry her tears and look at the spider in the box. It was quite small really.

'Not bad,' he said, 'not bad at all, I think we're making progress.'

She sat in the kitchen and looked straight at the Widow. She could see what she was up to all right.

'These poor auld legs are killing me,' the Widow said. 'Ann, can you take the bread out of the oven? I don't think I can manage it, love.'

Oh, she could see what she was up to.

'Ann, I need a bit of help here, can you put the clothes out on the line?'

That's why she had kept her at home, made apple tarts and soufflés, bought her silky nightwear and good Italian leather shoes, that's why she petted and pampered her. To make her guilty, to make her owe, to put her deep in debt. The Widow wanted to be minded while she puffed and limped and grunted and ended up in a wheelchair.

Well she wouldn't do it, she wouldn't. Spiders spin webs as nests and safety nets, she remembered, not just to catch prey. She recalled the spider in its little prison on the doctor's desk. She could look now, she could look. The prison grew and grew, black bars and double-locked doors. The Widow sat inside, her knees apart, her legs all swollen in their surgical stockings. Her sticks beat loud against the bars, furious and helpless, demanding to get out. Ann feared the locks would not be strong enough.

'Don't worry, Ann,' her Mama whispered in her ear. 'I'll never let her harm you.'

Mama was here. Suddenly she felt exultant.

'I think we'll let it out today,' the doctor said. 'But first I want you to relax and breathe. Close your eyes ... remember your safe place.'

Under the stairs, by herself, she was safe in the dark. A low thunk-thunk above her head. It was the Widow. Thunk-thunk, coming down the stairs, thunk-thunk, coming down the stairs. And calling.

'Ann!' Thunk-thunk. 'Ann! Where are you?'

She wanted looking after, she always wanted looking after now.

Ann grasped her thumbs close to her chest.

'Mama's here, Mama's here, Mama's here ...'

'Take a deep breath, Ann. You're safe,' the doctor said, 'I won't let her near you.'

Thunk-thunk. Thunk-thunk. Thunk-thunk.

'She'll suck your guts out through your head,' Brian whispered from afar.

'Oh Mama's here, she's here, oh Mama's here ...'

The Widow reached the last step, Ann could hear her grunting down the hall. A stick rattled against the door, it opened. Ann shut her eyes tight and held her breath.

'You're safe, Ann, breathe, I'm here to help you.'

She glanced sideways and there, standing at the open door, was her Mama.

'Yes, love, Mama's here, your Mama's here.'

She felt her cheek against the pink-flowered apron.

'Mama's here, love, Mama's here.'

'Take your time, Ann,' said the doctor, 'don't look until you feel ready.'

She watched the spider crawl around the doctor's hand and creep across the surface of his desk.

'Can I touch it?' she asked.

'Why certainly,' exclaimed the doctor, 'but is it not a bit too soon? Do you think that you are ready?'

'I think so, if I wear rubber gloves.'

'Of course, of course,' he said. 'I have a pair right here for just this eventuality.'

Ann crept her hand across the table, Mama's here, and stretched a finger towards the spider, Mama's here. It ignored her for a while and then climbed slowly up the tip of her glove. Her breath got caught, she couldn't breathe or grasp her thumbs. Mama's here, oh Mama's here …

'Take it away,' she squeaked and shook her hand violently. The spider clung and clung.

'Oh get it off, please get it off,' she sobbed, 'please, please!'

The doctor put the spider back in its little prison.

'Don't worry, I'll look after you,' he soothed.

'Oh Mama's here, yes Mama's here, she's here …' She could breathe again and even laugh a little at her panic.

Dr Bishop was in high good humour.

She practised every day, facing them. She bought industrial rubber gloves, a long mac with a hood and wellington boots and every day she practised. She felt invulnerable running the nozzle of the vacuum round the ceilings, into corners, nooks and crannies, sucking up the spiders and their webs. Every day.

'You really needn't do all that cleaning,' the Widow said, 'but it's nice to see you active.'

She practised in the bathroom, too, drowning them in water. Spiders could trap air, she knew, in the hairs of their body. They could go down the plughole and stay afloat and when the water stopped they'd crawl back up. She turned the showerhead to max and let it run till the water scalded. Then they'd crumple into a ball and die and flush away like so much dirt.

She was very nearly cured.

Dr Bishop was delighted.

'Do you think you need to continue coming?' he asked.

'I don't know,' she said.

'Well, how about a little break to see how you get on?'

'I don't know, yes, maybe.'

'Let's leave the next appointment for a month.'

'All right.'

There was a massive thud upstairs.

'Ann … come here … come quick,' the Widow called.

She stood paralysed in the hall. Breathe, breathe, she told herself and held her thumbs.

'Mama's here, love, Mama's here, yes Mama's here.'

There was another thump and the sound of water sloshing. She put on her mac and wellies and the industrial rubber gloves and went to the bathroom. The Widow was naked in the bath. It unnerved her. Somehow she never thought of her without black clothes.

'Mama's here, yes Mama's here.' She took a deep breath and didn't run away.

'Help me,' the Widow said faintly, 'I slipped. I think I've broken something.'

Ann stood at the edge of the bath looking down. The Widow was twisted sideways, her flesh all soft and white and wobbly. One arm was pinned under and she tried to keep her head above the water.

'Take the plug out,' she gasped.

'Mama's here, yes Mama's here …'

The web acts as a safety net. No longer … no … no longer.

Ann stretched to the showerhead and turned the water on full blast. The Widow screamed and struggled, slipped further down. But the plughole was too small.

'Oh Mama's here, yes Mama's here …'

She took deep breaths like Dr Bishop said, reached for the Widow's head and pushed.

'Mama's here, oh Mama's here, she's here, my love.'

She held her under. The legs flailed, the body heaved and flopped. Water sloshed all over her mac and wellies but she held on, jaws clenched, breathing through her nose. It struggled and it struggled but it didn't curl up tight like most spiders. It just went limp with its eyes and jaw wide open.

'Thank you, Mama,' Ann said aloud.

She removed her wellingtons, her raincoat and her gloves and put them away carefully under the stairs.

'Thank you, Mama, you can go. I'm better now, I'm cured.'

LEVERETS THROUGH
THE HOLE IN THE HEDGE

GRAHAM TUGWELL

(2011)

This story intrigues and terrifies me on many levels. Any diehard Lewis Carroll fan is bound to have a soft spot for hares, and for the adventures of little girls. But how quickly this tale tilts from the cosy adventures of two pals munching their ham and cheese sandwiches to a very scary alternate world. The little broken leveret takes me back to the horror of myxomatosis, which nowadays appears to have jumped species. The everyday tone, the fantastical core idea, the repetition of the eternal question, 'Are you happy?' – it's a world away from tea with the Mad Hatter and the March Hare and a very sleepy dormouse!

ATE AUGUST.

And here is summer, in one last handful:

Blades of grass for whistles.

Daisies for plaiting into chains, to wear around our wrists and necks.

Buttercups to hold under our chins – smiling, we twist their stems; we make the golden flowers spin.

'You *must* like butter,' Dympna laughs. Her eyes are moons behind pink-rimmed specs; her freckled face is dimpled with a grin.

'Nowhere near as much as you!' I say. How golden the glow upon her chin!

We kick our heels behind our backs and both of us wear ankle socks and little patent leather shoes, black and polished and buckled with straps.

(We pestered our mothers to buy them for us – we could be twins, Dympna Quigley and me!)

This is happiness – on stomachs side by side we lie, on a woollen blanket red and white, with elephants dancing about the edge and as I slide a daisy chain onto my wrist, I catch sight of my Snoopy watch. (Woodstock is hovering over the kennel.) 'Five to three,' I gasp, 'Dympna, the leverets will be *out* by now.'

'Let's go,' she says, fixing glasses on her nose. 'Don't want to miss them!'

We rise – the blanket gathered in my arms, and it's a lolling awkward thing, while Dympna lugs the hamper, to one side slanted with the weight of it. We make our way across the field – further in the grass is longer, rising roughly over knees, and we wade through in single file.

Dodging stinging stands of weeds and the clinging streamers we call Robin-run-the-hedge – it snares our socks and the hems of our dresses, leaves furry fruit upon our sleeves – I follow slow in Dympna's wake.

Ice-breakers in a wide green sea.

In the furthest corner of the field there is a leafless, lifeless tree, a thickened twist of rotten wood, jabbing fingers into sky, and round its cleaved and swollen trunk there is a stretch of dark green hedge and this is what we move towards.

Near the hedge the grass runs out – we smooth the blanket on stony ground and Dympna puts the hamper down and shows me where the handle has made her palm-skin white.

Side by side we settle. From here we can see through the hole in the hedge. Just wide enough for a crawling child, it *gapes* – a puncture in the green, trimmed with purple thistle crowns, the fried-egg splashes of ox-eye daisies.

The hole looks out upon a ditch. It isn't wide – at full stretch, with aching limbs, I could almost reach across – but it is deep and sheer and there is filthy water at its base, stagnant, haunted by aimless drifts of flies, rainbow-skinned with effluent.

Through the hole, on the far side of this abyss, we can see the field beyond – the grass is short and lemon-green, with cowslips flecked, with dandelions, where fat bees bumble through the air, where ladybirds are drops of blood on blades of grass.

Down we get on our stomachs again, propping faces on our hands and kicking feet behind our backs.

The sun so warm upon us and wind brings us the scent of grass; we wait to see leverets through the hole in the hedge.

Dympna points excited – 'Look!'

A smooth pink head bobs above a bower of grass and we softly coo as it sniffs the air, as it twitches its whiskers and slender ears.

One by one, from out of a dozen bowers, leverets are lifting heads.

Frail and skeletal things they are, heads and bodies hairless, with long pink ears and tails like little lips of skin. They step on grass with broad flat feet, their front paws bent against their ribs.

Looks like they've been skinned with knives.

Looks like they've been boiled.

The raw beasts hop and shuffle and movement is an agony, back legs stretched to ludicrous lengths they hobble past the hole in the hedge. More are rising – quickly we lose count – now there are hundreds of the things, stumbling in awkward, silent procession.

Always at this time, in this place …

Unpacking the hamper we eat sandwiches Dympna's mother made for us – ham and cheese and mayonnaise. Nibbling around a bitter crust, I point – one of the creatures is shambling softly into view. 'Who d'ya think *that one* looks like?'

Dympna peers through her lenses. 'I think …' she says slowly, 'I think that's the Tallun boy. The one who drowned in the reservoir.'

I squint.

'It has his eyes,' says Dympna, in decisive tones. 'And see, the skin's a bit bluer than the others.'

I nod. 'I think you're *right*, Dympna.'

The leveret with the face of the Tallun boy crosses before the hole and shuffles slowly out of sight. Then it's Dympna's turn to point. 'Look,' she says. 'There's Mrs Cleary who burned herself.'

'Are you sure?' I say, trying to remember Mrs Cleary. 'Didn't she used to cycle to mass?'

'Yeah,' says Dympna. 'See … the side of her face is all melted.'

'Oh, it is too.' The left side is purple and prune-skinned.

Wide and bright are Dympna's eyes. 'That's from when she fell asleep against the radiator. After her husband … you know …'

I knew – the whole *town* did.

The leverets, Mrs Cleary amongst them, hobble past the hole in the hedge.

Finishing our sandwiches I give my crust to Dympna, who likes them more than I do – then from the hamper we take a heel of bread and Dympna cuts it into squares and she is busy buttering as I go off along the hedgerow, looking for a stick long enough to use.

I find a long, straight branch and wander back, the bread squares waiting on a paper plate. I hold the stick and Dympna spears a buttered piece. With bread in place and barely daring to breathe, forward we lean – slowly, ever so slowly, we guide the stick through the hole in the hedge.

And we wait.

'Come on now,' whispers Dympna. 'Don't be scared,' and she makes a noise like she's calling her cat – '*Peeshweeshweeshweeshweesh … Peeshweeshweeshweeshweesh.*'

Hearing the call or scenting the bread, one of the leverets leaves the line, inching slowly towards the stick. We try to hold it steady – my hands are over hers –

As it comes close we see the face of Willie Clusker, whose son Dermot is in our class. (He had a heart attack at his building site, just when the roof was going on.)

Mr Clusker sniffs with his short and whiskered nose.

And then, tentative, experimental, he takes a tiny bite.

Dympna shouts through the gap: 'Mr Clusker! Mr *Clusker*! Is there anything you want us to tell your son? Have you got a message of us?'

I join in: 'Are you happy, Mr Clusker? Are you happy?'

Almost we collapse in giggles; it takes all our strength to level the stick.

Mr Clusker finishes the buttered bread, his blank eyes focussed on some point in the air between us. When the bread is gone, he licks the stick with a ribbon tongue and absently scratches the skin of his chest.

'Look, Sorcha,' Dympna cries, '*Look*. Mr Clusker's washing himself!'

Sitting erect on the lip of the ditch, the leveret grooms his long pink ears, dragging those sharp lengths down his face with a tiny hand.

'Aw,' sighs Dympna Quigley as he stretches out one long back leg and nibbles the muscle with his teeth. We slump against each other, tittering again – the stick withdrawn Mr Clusker wanders off, rejoining the parade of leverets.

'Good luck, Mr Clusker!' cries Dympna Quigley, waving the stick in giggling salute.

We feed another six the same way, and that's the end of our heel of bread. Dympna sits on the blanket, knees tucked up to her chin, hands clasped around her shins. I'm wittering on about something

– I don't remember what – but out of the blue she says: 'Do you think we could bring one home?'

I'm caught off guard. 'Maaaaybe,' I say, after a while. 'But I don't think we *should*. They look …'

(I was about to say happy, but … that wasn't right.)

Dympna's eyes are waxing moons. 'We know what they eat,' she says, 'and we'll give them lots of room to parade, they'll be grand in the back garden, Sorcha.'

'I don't know,' I say. 'I don't know.'

But there was never any arguing with Dympna when her mind was made up.

I help her – I don't want her to hurt herself, I don't want to lose her in the ditch. I hold her hand as she stretches away, as she leans across –

'Just a bit further,' she gasps, 'just a *biiiit* further. I can almost …'

I can't see a thing – the hole in the hedge swallows her completely –

'Got one!' she yelps and with all my might I pull her back – I lose my footing on the stony ground – 'Look, Sorcha, look!' – the leveret she holds has the face of Josie Whelan.

'Dympna …' I whisper.

It struggles but Dympna closes hands across its chest, gritting teeth and holding it. *Holding it.*

'Let it go!' I scream. 'It'll *bite* you!'

The leveret bucks, knocking the glasses from her face, and it screams, the high and toothless quiver of a newborn freshly pulled loose.

Dympna wails.

I cover my ears and I scream too.

She lets it go.

It hangs for a moment, a thin and bony thing, turning softly in the air.

It bursts upon the ground.

Dympna looks at it, then looks at me.

Disgusted.

'It was cold,' she whispers. 'So cold.'

And as she wipes her hands upon the grass I say 'Let's not do that again.'

I look at my Snoopy watch – time for dinner.

We go home.

Neither of us in the mood to eat.

Not after that.

So summer went, and autumn came, and with it school and darkening days and our time with the leverets grew less –

And Hallowe'en came, and we both dressed as leverets – two girls in pink, with matching patent leather shoes.

(You'd think we were twins, Dympna Quigley and me!)

Our mothers took photos of us nibbling buttered bread off sticks.

And we held hands and went from door to door, until I got tired and Dympna went on ahead, until Mr Cullen's car flung me across a garden and trapped her, broken, against a wall.

With one of my legs hanging destroyed, I crawled across the grass to where the car was pinning her.

She looked at me, eyes bright moons behind her glasses.

Her mouth opened.

Her mouth closed.

She was trying to tell me something.

I tried to listen, but Mr Cullen was screaming.

I couldn't hear what she wanted to tell me.

I couldn't find her hand to hold.

And I go there still, though nine long years have passed.

The grass is shorter and the rotten tree long felled, and all around the fields are lost to housing estates.

But the hole in the hedge is still there.

I sit upon the blanket we always used to bring and reach across with buttered bread.

The leverets parade – I can always tell which one she is.

'Dympna,' I whisper, 'Dympna. Here's some bread for you.'

Sometimes Mr Cullen comes but I push him away with my walking stick.

'None for you, Mr Cullen,' I say, 'you'll get nothing from me.'

He looks past me with dead black eyes, and I jab him again and he wanders off, rejoining the leveret procession.

Leaving me and Dympna alone.

And as she nibbles on the bread I remember how, on that last night, her mouth opened and closed without a sound.

I bend my head and whisper: 'Dympna … have you got a message for me?'

But she just stares into the air between us.

Her eyes are bright and round.

Like moons.

And I say to her, I say 'Dympna …'

'Dympna …'

'Are you happy?'

'Are you happy?'

TRACING THE SPECTRE

TRACY FAHEY

(2016)

Perhaps some ghosts want to remain alone, but human beings are nosy. If a group embarks on a ghost hunt in a grand but freezing castle, what could possibly go wrong? Not all ghosts are easily recognised, nor do we understand what they may presage. I am reminded of a story heard as a child, of the ghost of an English captain, whose appearance was always an omen of death or disaster. One local sceptic dismissed the tale until, one moonlit night, pulling hay from a rick, he found he was tugging the captain's sandy beard. No death followed except the annihilation of the sceptic's former disbelief!

AFTERWARDS IT'S HARD TO recall the exact sequence of events. Some stand out, light-bright, like what happened on the stairs. Others recede into shadows, so that they're confusing to remember. And some of them can never be forgotten.

But I'm beginning in the wrong place. Let me get it in order. I'll tell you about the drive there.

It is a cold drive down through the flat Midlands. The sky glows a sullen dirty grey through the rain-blotched windshield. Ahead are vistas of spiky, mud-coloured trees, their branches hacked into uniform length. The screech-squeak of wipers sliding on the greasy windscreen is rhythmic, atonal, endlessly annoying. All conversation has stopped miles of muddy road ago, the passengers subdued and quiet as the chill of mid-morning subsides into the warm fug of crowded bodies. In the front, the annoying Californian woman Skye is fidgeting irritably with the radio dials. She's already insisted on sitting in front – 'If I don't I get real nauseous' – and complained bitterly about the quality of the airport coffee. I could tell her the radio doesn't actually work, but a mean part of me lets her continue to fiddle with it. She gives up eventually, after producing only static. I keep steering the car down the wet roads, eyes aching from the queer unrelenting brightness of the sky.

And still the rain continues, driving, relentless.

A dirty rain spatters like snow on the windshield. Whirls of water spray ahead, ricocheting off the road to form a solid layer of mist. It has been a sludgy crawl through wet, grey, low-set towns with their abandoned roadworks, great pools of water stippled with raindrops in torn-up tarmacadam. Though the streets are thronged with parked cars, the towns are curiously lifeless, with only the odd lone, hunched figure hurrying through the spitting rain. Inside, the windows slowly cover with condensation, reducing the visibility even further. And so it goes on, town after town, field after field, wall after wall, until finally, in the late afternoon, the car swings in between the tall grey pillars that stand at the end of the muddy drive of Knocknamara Castle.

'Man. That's some driveway.' Bill, the laconic guy from Texas has woken up. He peers forward, head almost on my shoulder. We bump down the rutted lane with a series of body-jarring jolts.

'Ow,' complains Skye, her face drawn into a frown. 'Watch how you're going!' I say nothing. *Why didn't you offer to drive?* I think savagely, swiping at the condensation on the windscreen. But even I relax when Knocknamara itself comes into view, outlined sharply against the dull white-grey sky. It is a great, vertical mass, built solidly of dark stone, its mock-battlements and decorated pinnacles creating a spectacular Gothic silhouette. Bill emits a low whistle, Skye cranes her neck forward to take it all in, and even quiet English

Mark is moved to murmur appreciatively. I pull up in a crunching swirl of gravel and stop. The vast wooden door swings slowly open and I see a woman there, waving at us.

We have arrived.

The caretaker, Mary, leads us in. The entrance hall is impossibly grand, with an immense double staircase rearing up before us. I gently touch the dark, carved wood of the newel post. Mary shows us the library, the grand saloon with its large, pointed windows and glorious fan vaulting, and pauses as we descend the staircase again. 'Now I recommend you stick to the areas I've shown you. You can't go up on the second floor – that's the family's private quarters.' We nod obediently. 'There's no light on the staircase above the second floor, and the third floor has a lot of issues with the roof.' Mark is making notes. Bill, I notice, is shivering visibly. The endless cold of the house is a constant unpleasant surprise, tipping my nose with ice, numbing my toes and breathing blasts of chill air at my face. Skye shivers ostentatiously, despite being wrapped in what seemed to be a belted sleeping bag. Her raw-boned, red-nosed face peers around, sourly. 'Goddamn it, that curator said this place would be HEATED!' Her voice echoes against the tall walls. 'Well, the kitchen is down here; it's the only warm part of the house at night,' says Mary, ignoring her rudeness and pointing to the left of the staircase. 'We'll light a fire upstairs too, but the ceiling's too high for you to really feel it.'

'Thanks,' I say, as no-one else seems about to. 'Is it OK if we bring in our equipment and set up? Did you say you were lighting a fire in the library?'

'Oh yes. I'll call Jane up to start the fire. I'll be in the kitchen for the next while, but after that she'll be available to you if you need her. She's sleeping here tonight. Well now, in case I don't see you later, good luck to you all.' She scowls briefly at Skye (who is obviously left out of the good wishes) and shakes my hand with a vigorous warmth. She joins the men who are already making their way out to the car, calling to each other across the hallway. Skye digs her hands into her pockets and rocks gently on her heels. 'Let the fun begin,' she says lightly.

We are, as our arts grant application says, '*an interdisciplinary team of international artists collaborating on a twenty-four-hour project based on artist-led paranormal investigations in Ireland and the US.*' It's the second part of the project; the first has already taken place in Tennessee earlier in the year. The project is not my idea – I got drafted in at the last moment, when Carol the Irish photographer decided that being eight months pregnant and spending the night in a dark, haunted castle would be mutually exclusive. So here I am. My job is simple. I am to set up static cameras on timers around the castle – here, in the entrance hall – I put down the camera and carefully check that it is functioning properly – here, in the library – I gently put down my second one. There are two more. *One on the staircase, I think, the other in the ballroom?* Finally, with my trusty Nikon, I'll be patrolling at night, at irregular intervals to capture images of transition, from light to darkness. I sit on one of the cold, lumpy chairs in the library and congratulate myself on my solo part in this team project. Nothing to do with the others, thank goodness. I watch them, as they come up the stairs talking. Skye is just a pain in the ass, a born complainer. She is a performance artist – *of course she is, I think resignedly,* who is going to perform a series of interactions with the castle that Mark will film. Mark is OK, I concede, he's just very serious and a little off-putting. I watch his ungainly bespectacled frame as he drags equipment up the stairs. Bill helps him. I have warmed to Bill most of all, partly because of his marvellous Southern twang, but also partly because he has not annoyed me yet. Granted, he slept all of the way here, but he has a drowsy, benign air about him that bodes well. He is a sound artist, he told us, yawning, at the airport. Like me, he is opting for the stealth approach – he wants to set up equipment to monitor and capture different sounds around the castle. In fact the whole project is his idea – a tying together of witch legends from Ireland and Alabama. Outside, the sky looks particularly Irish, a blanket of rough grey hemmed on the horizon by a rim of dirty white light. The light is failing fast.

Once I've installed my last two cameras, I ramble down the stairs. Mary has packed up to go. She nods cordially at me as she picks her handbag off the staircase. 'You'll be fine,' she says kindly. 'Now Jane sleeps through here, down the corridor at the back –' she points towards the kitchen '– so if there's anything you need or if anything happens, just give her a shout.' She ties her coat belt tightly around her middle and calls a goodbye behind her. The huge door bangs to, and she is gone.

Skye is upstairs in the library in front of the fire. She is cross-legged, her eyes closed. Mark sees me looking at her. 'Getting in the mood,' he says with a faint smile, adjusting his film camera. 'Attuning to the building.' In the background, a slight, elderly woman – Jane, I presume – is crouched over the fire, which is crackling furiously and emitting sharp bangs. It may be my imagination, but I think I can feel the heat starting to radiate out and minimise the startling cold. I raise my camera and shoot some photographs of Skye. I focus on her pale, freckled face, her almost translucent skin. Jane wanders by me, nods a hello and moves out of the room just as Bill comes in. 'Well, now, y'all,' he smiles. 'Here we are. All ready to go.' His grin is broad and friendly.

Skye stretches elaborately. 'Thank Christ this room is heating up a little! What are they thinking of, not to bring in heaters? We could get seriously sick here.'

'Oh now,' protests Mark. 'I think we're made of stronger stuff than that.'

She looks down her long, narrow nose at him. 'Fine for you,' she says coldly. 'But I have lung issues. I need to ensure that I am always at optimum temperature.'

'Right.' Only a polite Englishman could fit so much disbelief into one small syllable.

She ignores him, instead setting out small cushions in a circle. 'I need you all for this bit,' she calls over her shoulder. I look eloquently at Bill and Mark. Mark is openly smirking. In a weird way, it's almost fun, having someone to gang up on. And Skye is truly awful. She continues to bully us, her strident whine cutting across the cold room. 'Now I want you all to sit down, yes, cross-legged if you can. Then I need you to empty your minds of clutter. I want you to focus on the room itself. On the history of the castle. On the presence of the witch, Bridget Ryan. Or, rather *alleged* witch and probable Gaelic healing woman,' she adds piously. I sit down obediently, trying to recall the briefing notes. According to them, the woman, Bridget Ryan, was stoned to death outside the castle in the early nineteenth century for the crime of setting a curse on the landlord's cattle. I look out the window at the bleak landscape and shudder.

'Eyes closed!' This is directed at me. I hastily shut my eyes and to my surprise find the sensation is relaxing. The silence is almost perfect, the tiny wheeze of our breathing the only audible sound. A thin chill breezes up against my face. The vast room is silent. Then, faintly there is a 'ting' like glass being struck lightly, a pause, a footfall, a pause, a light scurry of steps. Skye's eyes pop open instantly, she grabs my sleeve. 'You heard that?'

'Yes,' says Bill, and then, seeing her fright, 'Hey, don't worry, it'll just be that old lady!'

Skye's pupils are dilated. 'Jane!' she calls suddenly.

'Ah, Skye, don't.' I pat her arm. 'Don't call her up all these stairs again.' Skye doesn't listen. 'Come here!' she calls. She is clearly upset, her cheeks and neck are a mottled purple-red.

There is a silence, and then we hear the slow, creeping footsteps come up the stairs. The door creaks open. Jane looks at us, her face uncertain. 'You called me?'

Mark stands up and apologises, tells her it was a mistake. She nods and disappears again. I check my camera, and decide to walk around by myself for a while. *Group hysteria*, I think knowledgeably. I will be safer on my own.

Much later I wander down to the kitchen. Bill is there, stirring soup on the stove. It smells marvellous. 'Here,' he offers, ladling it into a bowl. 'Campbell's finest, ma'am!' I savour the heavy, delicious scent of tomato. Everything is flavoured with a surreal edge of tiredness that makes the panorama of pots and bowls twist and buckle as I yawn.

'So, how you doin' up there?' Bill pours out his own soup.

'Grand,' I reply, stretching my arms above the armchair in a bliss of warmth. My skin is now heated on one side from the open fire, the other still chill to touch.

'No sign of the witch?' He is smiling, but his voice is grave.

'Nothing yet. Those noises were weird, though, earlier. Did anything odd happen when you were working in Tennessee?'

'You could say that,' he says quietly, then pauses. I nod eagerly, mouth full, to encourage him to keep going. 'Well, we were in Bell

Witch Cave in Adams, Tennessee – you've heard the story, about how she haunted a farming family there in the early years of the nineteenth century, and, so folks believe, for a long time before that. In fact they say her legend might derive from the Trail of Tears, the dispossession of the native Americans and how their souls haunted the land claimed by the settlers. I grew up round those parts, and I'd been recording in the cave on and off for years. Let me tell you, I heard some weird sounds in that time. But it wasn't till I met Skye that she persuaded me that there might be a whole, big project in it. So we did the filming there. Some strange stuff, alright. Carol wasn't too happy there.' He is almost speaking to himself.

'Carol, the other photographer? The one who dropped out of this project?' He looks at me, an odd sideways glance.

'Yes.'

'She *really* didn't like it,' chimes in Mark from the doorway. Both Bill and I jump.

'Jesus!' I say good-naturedly. 'Don't creep up on us in a haunted castle!' Mark laughs.

'Poor Carol. She claimed it made her feel sick – the place, the atmosphere. I think she felt that doing it all again here would be too much for her.'

'So did you see anything there?' I am curious.

'Not really,' says Bill, rinsing the soup saucepan with hot water. 'Some shadows. Some odd noises. We went astray for a bit, got disorientated.' He clears his throat, obviously wanting to change the subject. I imagine being with them in the dark cave and shiver. While Bill and Mark discuss the technical details of the US leg of the project, I feel the welcome warmth begin to thaw out my ears and nose. I trace a finger over the worn floral patterns on the armchair, patches faded on the arms to expose rough stitching below. I finish my soup and sigh. 'Right, so, back up the stairs with me, then.'

I go from room to room, checking all the cameras are still on the timers. It's dark now – *dark as the hobs of hell*, as my mother would say. I feel like a proper paranormal investigator as I flash my torch around. Those shows always look so action-packed on TV, with their edited highlights. No-one tells you about the long waits, the intense boredom, and the biting cold. I have positioned myself on the stair-case, with a sleeping bag for warmth. One o'clock. Two o'clock. I traipse down every hour to make myself a cup of tea. Bill has set up his equipment but seems to have abandoned it to have a nap in the warmth of the kitchen. I debate joining him, but then am tempted by the thought of getting some more photos. Three o'clock. I'm just shooting a roll of film to capture my torch's reflections on the wooden stairs when several things happen at once.

There is a shout – *Mark?* I think, confused. 'Something bloody touched me! It did!'

It is Mark. I can hear Skye crying downstairs. I freeze, confused, then I hear it, the sound of slow deliberate steps coming down the stair-case towards me. I don't even think, I just scream and run, trip-falling, stumbling, running again till I reach the bottom of the stairs.

'Jane!' Skye is sobbing, loud, harsh sobs, as she throws open the kitchen door. 'Oh Jane!'

Mark is just behind us, breathless. He is shaking,

'What the hell?' Bill sits up straight in his chair, dazed, hair crumpled on one side of his face.

The door at the back of the kitchen opens and a girl appears, blinking, in a t-shirt and shorts.

'What's all the bloody noise?' she says in a strong Australian accent. We look at her, then at each other.

'Where's Jane?' blurts out Skye. The girl knuckles her eyes, and frowns, standing with one bare brown foot on top of the other on the rough stone flags.

'I'm Jane,' she says, bewildered.

'What about the old woman? She was up with us earlier in the library?' says Mark. He is clutching his coat around him convulsively.

'Jeez,' says Jane blankly. 'Sorry mates. No-one like that works here.'

And that's how the night ends.

When Mary comes in the morning, we are all in the kitchen, huddled around the fire. Skye is chalk-pale, freckles standing out like marker dots on her face. Mark looks tired and ill, and even Bill is subdued. All of our equipment was gathered up at first light. Mary unbelts her coat and puts on the kettle. She is clearly curious about our night and even asks us about it directly.

'It was great,' I say, 'but we're on a tighter deadline than we anticipated. No time for tea. Thanks for everything.' She says nothing else, but her shrewd glance follows us as we pack up the car.

That's it, I guess. I don't think the project was ever completed. I shared my images with the others on Dropbox as per the agreement. That was the last I heard of the project. I never heard anything about the promised launch. We never collaborated as artists again.

I heard Carol had her baby. A little girl, perfectly healthy. I bumped into her at an exhibition recently, but she didn't want to talk about the Tennessee shoot, just like Mark told me. In fact, when I brought it up, she looked at me like I'd just vomited on her shoes. Then she walked away.

Mark? I have no idea where Mark is. I think he's still based in London, making fastidious, detailed work. I'd say he probably finished his film of Skye's performance, he was that sort of person.

Skye is dead. I saw her obituary notice in a visual arts newsletter. It seems odd that someone so spiky and *present* should be dead. I feel bad. I never really believed in her proclaimed lung condition.

Bill still writes to me, diffidently and intermittently. He never mentions Knocknamara. His occasional emails are comfortable anecdotes of farms and canyons and the sounds he's captured outdoors.

And me? I'm fine, for the most part. I didn't send them all the photos you know. I kept some back. There are some of us in the kitchen, drinking tea, laughing. I like those.

There's a few I don't like. They're the photographs of Skye I took in the library.

Here, look at this one. It's a good portrait, a close-up. I've captured her haughty, patrician face, the atmosphere of stillness she could evoke. I've also captured something else, something that keeps me awake at night. Behind Skye, there is a shadow. Look closer and you can see – if you squint a little – it looks like a dark shape. Look at the next one. Now you can clearly see what it is – an old woman standing by the fire. And in this one – the last photo in the sequence – you can see her wrinkled face in the firelight. She's looking right at Skye, and her face is twisted in a bitter smile.

I can't bring myself to destroy that photo. Sometimes at night I'll take it out and look at it. Who was she? Why did she come to us?

And, on the darkest of nights, I wonder – *can she find us again?*

THE SEVENTH MAN

ROISÍN O'DONNELL

(2016)

Would you give up everything for love? Maybe? What if everything included nine thousand years of a life in which you grew ever stronger and more beautiful on the life force of a husband — or six? A life in which you loved them to death and replaced them as needed? A story old as love itself yet as young as Tinder must make you think twice. Think more than twice! You'll be a scatter of bones, and he a living, loving man who won't remember you ever existed. Ghosts are scary, but love is scarier still.

BB-TIDE HAS COME TO ME, as to the sea. I am no longer immortal.

Here in this place, autumn light falls through the hospital window and outlines everything golden. It picks out my husband's fleece-lined lumber jacket on the back of the door, slung there casually as if on a passing visit. It glints on the yew-red prickles in his stubble, and burnishes the shadows that cup his sleeping eyes. It illuminates the tubes through which they feed him his enchantment. It gilds the brass clipboard at the end of the bed, on which our consultant Doctor Furlong has written the painfully legible words 'no change'. And as I look on the new narrowness of my husband's blanket-outlined shape, I feel it in my pores; the crinkling of my humanity. With the six others, it was never like this.

I seduced each of them from the rocks of Beara, starting with the Spaniard I dragged up from the deep. Spluttering brine, he let me haul him from his sinking Milesian galleon. His fingers locked in the ropes of my hair. My lips blew life into his.

I could have saved hundreds of others, but I only needed one. I kept this skinny skipper from A Coruña in my cottage on the cliff, strengthening him with hearty broth, honeyed words and home-brewed poteen. He saw me as the Madonna; a black-haired seraph, crackleware skinned. *Santa Maria!* he'd yell, when he stumbled from bed in the small hours, sending the storm lantern swinging. For the waves that had swept him to Ireland had stayed inside his skull, leaving him forever listing; the world a tilting deck.

'Would you ever look,' the locals clucked. 'The kindness of that girleen.'

'The way she looks after that man of hers.'

'It'd put the heart across ye.'

Bewitched, those locals were. During that time, my magic was strong. My slate eyes were the grey of the Beara cliffs. My voice was fierce as the wind that rummaged through the peninsula. My lips were the red of the storm-battered trawlers below on Bearhaven Bay. The spirit of one young man would allow me to survive another few hundred years. I'd never needed this type of tonic when I was younger, but it was a solution when I began to get old. Around crackling fires, the Irish wove yarns about 'The Hag of Beara, the oldest woman in Ireland', but they never suspected it was I, the sweetest girl from Sneem to Ballybunion.

As for the young Spaniard, his spirit was rich and plentiful, though his soul was wandering. Each Samhain, I magicked his speech so he couldn't tell anyone my secret. When he begged a local Spanish-speaking captain, *'Señor, por favor ayúdame. Estoy bajo el control de esta mujer loca.'* All the captain heard was a dolphin's clickering, while I grew fat and gorgeous on the young man's energy. Yes, that one served me well. He was my first husband.

'Cara?' The night-nurse whose name pin says *Blessing* touches my arm. 'Will you sleep in the Relatives' Room, dear? You'll get a crick in your neck.'

I shake my head. Her black eyes pitch their stubbornness against my own, knowing they will lose. You cannot win against insanity.

'I'll tell Doctor Furlong on you,' she pouts in mock offence.

'Doctor F. can eff off,' I reply.

'What are you like?' She shakes her head and leaves the room. Through the glass panel on the door, I watch her amble down the corridor towards the nurses' station. Her blue scrubs look like the comfiest and cleanest garment on Earth.

The silence seems louder after Blessing has gone. Orange street-light falls through the metal binds, laddering my husband's bed with barcode shadows. I rearrange my legs in the bedside chair, and the creak of the springs could be that of my aching limbs.

For twelve nights, I've slept upright with my leather jacket wrapped around my shoulders like wings. Each morning, I've binned the dead chrysanthemums in the plastic Ikea jug on the bedside locker, and I've bought new ones from Nancy's Blooms on the corner. They never last more than a day. My nervousness kills them off. The flowers don't so much wilt as internally com-bust, scattering petal-debris across the sill.

During the day, I sit on the radiator by the dust-opaqued window, sipping cups of plastic-y coffee from the hospital vending machines. Searching for something safe to look at, I've counted the number of lampposts on the street below and the number of silver shamrocks on each one. I've counted the number of beeps from the traffic lights each time a pedestrian crosses the street, and the number of times my husband's heartbeat peaks per minute. I'm not sure what else to do. His chest rises and falls slowly, like a stingray's wings. This feeling is unchartered. My husband is dying, and for the first time in history, this has nothing to do with me.

I snatched my second husband from the Skelligs while he was kneeling, trying to find words with which to adore his God. His brown cassock grazed my thighs, and his rosary beads clinked cool as pebbles from a mountain river bed. He'd come from the island of Iona, and he believed in me as if I were a deity. In his eyes my hair was hay-blonde, and my features were soft. This kind man saw me as a quiet redemption. In a stonework beehive, I sated my thirst on his soul.

How many times have I re-cloaked myself over the centuries? Sometimes I've been feral and sharp-witted; other times, tame and homely. I have metamorphosed so often to suit each husband's fantasy, I no longer know which version of myself is real.

Magicking myself was easy, and I magicked the locals too. In Castletown, and as far away as Ballinskelligs, people believed my family were fishing folk who lived in Bearhaven Bay. For nuptials, I'd magick some bewildered ole fella into walking me up the aisle. There'd be a veil, a kiss on the cheek and a button-hole stuffed with a white carnation. It was smokescreen rather than sorcery. I didn't deceive them. I just created a spell that prevented them from questioning. They believed what they wanted to.

Third and fourth blur into a tangle of straw, whitethorn and sex. One was invading, the other defending. One was hiding from something, the other from something else. All I can recall is that I could have guzzled the serum of their youth indefinitely, and that a legend gathered around one of them once he was gone. They said that he'd been put under a spell and was sleeping under Lough Derg, and that he would ride forth on a silver-shod steed. These mortals are fools, for I'd slung his bones into the ocean and forgotten him immediately.

My fifth husband was fleeing, lusty with treason, when I seduced him on the sound off Bere Island. His Ulster aristocracy were so brimming with plots and scheming, they didn't notice the man weakening a little each time he lay with me. 'Kathleen,' the man said one morning, shirtless and frowning at the new hollows below his ribcage, 'Do ye not see how pale I've become? How thin?'

'Hush, *mo grá*,' I told him. ''Tis probably but a touch of the *féar gortach* – the hungry grass. Those cursed patches are common round here. Did you keep a loaf handy, as I told you?'

'Probably not. That could be it, I suppose.'

These husbands were gullible as rain-yellowed sheep. They didn't know what to believe. By the time the Ulster aristocrats set sail from the shore of Lough Swilly, my second husband was already dwindling, and I was bored and gorgeous again. Leaning over the bow of the ship, I watched Atlantic dolphins race the stern. It was unlike me, to wander so far from Beara, among people whose trickful sing-song accents befuddled my charms. As we sailed the Cork coast, I dived overboard and swam homewards. I'd gorged myself on enough of my second husband's energy to last another century. The man fled across oceans, trailing his relics.

When my husband is awake, he talks about his body as if he's already outside it. 'PSA levels have dropped a little, and the liver is doing well. That's grand news, isn't it?'

'Bloody brilliant,' I say. 'When will we get to go home?'

'Cara, don't be like that.'

He clasps at good news and rattles it like a toy. He sits up in bed and kills me with his fake smiles, his fever-bright eyes, his effort to look well. But I know better. My life stretches back to the last glacial maximum: Ireland covered in ice sheets. Through volcanic winters, past Mesolithic hunter-gatherers and the Viking raids, I've seen it all. I know when a man is about to depart this life.

Doctor Furlong pauses at the foot of the bed. 'Well,' he says, 'things seem to be fairly stable.' His nasal voice sounds as if something is trapped inside it. He carries his usual air of mild annoyance, perhaps at the strip-lighting polishing his bald head, or at the patients themselves. 'Yes,' he adjusts his small round glasses. 'All things considered.'

I glare at him, and he becomes fascinated by something beside his left shoe. This man will always tell me if the news is good, but he'll never say it's bad. He'll say it's *not so good* or *not as good as we'd hoped*. It's as if this precious body were a weather forecast or an election promise. *Not quite as good as we'd expected.*

Today, Doctor Furlong clears his throat, 'Mrs Connolly? If I might have a word?' And he takes me into the Relatives' Room and shuts the door behind us.

'How the chestnut horses shone,' my sixth husband said, 'and how our bayonets gleamed when we marched out from the Royal Barracks in Dublin in 1914. Along the quays, factory girls, dockhands and toffee-nosed clerks alike all stopped to lift their caps and wave their kerchiefs at us. The streets were a flutter with well-wishes.'

I stroked his head. 'Shh, *a stor*, the past is done.'

His first horse was shot from under him, somewhere at the front near Armentières. Three years later, he returned to a different country. Stepping off the gangplank, a crowd jeered from the docks;

the Irish Sea, the River Liffey and the sky over Dublin were an angry kelpie spitting in his face. Raw egg slimed his cheek. Egg shell littered the upturned collar of his great coat. Old friends turned, lowered their eyes and shuffled away, as if he were a bad omen. He lingered in his hometown for as long as he could bear it, and then he stepped out into the howling night.

Many men were on the run in those days, caught on the wrong side of history. Shapes darted between dry stone walls. Ireland was an anthill teeming with men trying to outrun their own shadows. That was a good time for finding husbands. My sixth knocked on the door of my cottage one growling December night, 'Sorry, Miss, if you'd happen to have some shelter? An outhouse? Anything?'

I kept him with me.

Between six and seven, a long time passed. Men no longer came praying or invading or fleeing or hiding on the coast of Beara. Sometimes I'd see a fine-looking young man in a bright rain-proof coat, but he would normally be accompanied by a woman in a matching coat who shouted, 'Look, Babe, let's take a photo over here!' Those rare young men who ventured out here alone had hand-held GPS devices and were so hell-bent on hiking the three peninsulas of Kerry that they were oblivious to my enchantments. Meanwhile, I grew weaker, with only the wind for company, and in the bubbled mirror with the crazed and flaking edges, my reflection aged. I spat into the merciless salt-spray of the Atlantic gales. 'How are you meant to seduce a husband these days?'

I liked the sound of *Tinder*. It sounded like *timber*: things being chopped and tossed onto the fire. Smouldering, sparking, cracking. An excellent start to a marriage. When the man onscreen asked where I'd like to meet up, I replied, 'the Beara Penninsula,' and he replied, 'A woman after my own heart. A hiking date it is then so.'

After that, what happened was a navy jeep with a bumper sticker that said GONE FISHING, a checked shirt and a rough-bearded smile. 'Now I know what you're thinking,' the tall man said. 'I'm a little older than in my profile shot, but so are you if you don't mind my saying so, and besides, you can't judge a person from a thumb-nail.' He inhaled a sigh, exhausted by this rehearsed sentence, and took off his cap to scratch his head. 'If it's not too forward of me, how old are *you* anyway?'

'Nine thousand and twelve,' I answered truthfully.

The man laughed. 'I knew you'd be good fun.'

And so we set out to sea, on a gin-clear day, as the fishermen call them, two weeks before Bealtaine. A shift in clouds, a shaft of light, and the landscape appeared in a zenith of green and teal. As we walked round Cahermore and sailed his boat, the *Branwyn Morrigan*, out to Lambshead and Dursey Island, Ireland drenched herself in blinking sunlight and garlanded herself with rainbows. I tried to keep things normal, to follow my usual seduction routine. But the afternoon became scalded onto my retinas, like the aftermath of staring too long into a furnace. After that, I always kept my phone by my bed, waiting for some words from him, and that blue light got into my head, until I could think of little else.

The second time we met, he took me home to his bungalow outside Bantry, and I giddily noted the upturned currach by the front door, the sigh of nets on the lawn, and the lobster pots strung from his windows on slate-blue ropes, as if they had absorbed the sea's colours. I remember the sincerity with which he went about preparing dinner for me, while I sat on the corner of the kitchen worktop, swinging my heels against the cupboards. We talked while he chopped fistfuls of parsley and diced spuds and threw smoked haddock into the sizzling pan.

Conversation was as easy as breathing. He told me of sea-storms and doldrums, of opportunities missed or seized. He laughed and mourned for his mistakes. And he drew my past from me like venom from a wound, leaving me feeling *young* for the first time in history.

Am I afraid of his death or my own?

His hair is fine as fish wire; strong auburn in a certain light, other times light-softened to a mousy grey. In those early weeks after we met, I panicked myself into multiple kidney infections. Venusian dimples aching. Inner tract burning with an acid excess of love. I was soothed only by his hands; the timbre of his voice. 'He's just another husband,' I codded myself. 'Just another source of youth I'll guzzle until I am full.' But then, one bright morning before he boarded the *Branwyn Morrigan*, he bounded up to give me a bristly kiss, and as the boat pulled away, he shouted something into the wind; three small words which changed everything.

White lights and sliding doors. A stuffy heat that dries out your eyeballs. The aspidistra in one corner of the Relatives' Room has been dying for a long time. GIVE BLOOD, say the tiered leaflets on the magnolia walls, GIVE THE GIFT OF LIFE. Doctor Furlong looks at his hands, 'Cara. You know we're doing everything we can. But it's only a matter of time.'

Time is all I've had. From one era to the next. Endless, infinite, boundless time since before the mountains had settled. A banquet of minutes has left me on the edge of narcosis, as after an obnoxious feast. I'm tired of time, nauseated by it. After tasting the moments with my seventh husband, I want nothing else. On our wedding night, the clocks went back and neither of us noticed. Insomniac with happiness, for one night we were an hour ahead of the rest of Ireland. Living a future with only us in it.

'Cara, are you listening?' the doctor says. 'As I said, putting your husband's affairs in order might not be a bad idea. Cara?'

I stand and leave the Relatives' Room, shutting the doctor's voice behind me. My trainers squeal down the warren of magnolia corridors. As I walk, it occurs to me that perhaps I'll never find my way back to this ward again. I imagine the hospital as a cream-coloured Rubik's cube with my husband locked inside it, and me standing outside, frozen.

Night is coming. The cold autumn air needles my skin as I step out of the hospital. A few smokers huddle around a bin at the main entrance. Rush hour traffic is building; the motorway beyond the hospital entrance is a red river of taillights. Lining the carpark, fingerlings of leafless branches try to grasp the dying light. And on unkempt summer beds, the black heads of sunflowers nod their bright petals onto the tawny earth. I stop and close my eyes, running my hands through my hair. I could return to Beara and start over with number eight … But I can't leave this place any more than the wind can pick itself up and walk away.

Whenever I had ancestors, I don't remember grieving. Or walking across a hospital carpark towards the copper haze of autumn trees feeling as if I'd left my spleen behind me.

The most dangerous thing you can do on this earth is fall in love.

I have survived everything but this.

It's only ever occurred to me to use my gifts to steal time from my husbands. But what if I could give time back? What if I could summon the lifeblood of a captured Spaniard, the breath of an Ulster aristocrat, the pulse of a soldier caught between wars? The moment the thought occurs to me, I'm swivelling and flying a crow-straight route back into the hospital. The sliding doors gasp open. I swoop along the corridors without touching the ground, sending nurses squealing and scattering, causing metal blinds to chatter like teeth. Double-doors bang open.

Dr Furlong is standing near my husband's room, but with one blast, I pinion him against the wall, and he hugs his clipboard. On his glasses, my ghastly reflection swells. He sees me now as I truly am: a skeletal apparition with white streaming hair, surrounded by a black confetti of bats and plumes of noxious Beara sea fret. My marmoreal bones have been polished to the patina of ivory. And inside my ribcage, my heart is pickled to the texture of roast beef. The doctor's eyelids twitch at the approach of the inevitable. At this exact moment, he admits to himself that he always knew I was weird. My arboreal arms seem to reach and stem and branch towards him. His lips part in the process of framing a scream that never emerges. Hospital lights palpitate, fizzing as my reflection flies along black curtainless windows.

My husband is awake but not afraid when I enter the room. Tomorrow he'll wake up hungry and he'll wonder why the warmth has returned to his fingers, why his heartbeat has steadied, why his IV drip has been disconnected, and why there's a pile of bones under the radiator. He'll flex his fingers in disbelief, feeling the vitality surge through them, and he'll touch his side, where the pain will have vanished. And he won't remember sitting in a Mexican restaurant on a Cork side street, a hot city breeze drifting through the open shutters, and a comfortable quiet swishing between us like a secret. He won't remember the first night we lay together and how we stumbled into the shower afterwards, weak-kneed, drenched, leaving steamed-up love notes in the bathroom mirror. Or that weekend in Mayo, how the Fiesta gave up the ghost somewhere outside Mallaranny, or how racing each other across the beach at Achill, I got to the sea first.

I shut the door behind me and glide towards the bed.

FAITH & FRED

MAURA MCHUGH

(2020)

Even as a child I felt a little uncomfortable visiting museum displays of skeletal remains. Increasingly, as a gesture of respect, such remains are being returned to their native place. So, there is sympathy for a man grabbing at a chance to turn his life around, but more sympathy for the twins treated so unjustly by a cruel world. We hear of the horrors they endured. Others are hinted at. I'll never again look at Hallowe'en skulls and costumes in a lighthearted way ... two little voices might say, 'You'll come back. You, or another.'

HEY FOUND THE SKULLS on the third day of renovation.

Owen had just bashed in the plasterboard with the sledgehammer his contractor, Bald Jim, had handed him with a, 'Let her rip, lad.'

Owen had bridled at the 'lad', since he was nearing thirty, but the heft of the scarred sledgehammer in his gloved hands gave him a tactile joy, which overrode his pride. Assaulting the wall was deeply satisfying: the hard swing, the protesting sound as the pitted metal head smashed through the cheap panelling, and the aftershock down his arms.

Dust and chip fragments flew up and obscured the view at first. Gradually, daylight from the big windows behind them lanced through the widening jagged opening that Owen had created. They knew this had been a closet of some kind before a previous owner walled it up, but it was wasted space, and Owen was determined to use every inch of Caldwere Farmhouse. From its dilapidated rooms he would create a home for someone willing to pay a good price.

Bald Jim tapped him on the shoulder to indicate it was time to relinquish the weapon, and Owen reluctantly handed it back to the brawny older man. Brute force had done its job, now was the time for the finesse of experts.

Bald Jim propped the tool against the wall, and selected a smaller hammer. He pried at the opening, splintering it open further until he suddenly hopped back, alarmed.

'Flippin' 'eck,' he said.

'What is it?' Owen stepped into the miasma, squinting. Something gleamed white in between metal bars. He fished his phone out of the thigh pocket in his combat trousers and swiped on the torch app. He was aware of Bald Jim's solid presence behind him.

Two human skulls stared at him from inside an old metal cage fashioned from flattened iron strips. The cage sat on a simple wooden table.

'Holy shit!' Owen said, his voice hushed, as he directed the light around the space. He leaned forward, inhaling a mouldy reek, and immediately regretted not wearing a dust mask.

Sitting in front of the cage was a white card inscribed with fluid copperplate writing, obscured by a layer of dust.

He reached in warily and retrieved the card.

Here be Faith & Fred.
Keep them homestead,
Lest they wail.

'That's us buggered,' said Bald Jim after he scanned the text.

He walked to the double windows, dipping into the May sunlight, and pulled out an old-school battered mobile phone from one of his many pockets.

'I'll call the cops.'

'What?'

'Do you think this is the first frightener I've found in one of these old gaffs?' He shook his head. 'Occupational hazard.'

'What'll they do?'

Bald Jim tipped back his hardhat and stared through the glass, across the flat green fields, to the blue line indicating the distant shore.

'They'll take your new friends for tests. Ask questions. Bring in boffins. There'll be paperwork for sure. It'll be a right pain in the arse.'

The words stirred a panic in Owen. He imagined the room being shut down, and the disruption to their schedule. The news would get out in the area, and maybe become a viral story online.

He noticed that Bald Jim kept well away from the hole punched in the wall, and cast unhappy glances in that direction. If this bloke was nervous because of a spooky find, how would the other workers react? Or potential buyers?

Owen had little margin for mistakes. His new leaf had been turned over too recently, and there were plenty of people longing to see him screw up again.

'Does anyone else have to know?'

Bald Jim turned away from the calm vista, levelled a hard stare at Owen, but said nothing. Leaving a gap into which Owen rushed.

'It's probably a nineteenth-century parlour entertainment. We know from the plans that it's been shut up for at least a hundred years. It's not some CSI Holderness situation…'

Bald Jim nodded and let Owen continue.

'If I wrap these up and dispose of them, then no one need be any the wiser.' He reached for his wallet. 'Why don't you take the rest of the day off?'

He counted off six fifty-pound notes and held them out.

Bald Jim considered the money for a drawn-out moment. Owen oozed a fresh sheen of sweat.

'Aye,' he said, 'the missus would love a fancy meal out.' He pointed at the hole. 'I want no sign of those when I'm back, mind.' He slipped the notes into his back pocket, and walked to the door, his boots thumping across the bare boards.

At the entrance he paused and added, 'Thaddy – Thadeus – Ogram runs The Adder's Knot. His family's been hereabouts since the Ark. He might know something about ...' And he jerked his head at the problem.

From where Owen stood, mote-suffused rays slanted into the recess and illuminated the empty eye sockets of the dead couple, lending them shining new orbs. Gooseflesh erupted across his arms. The black gaps between their aged teeth grinned at him.

'I'll take care of it,' he promised.

Bald Jim left, and Owen heard him calling to Roger and Tall Jim. A mumble of voices ensued, followed by doors slamming, and cars driving down the long lane to the main road.

Owen strode to where Bald Jim had left the hammer, grabbed it and laid into the edges of the gap, cursing as he did, venting his frustration.

He was panting by the time it was wide enough to pull out the cage.

It was awkward, arcing his body into the hidden space and latching his hooked fingers into the sharp metal grid. His legs pressed against the remaining plasterboard as he strained to lift and negotiate the cage through the uneven rent.

A shattering *crack*: the rest of the wall collapsed and he pitched into the closet, slamming down into the cage, knocking it off the table.

He fell completely inside the cavity, his face and chest landing on the cruel edge of the cage. Fireworks exploded across his vision. Beneath him, the skulls knocked around like snooker balls. Perhaps rolling with mirth.

He yelped, in fear and in pain, breathing in the dank smell of a previous century and old pacts.

A fury erupted and he rose in a flurry of thrashing arms and yelled curses.

'Fucking typical!' he screamed and hauled the cage out of the broken wall, dumping it on the ground, and kicking it several times until it was on the far side of the room. The skulls had moved about, but he noticed something else on their ivory surfaces: splatters of red dots.

The stream of damp on his forehead alerted him to the cut. He reached up to touch it and his fingers returned to his view dripping with vivid scarlet blood. His old phobia surged alive at the sight of it. His chest constricted while his legs softened like loops of over-cooked noodles.

He needed to get away, desperately.

Owen wobbled a couple of steps towards the doorway before he fainted.

He woke to twilight and pain.

Moving cautiously, he tested his arms and wrists, which must have broken his fall: sore, bruised, but not sprained or broken, thankfully. He sat up. His legs and feet checked out, but his forehead thumped an agonising beat, and his right collarbone radiated trouble. Gingerly, he touched his temple and felt the crusted scab. He whooshed out a few breaths, feeling the horror rise in him again, which was rapidly pursued by his disgust at his weakness. It prompted a maelstrom of memories replaying his worst moments:

his younger sister Poppy defending him in school because the bullies learned they could make Owen faint if they cut him; avoiding any chance of conflict by playing sick and hiding; warping into a cynical little prick who mastered mimicking others and performing idiotic stunts to make his 'friends' laugh; picking on Poppy relentlessly as a teen, trying to wear down her strength so they could be equally frail.

He clutched his hands to his head and moaned a little, because that sin hurt him more than anything else. He banished the past to deal with the present.

The room was deeply shadowed as the world dimmed into a rose-violet hush. The birds were not singing their farewells to the sun.

Owen looked over at the crevasse in the wall, a slash of black that seemed to bleed darkness into the room. He did not know what constituted concussion, but he wondered if he had it. It never sounded good when the concerned doctors talked about it as they shone a flashlight into the eyes of their patients on the telly.

He got onto one knee and levered himself off the floor at a sedate pace. The room tilted and distorted for a moment and he heaved in a breath to steady himself. The cage lay in crooked darkness, only visible due to a patch of white lattice.

A skull doily, Owen thought, and a fizz of weird laughter tickled his mouth, but he kept it contained rather than break the suffocating silence.

A city boy, Owen had trouble with the pervasive quiet at the farmhouse, especially at night. Worse still were the erratic unfamiliar noises that startled him out of the oppressive lull at odd moments: a fox yipping; the squeaking of hunting bats; owls hooting to each other. Whenever he went outside for a smoke break, and was engulfed in a soothing cigarette pall, dark shapes could suddenly flit about in the sky or zip low to the ground. The countryside was too full of unruly, strange life for him. He had set up a monastic existence in the bedroom upstairs, but he kept his wireless headphones on most of the time, listening to music and podcasts, or watching films. Anything to avoid confronting his jittery solitude.

He approached the cage and dragged it from its concealment and into the starlight squares cast by the windows. There was a latch at the front, and it lifted easily. Owen opened the door and considered what to do next. The idea of touching the skulls made his fingers draw back towards his palms involuntarily.

'Man up,' Owen whispered, and immediately hated that the phrase had passed his lips. It was a spiteful invective that had been thrown at him by his old man on many occasions.

He reached in and pulled out one of the skulls: it was cool to the touch and surprisingly solid. The bottom jawbone was attached to the skull by twists of copper wire. For some reason he thought this one was Faith. He left her on the wide window seat and retrieved her brother.

He sat Fred beside her and wondered why he thought of them as siblings.

Owen stood in front of them, looking at their dark sockets, brimming with secrets.

'What's your story, then?'

They stared at him, smiling, steadfastly mute.

Behind them, through the window, two shadows flapped by.

Turn on a light, you idiot!

He darted to the switch, but the yellow light of the lone bulb dangling from the ceiling made it worse. A jaundice afflicted the space.

But it showed him the hammer lying on the ground where he'd dropped it earlier. He picked it up and its weight gave him confidence. Owen approached the skulls and made a practice swipe in front of them. As if to threaten them.

They were unimpressed.

He hesitated, wondering if there was a better way to deal with this problem, and considered that these long-dead people probably deserved better treatment. But plenty of people die alone, forgotten, and unburied. His own Great-Uncle Spencer had died in this house and had not been discovered for a month. Which was how he came to inherit the place.

They'd had their life. Now he wanted his, the one where he became an older brother Poppy could respect.

He raised the hammer and brought it down on Faith's crown. She burst apart into skittering shards.

He laughed, and pulverised Fred.

He fetched a dustpan, swept up their pieces, and dumped them into a black bin bag. Afterwards he moved the cage into his bedroom, covered it with a dust cloth, and sat his secondhand lamp on it. Then he went outside, under the pitiless vault of stars, and walked to the skip. Owen pushed the bag of bone bits deep under the assorted rubble, and strolled back to the house, whistling.

In his dream Faith and Fred were teenaged twins with black curls, dark eyes, and deeply tanned skin that bore the marks of torture and beating. They stood upon a makeshift gallows, the noose around their necks. Hatred burned in Faith's bruised eyes as she glared at the Magistrate standing in the throng of baying townspeople.

'Obadiah Creaser: none of your line shall prosper. You, who swore to care for and shelter us, will never be quit of us now. We shall call out your sins to the Almighty forever.'

Then the terrible sound of two snapping necks followed by howls of jubilation from the crowd.

The shrieks continued as the faces of the watching people twisted and morphed into distended caricatures. It was a cacophony of righteous wrath.

Owen bolted upright in his bed, sweating, the sound ringing in his ears, and his heart thudding quickly.

The screams continued. Two voices sounding their anguished fury.

Owen leapt up, disorientated but desperate to end the horrible din. It was close, but not upstairs.

He slammed on the light and found shoes to slip on. Owen stumbled downstairs, flicking on every light switch he passed, urgently needing to push back the darkness. All the time the screams assaulted his ears, and kept the images of the twin children dangling, dying before an audience vivid in his mind.

He had to make it stop.

Owen nearly tripped over a box of tiles in the disassembled kitchen, but he noticed at the last second and jumped it before flinging open the back door.

Here, the noise was a piercing pain.

The reassembled skulls of Faith and Fred sat on the doorstep, screaming.

Owen reeled as reality crashed into disbelief.

They continued to voice their anger to the heavens.

Panicked, he ran over, gathered them up, and stepped back into the kitchen.

They fell silent instantly.

Breathing hard, he stood inside the threshold and looked out the door at the forbidding night. A chilly breeze swept past his bare ankles.

He glanced down at the skulls cradled in his arms, and walked through the doorway into the yard. Their cries pealed out again.

Owen marched back into the kitchen and laid the skulls upon the small, paint-stained table he was using until the room was kitted out properly.

The skulls locked their protests behind their teeth.

For a long time Owen stared at the de-fleshed heads and pondered his next move. Finally, he scooped them up, carried them to his bedroom, and put them back in their cage.

He covered it again with the thick cloth and returned to the kitchen to brew coffee and wait for the dawn.

Bald Jim didn't discuss the previous day's events with Owen again, although he asked about the plaster on his forehead. Owen described falling over the box of tiles in the kitchen during a midnight foray for snacks, and Bald Jim promptly moved the obstacle and lectured Owen on tripping hazards. Satisfied he had taught Owen a lesson, Bald Jim and his crew got back to work, moving through the tasks on their schedule. They had weeks of work left to do, and every day there was a new minor crisis or bill to pay. Owen had little time to dwell on the skulls' unnatural behaviour, but whenever his thoughts idled their cries reverberated in his mind.

He startled when a table saw shrieked, thinking it was the skulls again, but instead it was the reassuring sight of Roger, wearing protective earmuffs, cutting floorboards. He thought of the twins' skulls, sitting covered in his bedroom. Listening to a new generation of people readying the house for occupation. He considered all the various families they had haunted, until they were boarded up. How many people had they eavesdropped upon? How many people had gone about their daily business unaware that the dead twins spied upon them?

That evening he drove to The Adder's Knot in the nearby hamlet. It was a small but well-appointed pub that had made some concessions to the twenty-first century. It had wi-fi and a good local cider, but the few regulars in that night were elderly couples and bachelor men who were territorial about their seats.

Thaddy was in his sixties with a huge pock-marked nose and red cheeks. He eyeballed Owen as soon as he entered, and moved along the varnished oak counter to greet him.

'What'll it be?' hxe asked, a touch gruffly.

Owen ordered a soft drink, and quickly added, 'And whatever you're having for yourself,' once he saw Thaddy's spectacularly bushy eyebrows rise in surprise to meet his unruly hair.

'You're Spencer's nephew?'

'Ah, great-nephew. Owen, pleased to meet you.'

Thaddy placed the glass clinking with ice in front of Owen. 'Not a drinker?'

Owen considered being evasive but guessed Thaddy wouldn't abide bullshit. 'Yeah, I'm sober. It doesn't agree with me.'

Thaddy nodded solemnly as he poured himself a whiskey. 'A man should know his limits.'

Owen imagined this was a subtle warning that The Adder's Knot wasn't a place for a heart-to-heart. Instead they discussed rugby for an hour.

Eventually they got onto the subject of local legends and folk tales. Thaddy had a couple of whiskies in him and the customers had thinned out. There was only a tiny wizened man in a cap nursing half an ale at a table in front of the telly.

'Spencer knew plenty about local history,' Thaddy said. 'He was an old git – rest in peace – but he liked reading.' Thaddy shook his head as if this was a shocking habit. 'He even wrote a couple of pamphlets.'

'What?'

Owen had only met Uncle Spencer once, when he was ten, so he knew little about him.

'There's got to be some of them knocking about in his – your – house. Library might have a copy. Spencer was right proud of them.'

Thaddy rose stiffly from his stool behind the bar and reached for the hanging bell. He rang it twice. 'Time, gents! Finish up, please.'

Owen drove through the deserted, hedged lanes to his house, and after a quick sandwich headed up to bed. He tugged back the cloth to peer into the jail and check on the prisoners.

They didn't appear to have moved. They made no sound.

He sat down in front of them, cross-legged, and told them all about his pub outing.

That night he dreamed of Faith and Fred as children, living with their mother in a small house on a farm near a copse. The children played in the woods in a little lean-to they built, and in it they hung a variety of trinkets and tokens they had found or crafted. Fred had a talent for carving figures in wood. They were uncannily like the subjects he chose: a badger, a crow, a toad, his sister and his mother. Their woodland father. Faith's voice was unearthly divine. When she sang, the birds marvelled.

The twins devised special games and chants. They charmed the moths and snails. They played with their huge, grey cat, which was a cunning mouser. She often brought them mauled birds and rodents as offerings. The children buried them in a little graveyard they created and erected twig crosses as markers. They conducted their own burial rites in their green cathedral, singing odd hymns with angelic voices.

And when the little family visited the village, which was rarely, a stream of whispers followed them.

Owen woke up, his head muggy, his shoulder tender, and his mood poignant. He knew some of the tragedy waiting for the family. They just wanted to be left alone. Why couldn't people let others be?

Later, to the tune of hammering and banging, Owen dug through the boxes of books and knick-knacks he had ear-marked for charity shops. He hadn't looked too closely at any of their titles since to his eyes they were a bunch of boring history books, a subject he'd failed in his GCSEs.

He almost missed the slender volume despite his thoroughness. It was slotted inside a large hardback book about the history of the Viking invasion. It had a woodcut print on the cover depicting a couple of crooked imps playing the drums and fiddle for dancing hags in pointed hats. It was titled *Tales of Vanished Villages* and there was his grand-uncle's name: Spencer Creaser.

Owen brewed a mug of coffee, heavy with milk, and retired to his bedroom to read. He'd left a corner of the cage uncovered so Faith and Fred could get some air while he was out of the room. He pulled the cloth back further so the pair had a better view. He showed them the book.

'Spencer was an author. Fancy that.' He felt strangely proud of the man. As if his relative's literary achievement somehow opened a possibility for his future. Like he could have that same talent in his veins.

He read the preface, in which Spencer credited his grandmother for his interest in history and folklore: *She had a story for every croft and bole, and none were the same. She collected the skeins of the past and wished them rewoven.*

Owen regarded the index. One category was 'Fairies, Boggles, and Wee Folk'. But the section that arrested him was 'Screaming Skulls'.

Much to his surprise there were several examples. Skeletons that were restless and loud in graveyards were disinterred and returned to their homes, and over time, most of their bones were lost, until only the skulls remained.

Some of the early peoples of England were head-hunters and kept skulls as trophies. Many cultures consider them the receptacle of the vital spirit. The practice of pilgrimage to visit decorated saints' bones in jewelled reliquaries remains popular. In other lands they are brought out each year, to be fed and feted. Sometimes they communicate prophecies or act as guardians of ancestral knowledge. To hear their voices is a sign of someone attuned to a peculiar realm.

Owen looked up from the pages and regarded the skulls. They looked back at him. He frowned. *What a shite superpower.*

He skimmed through the stories until he spotted an entry that caused his pulse to speed up: *Caldwere Farm.*

It is said that Caldwere Farm became the property of a widow of striking beauty, who had twin children called Faith and Fred.

Owen blinked and read the words again. They were real. He glanced over at the skulls in their draped shrine. From below he heard a barrage of hammering, and voices raised. Something shifted, as if the house's axis had moved minutely. 'That's got it,' he heard Tall Jim shout. Then all was quiet again.

Owen returned to reading.

The family lived quietly, a day's walk from the seaside village of Withensea (long since fallen into the waves). The children played in the woods and rarely went to church. In the evening lights were seen flickering through the close-knit trees. Strange songs floated on the air. They had an eerie way of speaking as one and were reported to ask impious questions. As innocents, they must have been damned by their mother. Something had to be done to save them.

Their mother was taken, tested, and confessed to being in league with Satan. She was hanged, and the local magistrate, Obadiah Creaser, ensured the twins witnessed their mother's wrecked form led up to the gibbet and her neck stretched.

Obadiah was granted guardianship of the children and their land, but no amount of godly care could reform their wildness. The girl was particularly obdurate. The Magistrate prayed privately with her every evening, but the child's screams of defiance were heard by all in the fine new farmhouse he built upon the land.

Several people testified that she became wanton and led her brother into terrible betrayals against God's natural order. During their trial the twins protested this vehemently, although the girl was no longer a maiden. Seven years after their mother's hanging, the twins were dragged up before the village and hanged by the same noose.

Owen stopped, his face wrinkled with revulsion. This man, Obadiah, was an ancestor who had profited from a terrible abuse of his position of authority. Owen did not want to look upon the twins again, so he returned to the final paragraphs.

Faith cursed Obadiah and all his line from the gallows. 'You, who swore to care for and shelter us, will never be quit of us now. We shall call out your sins to the Almighty forever.' Their bodies were buried, unmarked, outside the graveyard, but people nearby complained of rending screams every night, until finally the exhausted neighbours gathered, dug up the decaying twins, and dumped them on Caldwere Farm.

Over the years only the skulls survived. The Creasers never declined, but never prospered. And each time a relative attempted to sell on or destroy the skulls, they returned to cry their bloody truth until they, and their caretakers, returned home.

Owen gasped, and glanced at the skulls. He knew he could not remove them. But, surely he could *leave* them? He had been considering digging a special grave in the cellar, where he could bury them so he could move on.

He knelt in front of the two skulls and placed his face close to their hard features.

'I didn't do this to you! You can't take it out on me.'

They regarded him silently. Judging him, Owen felt.

He flipped the cloth back over their cage.

'It's not my fault!' he hissed at them.

He stood up too fast and his head ached.

You will take care of us.

Owen froze.

You, or another.

His breath hitched in his chest, and he took a step back, as if he could evade the thought.

'No,' he said, softly.

You'll hear us always, lad, no matter how far you run. We'll sing our special songs. The ones that charm snakes and spiders. That attract ill luck and ill will. You'll come back.

You, or another.

He had planned to sell the house and split the money with Poppy. And then he'd travel and move somewhere far from those who knew his old, weak self. He'd be a fresh person, someone freed from expectations and old stories.

It felt as if giant chains had fallen from above and landed upon his shoulders to anchor him in his past. He would be fastened forever in fucked-up, irresponsible Owen.

He dropped to the floor with a thud.

Owen reached forward with unsteady fingers and drew the curtain up.

Inside their shadowed cell the two skulls gleamed with pleasure.

'Please,' he entreated.

You, or another.

A SCREAM AWAY FROM SOMEONE

DEIRDRE SULLIVAN

(2021)

A wonderful ghostly tale with a twist to one of my favourite terrors: the fetch, or doppelgänger. You can almost taste the dust of the ruins of the Blitz, the greyness that pervades. A wonderfully drawn portrait of a gay man negotiating a hostile world, one I remember like yesterday. And the sound advice always to be a scream away from someone. But what if that someone is wearing your face?

URING THE BLITZ, MY uncle moved to London. He was a gay man and it wasn't easy for them here at the time. It probably isn't easy for them now. I wouldn't know. He was the only one I ever had any contact with.

My uncle was a tall, thin, soft-spoken man. He had a fondness for pale colours – dove grey, bone, that sort of thing. They blended better into a big city like London. People got away with things there that they couldn't in other places. That's still true.

He was an able-bodied man and he found work. He had been worried people over there would call him a coward for not fighting. He'd heard things from men who hadn't fought in the first one, soft feathers pressed into their hands like little knives, stabbing looks from patriotic women.

It was all right though, he was left alone to find his way. There was a calmness about him, a sort of peace. A blankety thing like him wouldn't do too well in combat and people sensed that and left well enough alone.

My uncle liked the night-time. It had been calmer and emptier than the day back home but here the night was different. The sky was different. Different shaped clouds and the stars were hard to make out in the distance. Hauling bodies was what he worked at. Long after people had been rescued, brought to hospital, he'd trawl through what was left to find the dead.

I have very few memories of him. I was born when he was older still, long after the war had ended. Back in those days women had litters instead of families and my mother was the runt of hers. She had me at fifteen, and they sent her over there to live with him. Otherwise, she would have had to go into a home for the unmarried.

I never found out who my father was. 'A man,' she'd say, which wasn't very helpful. She knocked six months off my age when she moved home. And added in a husband. With TB. She modelled him on my uncle's friend. Not that he got TB and died. He didn't. But in the looks and personality of things. She needed someone who'd be in a photo she could show them. She didn't know a lot of other men.

I believed the lies she told for ages. About the husband, about where I came from. It was only later, safely married, that she started to let pieces of my early childhood spill out at me. Stories about my uncle and his friend. The life they had together. The friend had a wife as well as my uncle. But he'd had my uncle first and they would stay friends till one of them was dead.

They had an arrangement about that as well. If my uncle died first, his friend was to go to his funeral. But if the friend died first, my uncle was to avoid the service at all costs and mourn him privately in his own way. The friend loved the wife, you see. But like you'd love a sister. My mother often wondered if the wife knew. And – once my mother married – how she didn't.

My uncle had a two-bed apartment that he owned, and she stayed there till I was two or three. I was small. She cleaned the place for him and made him dinners. Told him when he had toothpaste in the corner of his mouth. For a man who took pride in his appearance, there was always a little bit of dishevelment about him. A little flaw. A tattered patch of furze he'd missed while shaving, a piece of lettuce stuck between his slightly bucked front teeth.

He would have liked the pair of us to stay, my mother told me. He never asked, nothing so direct, but he told her we would always be welcome, more than welcome, when she began to make her plans to leave. Which might have been politeness, but my mother was perceptive. She knew things about people instinctively. She hated my first husband, made him put the milk in his own tea.

My uncle's soft hands became callused and scarred from the cement and brick and wood and dusty plaster debris. By the time my mother lived with him, he wore leather gloves with soft wool lining when he left the house, and always carried hand cream. It had a very particular scent, something between Vicks VapoRub and cedar. I've smelled it since. Brought water to my eyes.

My uncle found babies roughly twice a week. Children were scarce – a lot of them had been sent to the country. The ones that were too loved stayed in London. Rarer than babies, but not uncommon. A lot of people want their children near them. My mother wanted me. She could have given me away but kept me close instead. I'm glad of that. A lot of women didn't get the choice.

My uncle would find photographs in frames or wallets, sometimes in the gutters or blowing through the streets like dirty leaves. He would always try to pair them with their owners. Leave them in nearby shops or post offices or with the police. He would return to ask if anyone had found them, and if not would take them home, file them away, leaving his address. We found boxes of them when we cleaned out his house. Pictures of his family and friends all mingled in. It was hard to tell the strangers from the blood.

The worst thing that ever happened to my uncle didn't seem that bad to me at first. I loved this story when I was a child, and so did my mother. She was still a child when she had me. She shouldn't have been let. I mean, she didn't know what sex even was until she had it. Even then. She said that once and when I asked her more her mouth got tight and she emptied a drawer full of keys and receipts and bits of string and cleaned it out and made it tidy.

I helped her, tying all the string together, winding it into a ball the size of my fist, still smaller then than hers. She was a big woman. Not fat, but tall and wide. She must have developed early. Women shaped like that so often do.

My uncle only told it to her once. The night before she left. They were sitting down on his uncomfortable sofa. He loved old furniture with wooden legs and velvety upholstery, and it always looked beautiful and felt horrible, especially on bare skin. She was all packed and ready to go back and he told her she didn't have to.

He was drinking a large glass of red wine. He called it that, 'a large glass of red wine', and she had a smaller one to sip. Her special one. She didn't like the taste, but she wanted to keep trying it because it looked so elegant. And they sat together on the uncomfortable furniture and she had me – at that stage a little sleeping toddler – in the box room and they sat together and they sipped and he told her a story.

Sifting through rubble is hard work and hauling corpses out is harder still. You keep a scarf over your nose so you don't breathe powder in and even so your handkerchief fills up with grey and black. After a while, you start to see pieces of people you know.

Your father's nose on someone else's face. Your mother's knuckles. The forehead of your schoolmaster. It's like a jigsaw that makes the wrong picture. Not the one that's on the box, but something only slightly like it. This is what my uncle told my mother and I do not disbelieve him.

He didn't want to work with his hands, he wanted to do brain-work and he got that later, translating texts. Before that though, the hours he had to keep were strange and irregular. You take what you can get when you're an immigrant. You do what you need to do to keep your head above water.

Some nights, there'd be very little to do; they'd wait around. And others, they could work into the morning, afternoon, until they couldn't move. He always hoped to find somebody living. Every now and then that happened. Once he found a nest of kittens in the stuffing of an old armchair. He kept one but it died before my mother lived with him. Probably for the best. Cats don't like babies. Noisy things, encroaching on their space.

One night, my uncle found a shoe, sticking out of the rubble. It was a soft, tan, leather shoe. He knew the sort. They came from Woolworths. He had seen them. They were more expensive than what he wore. This was in the days before the good job and the rich friend.

The building, or what had been a building, was in a good area. Leafy, white houses with steps up to them, and wide streets. Big houses for big people, my mother used to say. I think her mother said it before her. And the shoe was attached to a foot, which was attached to a leg and something about the leg was quite unsettling. He couldn't put his finger quite on what. The angle or the shape. It bothered him that he did not know why he felt so awkward looking at it. Trepidation, or the birth of fear.

My uncle noticed things about people. He was observant, fond of music, art. A decent listener. Sensitive. You wouldn't put him rooting through the dirt for bits of people. But he got down to it. He did his best. With the Luftwaffe in the forefront of your mind, there wasn't a lot of time to be bothered by the job at hand. Finding little children, especially inside their mother's arms, would do it. Grown men were rare enough; a lot of them had gone to fight the war. My uncle pulled hard at the leg but the pieces of house would not dislodge and so he had to pick and pick for ages.

The men who found the bodies worked in pairs, two of them in the one place. Some people worked in tandem, digging and chatting. My uncle and the man he generally worked with would go to separate areas and tease a body out, only helping each other if absolutely necessary. My uncle was a quiet man, not much for chat unless he knew you. He found the women easier than men. He liked the gentle people. His workmate was a rough sort, with a fancy voice. My uncle reckoned he might have come from bigger people once. He never asked, the workmate never offered.

In the blitz-lit darkness, there were always scavengers around as well. If you asked them, they'd pretend that it had been their house but they were lying and you had to run them. They were only out for things to steal from other people's dead. Scum, my uncle called them.

It happened on a cold night, and my uncle's workmate (respiratory issues and flat feet) wanted to get back to his wife who'd had a baby. He called her 'the missus' and the words sounded strange on his posh tongue. There was grime all over them, not black grime like miners get but a matte white pallor. 'We looked like ghosts,' he told my mother. 'The skin and in the eyes.'

My uncle kept on digging. And digging. Soft wool trousers, charcoal grey. It's hard to tell in the dark, but they had a flashlight, and they looked charcoal grey. They felt expensive. My uncle pulled them back over the leg and smoothed them down. The body had been dead a while; it was stiff but pliable. Rigor mortis had been and gone. The building had been bombed the night before. Looking back, my uncle thought it strange, but at the time he didn't know enough to put a name on his unease.

Digging and digging. A slim, soft stomach covered by a waist-coat. Mother-of-pearl buttons. Thin and delicate. Tasteful. No jacket, in his shirtsleeves, rolled up. The arms were outstretched, and it took the length of torso to uncover them. The corpse, it seemed, was completely upside down, splayed unnaturally. It was peculiar.

My uncle didn't like it. His partner smoked and sighed, not offering to help while my uncle scrabbled at it with his two big paws. Pulled the arms out by the elbows, awkwardly.

Eventually, his workmate came to help haul the body out with him. It's hard to lift a man's weight by yourself. Men are heavy things. When I was little my mother told me to be careful of all men. Strangers and the ones I knew as well.

'If you are in a room beside a man,' she said, 'keep the door open, love. Always be a scream away from someone.'

When the body was stretched out, my uncle found himself examining it. It reminded him of someone, but he couldn't put his finger on who. He wiped the dust off the man's face with his sleeve. The small eyes, widely spaced, the high sharp cheekbones, the little port-wine stain upon the chin.

His workmate eyed the corpse, and said: 'It's you mate, only older.' The more my uncle stared, the more he saw the truth in that. It had his face, but didn't have his life. They lumped it on the stretcher, sent it on its way to a decent burial.

My uncle never found out who that man was. The one that sort of lived inside his body. Like townhouses, they look the same but you don't know what's inside until you peep. Condemned, my uncle thought, filching through the silk-lined empty pockets. There was no wallet. No man had lived inside that house, a neighbour told him later. Only spinsters, and their little niece. My mother always gave that girl my age, when she told the story. To make me feel a part of it, I think.

Not a scratch on him. Dust but not a scratch.

The story wasn't scary enough to stop me sleeping as a child, but still it gave a pleasant nervous feeling and she told it to me quite a few times. The ending never changed. Her brother sad, and staring at his wine and saying dully:

'When I look in the mirror, loveen, it isn't my face that I see. Not anymore. It's always his. Since that night. Never mine.'

I never really understood the horror of that until I was older and began to shy away from mirrors, taking better care of my skin but knowing it was quite a pointless endeavour. Sometimes I look at my own face and imagine it's a stranger far away. Someone I've discovered nearly dead. I wait for it to move and when it does, I get a sick little thrill. I've caught it out.

I lie awake sometimes, beside my husband, a scream away from no one. My two fled the nest as soon as possible. And I think of my uncle. We visited him twice, after that. Once when I was ten, for a weekend. And again, at his funeral. His friend long gone, and no one in the chapel knew our names. My mother in her little suit beside me. Knees together, hands inside her lap, staring ahead.

I scanned the faces in the crowd and wondered if someone here was happening upon his own face and body at the end of someone else's life. I wondered if I screamed who would hear me, and how many would come and would they help at all or make things worse. I held my tongue and counted the words in the Lord's Prayer. Twice. The answers were completely different both times.

AUTHOR BIOGRAPHIES

Elizabeth Bowen (1899–1973) was a Dublin-born writer who grew up primarily in England. She notably wrote about life in wartime London and books about the 'big house' of Irish landed Protestants. Her works include novels *The Last September* (1929) and *Eva Trout* (1968), the latter of which was nominated for the 1970 Booker Prize.

Catherine Brophy (b. 1941) is a writer and broadcaster from Bray, Co. Wicklow. She was educated at University College Dublin and has worked as an audiologist and lecturer. Notable works include her novels *Dark Paradise* (1991) and *The Liberation of Margaret McCabe* (1985).

Thomas Crofton Croker (1798–1854) was a Cork-born antiquary whose collections of songs and legends later formed a repository for the writers of the Irish literary revival. Croker was a founder member of the Percy Society from 1840 to 1852. His later works include *Popular Songs of Ireland* (1839).

Lord Dunsany (1878–1957), or Edward John Moreton Drax Plunkett, 18th Baron of Dunsany FRSL, was an Anglo-Irish writer of short stories, novels, plays, poetry, essays and autobiography. He was particularly notable for his work in fantasy, such as *The Book of Wonder* (1912) and *The King of Elfland's Daughter* (1924).

Tracy Fahey (b. 1971) is an Irish writer. Twice shortlisted for Best Collection at the British Fantasy Awards in 2017 and 2022, her short fiction is published in over thirty American, British, Australian and Irish anthologies. She holds a PhD on the Gothic in visual arts. Fahey's writing is supported by residencies in Ireland and Greece, and a Saari Fellowship awarded by the Kone Foundation, Finland.

Sheridan Le Fanu (1814–1873), full name Joseph Thomas Sheridan Le Fanu, was a prolific Irish writer of ghost stories and mystery novels during the Victorian period. He was a leading ghost story writer of his time. Le Fanu penned iconic works such as *Carmilla* (1872) and *Uncle Silas* (1864).

Dorothy Macardle (1889–1958) was an Irish writer, novelist, playwright and republican activist from Co. Louth. She is best remembered for penning *The Irish Republic* (1937) and gothic novels such as *Fantastic Summer* (1948) and *Dark Enchantment* (1953).

Charles Maturin (1780–1824) was an Irish Protestant clergyman, playwright and novelist born in Dublin. He is best known for writing *Melmoth the Wanderer* (1820).

Maura McHugh lives in Galway and writes prose, theatre, film/TV, video games and comic books. Her short story collection, *The Boughs Withered (When I Told Them My Dreams)*, was nominated for a British Fantasy Award. She also writes non-fiction and appears on podcasts and radio, where she reviews and discusses pop culture.

Mary Frances McHugh (1890–1955) was an Irish writer from Dublin. While McHugh made important contributions to the horror story genre, she is most known for her poetry, novels including *Thalassa* (1931) and *The Bud of Spring* (1932) and her autobiographical writing, which earned her comparison with George Moore in Irish literary circles in the early twentieth century.

Fitz James O'Brien (1826–1862) was an Irish-American writer, poet and Civil War soldier born in County Cork. He wrote notable short stories such as *The Diamond Lens* (1858), *What Was It? A Mystery* (1859) and *The Lost Room* (1858).

Flann O'Brien, pen name of Brian O'Nolan, (1911–1966) was a writer, satirist and Irish civil service official, the latter of which he worked as for eighteen years. He is known for his comic novels, *At Swim-Two-Birds* (1939) and *The Third Policeman* (1967). O'Nolan is widely considered a major figure in twentieth-century Irish literature.

Roisín O'Donnell's short story 'How to Build a Space Rocket' won Story of the Year at the An Post Irish Book Awards 2018. She is the author of the collection *Wild Quiet*, published by New Island Books in 2016, which was longlisted for the Edge Hill Short Story Prize 2017 and shortlisted for the Kate O'Brien Award 2017, as well as the International Rubery Book Award. Her first novel, *Nesting*, will be published in 2025. She lives near Dublin with her two children.

Charlotte Riddell (1832–1906), known in later life as Mrs J. H. Riddell, was a Northern-Irish writer from the Victorian period. She was also editor of the London literary journal *St James's Magazine* in the 1860s. Although she is the author of 56 books, Riddell's most memorable works are her stories about ghosts and the supernatural, such as 'The Banshee's Warning' (1867) and 'The Old House in Vauxhall Walk' (1882).

Saki (1870–1916), pseudonym of Hector Hugh (or 'H. H.') Munro, was a Scottish journalist and fiction writer whose witty and sometimes macabre stories often depicted the Edwardian period and satirised the social scene and attitudes to class structure. Notable works include his short story collections *The Chronicles of Clovis* (1912) and *Beasts and Super-Beasts* (1914).

Abraham (Bram) Stoker (1847–1912) was a novelist born in Dublin, Ireland. During his lifetime, he was known for being the personal assistant of actor Sir Henry Irving. However, posthumously, he is most known and celebrated for his influential Gothic horror novel *Dracula* (1897).

Deirdre Sullivan is an award-winning writer and teacher from Galway. She has written eight acclaimed books for young adults, including *Savage Her Reply* (Little Island, 2020), *Perfectly Preventable Deaths* (Hot Key Books, 2019), and *Tangleweed and Brine* (Little Island, 2017). She was the recipient of the CBI Book of the Year Award in 2018 and 2021, and the An Post Teen and Young Adult

Book of the Year in 2017 and 2020. Her debut short story collection for adults, *I Want to Know That I Will Be Okay* (2021), was published by Banshee Press. Her short story 'Little Lives' won the An Post Irish Book Award for Short Fiction in 2021, and has been optioned for film. *Weave*, a collaborative collection of short fiction and folklore, co-written by Deirdre and Oein DeBhairduin and illustrated by Yingge Xu was released in 2022 by Skein Press.

Graham Tugwell (b. 1983) is a writer, performer and educator. Over fifty of his short stories have been published across five continents. He is the writer and producer of Ireland's first horror audio drama *Down Below the Reservoir*, described by RTÉ Culture as 'ominous and impeccably produced'. He lives in the east of Ireland.

Oscar Wilde (1854–1900) was a Dublin-born wit, poet and playwright who is best remembered for his epigrams, plays such as *The Importance of Being Earnest* (1895) and his only novel, *The Picture of Dorian Gray* (1891). Wilde attended Trinity College Dublin and Magdalen College, Oxford and is associated with the late 19th-century Aesthetic literary movement.

W. B. Yeats (1865–1939) was a poet, dramatist, writer and politician of Protestant Anglo-Irish descent and one of the key figures in the Irish Literary Revival. He was educated in Dublin and London but spent his summers in the west of Ireland. Major works include the poem 'The Second Coming' and plays such as *The Countess Cathleen* (1892) and *Deirdre* (1907). He received the Nobel Prize for Literature in 1923.

ACKNOWLEDGEMENTS

The publishers gratefully acknowledge permission to reprint copyright material in this book as follows:

'A Scream Away from Someone' by Deirdre Sullivan from *I Want to Know that I Will be Okay* (Banshee Press, 2021), reproduced with permission of Banshee Press.

'Arachnophobia' by Catherine Brophy, reproduced with permission of the author.

'Encounter at Night' by Mary Frances McHugh from *Great Irish Tales of Horror* (Souvenir Press, 1997), reproduced with permission of Profile Books.

'Faith & Fred' by Maura McHugh from *Cursed* (Titan Books, 2020), reproduced with permission of the author.

'Leverets through the Hole in the Hedge' by Graham Tugwell, reproduced with permission of the author.

'The Demon Lover' by Elizabeth Bowen, reproduced with permission of Curtis Brown.

'The Portrait of Roisin Dhu' by Dorothy McArdle from *Great Irish Tales of Horror* (Souvenir Press, 1997), reproduced with permission of Profile Books.

'The Seventh Man' by Roisín O'Donnell from *The Glass Shore: Stories by Women Writers from the North of Ireland* (New Island, 2016), reproduced with permission of the author.

'Two in One' by Flann O'Brien, reproduced with permission of the Author's Estate.

'Tracing the Spectre' by Tracy Fahey from *The Unheimlich Manoeuvre* (Sinister Horror Company, 2018), reproduced with permission of the author.

'Where the Tides Ebb and Flow' by Lord Dunsany, reproduced with permission of Curtis Brown.